'So proud and so defiant.'

Conrad's gaze as he studied her upturned face was no longer mocking, but serious. 'I am here for a reason and my duty must be done. Until then I can allow you to do nothing which will jeopardise my plans.'

Eleanor gasped as his eyes narrowed and became cold.

'Then we are enemies.' Refusing to look at him, she sat on a boulder.

'Yes, Lady Eleanor Twyneham, we are indeed enemies.'

Dear Reader

With AN UNEXPECTED PASSION, Paula Marshall gives us a 'faction'. Written about real people, the story is inevitably different; no exciting moments can be created that didn't really exist. But this glimpse of actuality becomes compelling, and I think you will like Haryo and Granville as much as I do.

We also have Pauline Bentley with SILK AND SWORD, following the fortunes of Eleanor in the chaotic times of 1485 when Richard III lost to Henry VII. An exciting and very different month for you!

The Editor

Pauline Bentley has long been captivated by history. Born in Essex, she trained as a legal secretary, but always came away from visiting castles or manor houses with the desire to write about them. She now lives in Sussex, is married with two children and a growing menagerie of dogs, and finds inspiration walking over the South Downs.

Recent titles by the same author:

REBEL HARVEST
WOMAN OF CONFLICT

SILK AND SWORD

Pauline Bentley

First published in Great Britain 1993
by Mills & Boon Limited

© Pauline Bentley 1993

Australian copyright 1993
Philippine copyright 1993
This edition 1993

ISBN 0 263 78054 6

Masquerade is a trademark published by
Mills & Boon Limited, Eton House,
18–24 Paradise Road, Richmond, Surrey, TW9 1SR.

Set in 10 on 10½ pt Linotron Plantin
04-9306-84255

Typeset in Great Britain by Centracet, Cambridge
Made and printed in Great Britain

CHAPTER ONE

'FREEDOM is never more precious than when one has had it taken away!' Eleanor Twyneham addressed a startled fox drinking from the opposite bank of the river. She twisted the iron boat ring, set in the supporting timbers of the bridge, to close the concealed opening. Only she knew of the existence of the tunnel which led from the underground store-room in Highford Castle. Twenty years ago Highford had been given to her father, Sir Cedric Twyneham, as a prize of war after he had helped Edward IV crush a Lancastrian rebellion.

Eleanor climbed the riverbank. For a moment she crouched, glancing towards the castle. It was half hidden by mist. From its promontory high above the ravine it seemed to be rising out of a pearly cloud. Nothing stirred. As usual her escape was undetected. Eleanor relaxed and pulled the hood of her cloak over the braids of dark blonde hair wound like a crown upon her head. This summer of 1485 was proving unseasonably cold.

She was dressed in the guise of a page. Her long legs were covered by thick black woollen hose, though on close inspection the short green tunic concealed little of the curves of her slender body. She relied on the cloak for that. Five years ago she had first discovered the secret exit from the castle. Since then she had used it to escape the vigilance of the guards to visit her young brother. Daniel was no less a prisoner than herself. For seven years he had been in the care of the nuns at the priory. No one at the castle was aware of her visits. Discovery would have meant a severe punishment from her father. Daniel was a sickly, slow-witted boy, and, as far as Sir Cedric was concerned, he had no son. His name was forbidden to be mentioned at the castle.

A cockerel crowed the arrival of dawn over the castle, its cry taken up by several hounds in the kennels. Outlined on the battlements, the dark figure of a sentry started from his doze.

Ay, freedom was sweet. Eleanor grinned. Six months of being confined in the castle had not daunted her spirit. She would act in the same manner again if the need arose. Never would she allow the villagers to starve while there was grain within the castle. That she had opened the castle storehouse to provide grain for the people had sent her father into a rage. Her palfrey had been taken from her and she was not allowed outside the castle grounds. That she was still a prisoner did not surprise her. It was likely that her father had simply forgotten her existence.

The pain of his neglect no longer had the power to wound her. Sir Cedric rarely visited his Devonshire estate of Highford, dividing his time between his duties at Court and his main castle at Arnwood in Kent. The only interest he took in Highford was the amount of income it added to his coffers each year. The isolated fortress had been Eleanor's home for eight years, since the marriage of her father to the Lady Clemence. Her stepmother had refused to have the children of Sir Cedric's marriage to the Lady Isobel under her roof. Though Eleanor was old enough to be sent, as was customary, to a noble's house to be educated in the manners and refinements of a lady, she had instead been banished to Highford.

Older and wiser now, Eleanor saw behind her step-mother's motives. She wanted her children, not the Lady Isobel's, to inherit the Twyneham lands. Her vindictiveness had served the Lady Clemence ill. Two sons had died within a year and last Candlemas she had been brought to bed of another stillborn child. Daniel remained Sir Cedric's heir and Highford was to be Eleanor's dowry when she married. Not that Sir Cedric showed any inclination to see his only daughter wed, and, at seventeen, she was long past marriageable age.

Over the years Eleanor had drawn upon her pride and refused to let her pain at Sir Cedric's neglect show. It was Daniel she was concerned for. As far as the people of Highford were concerned, he was dead. Was Sir Cedric ashamed of Daniel's slow wits? Was that why he was shut away? Her father's actions were sinister and frightening. Upon his last visit to Highford, Eleanor, then fourteen, had overcome her fear of his volatile rages to challenge him.

When she had asked why Daniel had been sent away, Sir Cedric's heavy features had mottled with fury and he had struck her, blackening her eye and sending her hurtling against the wall. While she had been still stunned from the impact, he had screamed at her never to mention her brother's name again; and to emphasise each word had laid his riding whip across her back. That she had not died from the violence of his fury had been due to the intervention of Samuel, the steward. He had dragged Sir Cedric off. Worse than her beating had been to witness Sir Cedric fall on the ground, rolling about and screaming in his fury at being thwarted. He had stuffed rushes into his mouth as the frenzy had reached its height. Samuel had ordered Griselda, her maid, to take Eleanor to her room and tend her wounds. But the demented image of Sir Cedric stayed with Eleanor long after her scars from the beating had disappeared.

The next day Sir Cedric had left for Arnwood, his baggage train laden with Highford's money chests and the castle stripped of the last of its valuables. Samuel had been dismissed and banished from Highford. He was replaced by Bertram Le Gros, a brutal man who took pleasure in ruling the peasants by fear. Since his arrival, Eleanor had become the defender of her people from his cruelty. It had made her into a strong-willed woman who abhorred injustice.

Her blue eyes hardened with determination. She was

her father's vassal, bound to obey him as were the peasants. As such she could do little to countermand his orders. That did not stop her trying, no matter the severity of the punishment he ordered. Being whipped by Sir Cedric had not cowed her; it had made her rebel against his injustice. She was determined to help Daniel lead a normal life, and to rid the people of Highford of Le Gros's tyranny.

Eleanor tucked the small bundle of food wrapped in linen under her arm. Daniel had few comforts and he loved marchpane, a delicacy denied him at the priory. As she walked along the bank, she passed two families of swans feeding in the reed bed. She avoided the water-meadows shrouded in the morning mist, where soon the village goatherds and swineherds would be grazing their flocks. It was a quicker route to the priory, but her footsteps would leave a trail over the dew-covered grass. She left the riverbank and took the woodland track on the mile-long walk to the priory.

On her first visit five years ago, Eleanor had needed all her wits and resourcefulness to persuade the prioress to admit her. Mother Benedicta, who had been ill at ease throughout the interview, finally admitted that Daniel was under her charge, but that Sir Cedric had sworn her to secrecy. The nun had taken pity on the lonely girl who was so determined to be reunited with her brother. During her first visits Daniel had been sullen and uncommunicative, which was not surprising since the Highford nuns were under a vow of silence. It was a further injustice that Sir Cedric had condemned his son to live in a silent world. Was it any wonder that Daniel was given to fits of uncontrollable rages, his tantrums becoming more violent with each year? He was denied the companionship of children and family. Eleanor was resolved that the matter should not continue. No matter how great her father's wrath, she would confront him about Daniel's future.

The rays from the rising sun pierced like arrows

through the trees, dispelling the mist and dappling the ground in patches of light and dark. Ahead of Eleanor on the narrow track, a score of rabbits scattered. There was a crashing in the undergrowth and a roe deer broke cover. Eleanor paused to watch as it disappeared from sight. It was then that she became aware of the low drone of voices.

Outlaws! Her hand went to the dagger at her waist. They would cut her throat to steal the clothes from her back. Worse, should they discover she was a woman, she would be in danger of rape. Alarm quickened her heartbeat. She could only visit the priory once a month, when Griselda, who slept on a pallet in her room, visited her sister living in the next village. She always stayed overnight and returned mid-morning the following day. Time enough to get to the priory and back before Eleanor was discovered missing.

Eleanor frowned, aware of the need for caution. There had been no report of outlaws in the area, but any travellers of honourable intent would have sheltered the night at the castle. As she began to back away, a voice louder than the rest carried clearly to her.

'Why wait? Enter the castle disguised as a pedlar and hide yourself until nightfall. Then you'll have all the time you need to steal the. . .'

The last words were lost to her, but she had heard enough to stop her flight. Should she return to Highford to alert the sentries? The number of guards at the castle was small. The main force of her father's retainers remained with him at Arnwood. Therefore would it not be better if she learned the strength and plans of the men who would rob her home?

She laid aside the bundle of sweetmeats and edged forward, careful where she placed each foot, so that her passage was not detected. She saw the horses first — about a dozen of them tethered to the left of her. Hiding behind a tree, she strained to catch their words. The

men spoke in hushed whispers and to her frustration she
caught only odd snatches of their words.

'The oldest and least able of Sir Cedric's guards. . .
easy to overcome.'

'There will be no recourse to violence.' A calmer,
authoritative voice cut in. 'That's why I would enter
alone.'

'And risk capture!' the first man warned.

There was a confident laugh. 'Why should they be
suspicious of a pedlar? I know what I'm looking for.'

So they were thieves! It puzzled her that the second
man who had spoken had a voice which was cultured,
more like a knight than a brigand. Edging closer to their
camp, she could see the men clearly through the trees.
Several figures armed with swords and daggers squatted
on the ground or lounged against the oaks. They were
all dressed in dark colours to blend in with the forest.
Their leader was in the centre of the ring of men. He
was dressed in plain brown homespun, but his proud
bearing was unmistakably that of a man used to command. She studied him closely so she would recognise
him should he enter Highford. His back was to her. He
was above medium height, but not exceptionally tall,
and his light tawny hair hung thick and straight to his
broad shoulders. A leather sword belt rested on his
narrow hips and he wore long riding boots.

He was speaking again. 'I see no problem in entering
the castle.'

A loud crack from a twig snapping beneath Eleanor's
foot made her dart back behind a tree. Holding her
breath, she flattened herself against its trunk, her heart
thudding wildly. There was a pause from the speaker.
Had she been seen? Her eyes closed with relief as the
leader continued.

'The guards are lax from years of peace.'

Others murmured agreement. Eleanor's blue eyes
narrowed with anger. He might speak like a knight, but
he was clearly a robber-baron. How dared he attempt to

rob Highford? His complacence would be aptly
rewarded, she fumed, as she retraced her steps to the
track. Her visit to Daniel must await another day. Any
pedlar who entered the castle would be brought to her.
If it was the blond outlaw she would have him thrown
into the dungeon to await Sir Cedric's punishment.

As she was aware that any sound could still be detected
by the brigands, her progress was slow, and she continu-
ally scanned her surroundings. Suddenly an arm circled
her neck, a foot hooked behind her knee, and, with a
twist of an accomplished wrestler, she was sent sprawling
on to the ground.

The breath was knocked from her lungs and before
she could retaliate a man crouched over her, his figure
large and menacing. As her shaking fingers closed over
her dagger to draw it from its sheath, she glimpsed a
tawny head, a lean face with a close-cropped brownish-
tan beard and green glittering eyes which spoke her
death sentence. It was the robber-baron himself.

'Where have you come from, boy?' he demanded, his
dagger blade poised inches from her throat.

She braced herself against the expected thrust of the
blade, at the same time refusing to surrender to his
attack. Twisting her head, she sank her teeth into his
wrist.

'You fight like a damned woman,' he snarled as she
was roughly grabbed by the front of her jerkin, her
shoulders raised several inches from the ground as he
shook her. 'Damn your hide, boy, I'll. . .' Her mistreat-
ment had shaken the hood from her head. The words of
abuse were abruptly cut off. 'God's wounds! You are a
woman!'

The hesitation was enough. Not about to surrender
her life, or her virtue, without a fight, Eleanor freed her
own dagger and struck upwards. Iron-hard fingers fastened over her wrist, wrenching the weapon from her
hold, and her arm was forced back over her head. The

man straddled her waist to pin her securely to the ground.

'Lie still, wench, and I'll not hurt you.'

It was a command spoken in a voice which warned her he would give no quarter if she continued to resist. She glowered up into his tanned face, surprised that, though the beard made him look older, he was probably in his middle twenties. She had assumed an older man had delivered those assured and confident orders. The pressure of his thighs was like a clamp about her waist and the intimacy of the contact with his body alerted her to the threat of violation.

'Get off me!' she screeched in outrage.

'Are you from the castle?'

'Knave!' She began to squirm and kick. 'I'll die before I submit to your lechery.' Her nails clawed at his face.

With a snort of contempt he anchored both her arms over her head as she continued to twist and struggle. Fast becoming exhausted by her struggles, Eleanor realised she was wasting her energy, and, feigning weakness, she slumped against him.

'That's better,' he said gruffly. 'Hold still and you'll not be harmed.'

Her eyes blazed her hatred at him, her heart beating so fast that it felt as though it would choke her. The weight of his body remained covering hers, pressing her to the ground, restraining her, but not with such force that she was in pain.

'It's information I want—not your body.'

'I'll tell you nothing. Lecher. Brigand!'

'Your words make it clear you overheard our plans. A pity. For you must now be silenced. Though you speak too well to be a servant.' His green eyes narrowed. 'Are you then a lady's maid? What are you doing in the wood at first light, dressed as a page and unescorted? Perhaps you are the thief.'

'I'm no thief. I am maid to Lady Eleanor Twyneham,'

she lied, fearing that if he learned her true identity the brigand would take her hostage and hold her to ransom.

'Why are you dressed as a page?'

There was something disturbingly familiar about his features which tugged at her mind. Continuing her defiance, she scowled at him. 'That's my affair.'

'The circumstances make it mine. Answer me, wench.'

'This is my answer.' Eleanor wriggled and drew up her knee. Before it made contact, he twisted aside, rolling both of them over on the ground and coming to rest lying across her. She fought with gathering fury. His leg lay between her own in an intimate position, inciting her to toss her body in a frantic need to free herself. Instead of escape, she found her body moulded against his hard frame, her breasts crushed by his chest, her hips trapped by hard thighs. Immediately, she froze. Her wrists remained captured in his hands and as he stared down into her angry eyes she noticed the change in him. His green eyes no longer regarded her with murderous intent, they had darkened; his anger mingled with what even in her innocence she knew was desire.

There was a grunt of derision behind them. 'So it was a spy. And a wench at that. A comely one too. I'll leave you to teach her the lesson she deserves, Conrad.'

Over her attacker's shoulder, Eleanor saw the thickset figure of a dark-haired man who was also in his twenties.

To her relief her captor rolled off her and stood up. Her wrists were still held in his grasp and as he raised her to her feet his voice was edged with exasperation. 'There's more at stake than dalliance, Ned. The wench overheard our plans. She'll have to be kept prisoner until my task is done.'

'You mean until you've robbed the castle,' she raged.

Ned glared at her. 'She could do with learning to keep a civil tongue in her head. Any woman who speaks as fine as she does but dresses as a page will bring us trouble.'

'She can give us information,' Conrad replied.

'I will tell you nothing,' Eleanor said, pulling away in another attempt to escape.

He jerked her close to his body, his arms holding her tight while he spoke to his companion. 'She's a complication I could do without. A search-party could be sent looking for her.'

In reply she stamped her foot down hard on his toe and felt a grim satisfaction at his grunt of pain. It changed to fear as his green eyes narrowed with anger.

'If she's too much of a handful, my friend,' Ned laughed, 'I'll tame the baggage.'

'I'll manage. There's more than one way to bring a woman to submission.'

Eleanor blanched at the double meaning behind his threat. A chestnut destrier was brought to the brigand. He mounted and his arm circled her waist to pull her up behind him.

'No!' Eleanor screamed as she twisted to escape his hold. 'I'll not be your hostage.'

She hauled back from his arms, but there was no unseating her captor. The destrier pawed impatiently at the ground, threatening to crush Eleanor's feet. Conrad laughed at her useless attempt to escape him, and she was lifted effortlessly on to his lap. Again finding herself a prisoner in his arms, she continued her struggles. 'Let me go—curse you.'

The destrier reared. With a cry Eleanor clung to the mane, though her captor held her firmly to stop her from falling.

'Hold still, you little hell-cat. If you fall beneath Solomon's hoofs you'll be trampled to death.'

Reluctantly, Eleanor conceded that for the moment escape was impossible. She sat in mutinous silence as they rode to the head of the column of men. Each stride of the horse made her more aware of the strong arm around her waist and the touch of the man's hard, lean figure against her own. She sat stiff and erect, straining away from the heat of his body, and was instantly pulled

back against his immovable frame. At his chuckle, she
turned to glower at the knave, and found herself looking
into jade-green eyes which held an unnerving strength of
purpose. During their fight she had been too angry to
pay much attention to his looks. Now she had an
uncomfortable feeling she should know him. There was
something familiar about that bearded jaw and angular
face. The slender nose and dark blond brows were
commanding, and, in a rugged way, strikingly handsome. When she saw his mouth twist into a grin, she
realised she had been staring and jerked her gaze away.

She studied the riders behind them. They rode with
the skill of trained and disciplined soldiers. The destrier
she sat upon was a knight's horse. And certainly there
was much about her abductor's manner which was too
chivalrous for a common brigand. She eyed the horse's
plain trappings. Neither horse nor rider bore any insignia
proclaiming his knighthood.

Uncomfortable at his nearness and of the danger of
her situation, she refused to allow her fear to show.
'Where are you taking me?'

'Far enough from Highford so that you cannot be
rescued by a patrol of soldiers.'

'Abduction is a hanging offence.'

He smiled. 'Only if one is careless enough to be
caught.' As he spoke he pulled a silk kerchief from inside
his tunic. 'Now I must blindfold you. I would not have
you learn the route to our hiding-place.'

'Am I to know the name of my abductor?' she asked
bluntly.

He raised a brown arched brow. 'Since you proclaim
to be a serving maid, you may address me as master.'
The venom in her eyes brought a scowl to his face.
'You've called no woman mistress, have you? I regret,
my lady, I have no choice but to keep you prisoner.'

The well-trained destrier barely slowed its pace as he
dropped the reins to bind the kerchief about her eyes.
Unable to see, Eleanor tried to keep track of the direction

they took. Before several minutes had passed it was
obvious the troop was circling and doubling back, so
that she was hopelessly lost. Who were these men? she
wondered. Not common brigands, for sure. Her stomach
twisted with apprehension. These were unsettled times.
If rumour was true, then England was soon to be split
asunder by yet another bloody conflict between the
houses of York and Lancaster.

For many years, with Edward IV firmly on the throne,
there had been peace in England. All that had changed
on the King's death. Now, after a tousle for power, the
young princes were declared illegitimate. Evidence had
been found that prior to Edward IV's marriage to
Elizabeth Woodville he had secretly wed another. When
his love for the woman had waned, she had gone into a
convent, but was still alive at the time of the King's
second marriage. The Woodvilles were an arrogant
family who had risen high under the Queen's scheming,
and now the country rejoiced in their downfall. Edward's
brother, Richard, Duke of Gloucester, had been per-
suaded for the good of England to take the throne. Since
the accession of Richard III, the old feud between the
royal houses of York and Lancaster was never far from
people's minds.

Eleanor pushed aside her gloomy thoughts at the
prospect of conflict again breaking out between the
supporters of opposing factions. The Lancastrians were
already stirring up trouble, and many people were
becoming suspicious of King Richard's motives. She
knew enough of the struggle for power to realise that
soon the Lancastrians would make their move to put
their own claimant, Henry Tudor, Duke of Richmond,
on the throne.

Once Highford had been a fierce Lancastrian strong-
hold. How would the people react to an outbreak of
conflict? They certainly had little reason to love Sir
Cedric, who was Yorkist. Eleanor felt a stab of panic. If

these men were the supporters of Henry Tudor, she could be in dire danger.

Conrad D'Arton studied the blindfolded woman seated before him. He could not afford to let her go free, but with each passing minute in her company he became more certain that she had lied to him. She was no serving maid. If, as he suspected, she was the Lady Eleanor Twyneham, then the matter was grave indeed. A squire on the verge of gaining his knighthood broke all the rules of chivalry by abducting a noblewomen. The damned woman could cost him his knight's spurs.

He cursed the name of Twyneham. He had been brought up to distrust and revile the family of Sir Cedric Twyneham. Highford had been in his family for two hundred years before Sir Cedric possessed it. Sir Lionel D'Arton, his father, had been one of Henry VI's most trusted advisors. That was before the King had been imprisoned in the tower, his throne usurped by the Yorkist Edward IV. Sir Lionel remained true to his imprisoned King. He had planned a daring rescue to free the Lancastrian king from the tower. They had been betrayed by Twyneham, whose greed made him change his allegiance from Lancastrian to York. His reward had been Highford. Sir Lionel had barely escaped with his life, and only then by fleeing the country to spend his days in exile.

Conrad's hatred towards Twyneham burned deep. As the only child of Sir Lionel D'Arton, Highford was his inheritance. It was where he had been born. In its church were the tombs of his ancestors. Two days ago on his father's death-bed he had sworn that he would reclaim Highford or die in the attempt. One day Sir Lionel's body would be laid to rest beside Conrad's mother. Until then his father's heart, sealed in a silver casket, would be returned to his beloved Highford.

Now was not the time to lay seige to Highford. But he had vowed that his father's funeral would follow the

traditional family rites. For its performance he must
retrieve the Highford chalice, and the last touch upon
his father's lips would be the reliquary containing a
splinter of the true cross which his ancestor Sir Leofwine
had brought back from the Crusades. These were hidden
in a secret niche in the family vault, and it was there
Conrad would place the silver casket. This was the reason
why he sought to enter Highford.

He frowned. When he had seen Highford at dusk
yesterday it was just as he remembered it. The years of
wandering in exile seemed like an unpleasant dream. But
it was the blue Twyneham standard with its white
cockerel which flew over Highford. Conrad knew he
would not rest until the D'Arton wolf was raised in its
rightful place. That was in the future. Too late now to
undo the wench's abduction. He must follow the consequences through. What was the Lady Eleanor doing
tramping the countryside dressed as a page? By her
unconventional conduct, she had brought her fate upon
herself.

The scent of jasmine on the woman's skin wafted
around him and beneath his arm he was conscious of the
movement of her full breasts. He shifted his hold lower
to encircle her narrow waist, his gaze noting the long
slender lines of her thighs. He dragged his gaze away
from her body to study her face. Her hood had again
fallen back and her hair was the colour of pale golden
wine. Her brow was wide and intelligent, her nose
delicately upturned, and her mouth curved into a cupid's
bow—or would do if her lips were not tightly com-
pressed into white-lipped fury. Beneath the blindfold
those clear blue eyes would be snapping with an indigo
fire.

It was disconcerting that he should remember them so
clearly. But then they had been remarkable, their lus-
trous beauty changing to violet as she lay beneath him,
overpowered—subdued, but still defiant. The shock of
her beauty, when her hood had fallen back as she

struggled with him, had left a lasting impression. The way she had fought showed she had spirit and courage — qualities he admired. The memory of the curves of her figure pressed intimately against him on the ground played havoc with his emotions. Emotions which were further fuelled by the heat of their bodies thrown together by the motion of the horse.

The women's defiance was apparent in the frigid set of her shoulders, and he sensed that she was poised, awaiting the opportunity to escape him. There was much about her which intrigued him. Her beauty was bewitching and her spirit indomitable. But there was something else — a vulnerability carefully controlled, which affected him in a way he had never experienced before.

Conrad smothered the trail of his thoughts. Beautiful or not, the Lady Eleanor was the last woman in England he could afford to become entangled with.

CHAPTER TWO

THE warmth of the sun against her face told Eleanor they were upon open ground, and the horses slowed to a walk as they picked their way over rocky terrain. Close by was the sound of a waterfall. She had not known there was one this near to the castle. But then during her years at Highford she had never been allowed to ride far and was unfamiliar with the land. Blindfolded and held firm in her captor's arms, she was unable to do anything against her own plight, and her mind turned to the constant worry she felt for her brother. Unlike Daniel, at least she had been allowed those short rides accompanied by a groom. In recent years a horse of his own would have helped Daniel overcome his violent moods. What boy would not kick and scream at being shut away with silent nuns, and cooped up with no one to play with? If the boy had a temper it was no worse than Sir Cedric's. Once Eleanor had seen her father lose his temper to such an extent that he had smashed every piece of furniture in the room.

She chewed her lower lip, unable to understand the cruelty of her father towards his heir. Daniel was of an age when the boys of the nobility were sent to other households to train for their knighthood. By now Daniel should have received a rudimentary knowledge of arms and be proficient on a horse. Did Sir Cedric believe Daniel was too sickly to reach manhood?

And what of the neglect to Daniel's education? The nuns, unable to control him, had long since abandoned trying to teach him his letters. Though Eleanor knew that not all knights were literate, and were content to rely on clerics and scribes, it placed them at a disadvantage. Other young pages training for knighthood would

ridicule Daniel. Something must be done for him. Since
Sir Cedric showed no inclination to come to Highford,
then she must send him word.

Eleanor knew the advantages to be gained by learning.
She had been fortunate to have coerced Father Hubert,
the castle chaplain, to teach her. Not that the priest had
approved at first. What did women need an education
for? he had informed her sternly. Eleanor had smiled
sweetly and persisted in her request. Within a month
Father Hubert had agreed. When the priest had seen
how avidly she took to her studies, he had taken pride to
ensure that her Latin was as perfect as his, and that her
hand wrote a beautiful script. Nothing within her education had helped her to understand her father's attitude
towards Daniel. It was as though he had deliberately
chosen to forget his existence. But why? It made no
sense.

Inadvertently, the pain of her thoughts had brought a
droop to her shoulders. She straightened her back,
unwilling that her abductor should misinterpret it as
weakness. The destrier halted and the man behind her
dismounted. Firm but gentle hands lifted her from the
saddle. When he continued to carry her, she began to
struggle.

'Hold! Or you will have us both plunging to our
deaths.' The clipped command stopped her struggles.
Once her feet were on firm ground she would teach this
upstart brigand that she would not be handled like a
sack of corn. But he did not release her, and held her
body firmly against his own.

She heard the horses being led forward ahead of them.
The roar of the waterfall was close, and Eleanor felt its
spray as her captor took several long strides, once
pausing to steady his balance.

'If you put me down I am capable of walking,' she
snapped.

'Then I trust you have a head for heights. If you value
your life, make no quick moves.'

To her relief he let go of her legs, her foot slipping as she landed on a large, wet boulder. His arm steadied her and he kept it about her waist as he pulled off the blindfold. Her reaction was instinctive, her hand shooting upwards to slap his face. He caught her wrist before it met its target, the green in his eyes turning almost to black with anger.

'Do you fancy plummeting to your death? Trust a woman to put emotion before assessing the danger of her position.'

Her defiant stare bored into his. 'I'll not be bullied into submission. You do not frighten me.'

The spray from the waterfall was flattening the hair to his scalp and spiking his long dark lashes which made his eyes appear an even more startling shade of green. 'It was not my intention to frighten you,' he answered gruffly. 'Had you not better assess your surroundings before you proceed further?'

Eleanor turned away from his contemptuous stare, and was startled to see that she appeared to be on a level with the tree-tops. With a gasp she looked down. The veil of fog parted sufficiently for her to see that she was near the top of a craggy hill-face which fell sharply away to the valley some forty or fifty feet below. She glimpsed the churning white-foamed pool far beneath her fed by the waterfall. Then the scene below her began to revolve, her heart palpitated, and a sweat broke out on her body. She shut her eyes against the dizziness, but was unable to control her breathing, which came in panting gasps. As her knees began to shake, threatening to give way, she was pulled up against her captor's body.

Terrified, she clung to him as the trembling persisted.

'Open your eyes, my lady,' he commanded.

There was no mockery, only concern in his voice, which made her obey him. She swallowed, taking a grip upon her fear. It was humiliating that the man she regarded as an enemy should discover her weakness. She stilled the trembling to a slight quiver and her chin tilted with defiance.

'Do not address me as "My lady". I am a maid-servant.'

'Clearly you have no head for heights.' He supported her with his arms. 'I will not let you fall. It's only a few yards to the cave. Take my hand and I will guide you.'

She shook her head. 'I will never follow you, or in any way be a willing prisoner.' She had expected his anger; instead he regarded her thoughtfully. Something in his expression — the amusement apparent in his face and the assured confidence in his green eyes — told her that he was no ordinary brigand. Had he guessed her true rank? If he had, he made no acknowledgement of her superiority. The man had the affrontery to regard her as his equal.

'My lady, I usually only make a point of repeating myself to imbeciles.' His tone remained challenging. 'And besides, we are both getting unnecessarily wet.'

She had been too angry to notice that the spray from the waterfall had drenched her cloak and water was running down her face from her soaking hair. The horses had disappeared from sight and she realised that she was alone with her captor. Most brigands would have dragged her away by force. In the circumstance he had been extremely patient with her stubbornness. She risked a glance downwards and immediately the dizziness and trembling returned, her limbs paralysing with fear. It galled her to acknowledge it, but she was trapped on this ledge.

He stood calmly, allowing her time to see reason. When he held out his hand for her to take and be led to safety, she took it grudgingly. What choice had she but to follow him?

'You'll be punished for your crimes.' She maintained her defiance.

He shot her a cool, appraising stare. There was a

setness about his mouth which warned her that she would be foolish to provoke him too far.

Once off the ledge the path was easier, and a short distance further on they passed one of his men, burying the steaming horse droppings. They were taking great care that no one learned of their presence in the district. Her captor pushed aside a thick evergreen bush and Eleanor saw the entrance to a hidden cave. Little light penetrated past the first few yards, but she noticed that it was wide enough for two horses to pass side by side. Her captor struck a tinder and held the small flame aloft. To their left the cave curved sharply and at the corner Eleanor saw the distant light of a flambeau.

'Sit over there, my lady.'

She followed the direction of his arm and moved away from him, relieved to be rid of the close proximity of his presence. His commanding assurance disturbed her in a way she found uncomfortable. She remained standing, shivering in the cold atmosphere of the cave, her wet clothes unpleasant against her chilled flesh.

'Have you decided what to do with the wench, Conrad?' one of the men called to his leader.

He ignored the question and, going to his destrier, took a roll from its saddle. Returning to Eleanor, he held out a blanket. 'Take off your wet cloak and doublet and wrap yourself in this.'

'I will take nothing from you.'

He shrugged, the torchlight showing the twist of his full lips as his gaze moved slowly over her. 'When I give an order I expect it to be obeyed. I will not be responsible for your dying of lung fever. If you will not take off your wet clothes then either I or one of my men will do it for you.'

'I'll volunteer for that,' an enthusiastic voice offered.

Her eyes sparked with outrage at discovering herself at such a disadvantage. 'I shall not forget this indignity.'

Snatching the blanket from his hands, she retreated to the darkest corner of the cave. The muffled chuckles of the men kept her rage simmering as she tore off her wet garments, keeping on the damp shirt which clung revealingly to her full breasts. She wrapped the blanket firmly around her and spread her discarded cloak and doublet on to a boulder with little expectation that they would dry.

'When you have finished changing, my lady,' Conrad said, 'come back into the light. Give me your word that you will not try to escape and there will be no need to bind you.'

'You have it.' Eleanor did not hesitate. There was no dishonour in breaking her word to a brigand. She sat on the boulder at the edge of the circle of light, her thoughts dark with retribution. A month locked in her father's deepest dungeon would strip the arrogance from him. The men were huddled in a close ring, deep in debate.

'Your plan must be abandoned, Conrad,' Ned was arguing. He combed his fingers through his dark hair as his agitation mounted and it now stood out in spikes.

'Never.' Conrad was adamant. 'My duty is clear.'

'If, as you say, the wench is the Lady Eleanor, she would have been missed by now,' Ned persisted. 'There'll be the Devil to pay. Soldiers will be all over the place. Even the villagers will be sent out to search for her.'

'That does not alter the reason for my duty here,' Conrad responded with unwarranted heat.

Eleanor studied Conrad. So he had guessed who she was! But the knave still did not show her the deference due her rank. There was a tension in his lithe frame which came from something more complex than a thwarted robbery. It was echoed by the passion in his voice as he spoke. Whatever the danger to himself, Conrad would not be turned from his course. She stamped down a feeling of admiration. He did not deserve it. He was a thief and it was her home he planned to rob.

Her gaze roamed over the group of men, whose clothes

were not patched or worn as one expected of a robber-
band. Neither were their voices rough and uncultured.
A red-haired, freckle-faced lad with the gangling limbs
of an adolescent was handing round a wine-skin. Each
man in turn raised it to their mouths to drink. As the
boy approached Conrad, the leader tipped his head in
Eleanor's direction. The lad paused to pull out a horn
cup from a saddle roll and filled it from the wine-skin.

'My lady.' He knelt on one knee as he presented it to
her, as well trained as any page at Highford.

Eleanor was tempted to refuse, but the admiration in
the lad's face as he smiled at her made her take the cup.
He might prove an ally to help her escape.

'It is not "my lady",' she said softly. 'But thank you
for your consideration. What is your name?'

'Gauthier, *demoiselle*.' A blush spread across his round
cheeks.

'Your manners should be an example to others.' She
smiled, but her voice was brittle with a rebuke aimed at
his leader. 'Are you French, Gauthier? I can hear it in
your accent. In whose household were you trained as a
page?'

'My mother was French, *demoiselle*, but my father was
a friend of Sir——'

'Gauthier, get back here!' Conrad snapped. 'There's
to be no talking with the prisoner. She has a clever
tongue, and by it would seek to trick you into betraying
us.'

Gauthier's freckles disappeared beneath a fiery hue of
shame which covered his smooth cheeks. Feeling guilty
that she had used the well-intentioned boy to that end,
Eleanor smiled at him before he returned to the men.
'Thank you for the drink, Gauthier. I shall remember
your kindness.'

Ned scowled at her and scratched at his beard.
'Conrad, abandon this scheme. It's too dangerous. What
if you're recognised? You'd be playing straight into
Twyneham's hands.'

Eleanor's curiosity pricked. There was more to this than a robbery. Ned made it sound as if Conrad was her father's enemy.

Another man added his voice to the argument. 'At least let us see how matters stand at the castle. Perhaps the wench is the maid-servant she claims to be. Another day will make no difference. There's no reason why a pedlar should be suspected. But I agree that Conrad would be wise to avoid unnecessary recognition.'

Eleanor chewed her lower lip. Who was this Conrad? Had he committed other robberies in the district?

'I cannot afford to delay.' Conrad stood up to pace the cave. 'I give you until midday. No longer. I will honour my vow to Sir Lionel.'

'Perhaps there is no risk!' Ned stood up and gestured towards Eleanor. 'If that is truly the Lady Eleanor, she will be our hostage against your safe return.'

'No. I forbid it.' Conrad rounded on his companion. 'She is here merely to prevent her raising the alarm against us. If I am taken, she goes free. I want your word on it, Ned.'

The older scowled. 'You have it.'

Throughout their exchange Eleanor had searched her memory to make sense of the elusive facts nagging at her mind. Her eyes widened as the recall came to her. Sir Lionel D'Arton had been the owner of Highford before her father. He had a son, Conrad. It could be no coincidence—this Conrad was no other than Conrad D'Arton. He was not just her enemy but the enemy of the crown. Sir Lionel D'Arton had remained loyal to the Lancastrian cause throughout the years of King Edward's reign. It was plain to Eleanor that the villagers resented her father as their absentee overlord. Many still saw the D'Artons as their true masters. From her maid Griselda, who was a born gossip, Eleanor had learnt a great deal about the former owners of Highford. If she recalled correctly, Conrad had been sent as a page to the household of Jasper Tudor, who was uncle to Henry

Tudor, the Earl of Richmond. Later Conrad had shared Richmond's exile on the Continent rather than live in England once King Richard came to the throne.

Rumour spoke of Richmond raising an army against King Richard. D'Arton, like all Lancastrians, would believe that Richmond was his rightful sovereign. Had not Henry VI proclaimed him his successor when Henry Tudor was a boy of thirteen? That was before the Yorkist King Edward had defeated Henry VI and won the throne for himself.

From the inscription on the D'Arton tombs in Highford church, Eleanor knew that Sir Lionel's wife, Elizabeth, had died a few months before Highford was lost to the family. Griselda had informed her of that and more. Elizabeth had been thirty when one night she had complained of violent stomach pains and taken to her bed. She had died the next day, delirious with fever. Conrad had been a boy of six when Highford was confiscated from his family. That made him twenty-six. The vague recognition she had felt on first seeing him was because of his close resemblance to the D'Arton effigies decorating their tombs. The bone-structure of their faces, slender nose and square-bearded chin were all the same.

Had Conrad D'Arton, then, come as a spy to Highford to learn of any recent change in its defences? Did he later intend to lay siege to her home? Was he aware of the existence of the secret tunnel? She needed that way of escape left open if she was to continue to visit Daniel. Somehow she must devise a way of securing the door by the bridge.

The men were leaving the cave and she had been so lost in her thoughts that she had missed the end of their conversation. Conrad remained. Her first impulse was to taunt him that she knew his identity, but she thought better of it. It might be a powerful weapon she could use later. Why throw away the chance out of chagrin?

'Are you hungry, my lady?' He came towards her and

held out some dried meat. 'It's not very appetising, but I had not planned to entertain a beautiful lady.'

Eleanor ignored both the food and the taunt. She was too tense and angry to eat. 'I'm not hungry.'

He continued to regard her calmly. 'I take no pleasure in holding you captive. If it were possible I would let you go.'

'Yet you debase your knighthood by your actions.'

'I am no knight, but squire.'

'And by your conduct forever condemned to remain so.'

The torchlight threw the contours of his face into light and dark relief, but her words had struck a vulnerable spot. By the age of six and twenty most of King Richard's supporters had been knighted. Was Henry waiting until his men proved their worth in battle before he exercised his right as Earl of Richmond to knight his followers?

The chestnut destrier began to paw the ground with increasing agitation. Conrad looked across at it and frowned. When the horse continued to stamp its front leg he crossed the cave to examine it. The moment Conrad's attention was on the horse, Eleanor began to edge towards the cave entrance. She heard the squire speak to calm the destrier as he ran an expert hand along its leg and lifted its hoof.

Eleanor had reached the corner of the cave and could see the entrance ahead when Conrad exclaimed, 'Solomon, you've picked a bad time to throw a shoe.'

She threw a swift look in his direction and saw Conrad stroking the destrier's neck. Then, throwing off the cumbersome blanket, she ran for the entrance. There was an indistinct curse from the man as her escape was detected. She was reaching to push aside the bush which blocked the entrance when Conrad was upon her, his arm circling her waist to swing her round to face him.

'You gave me your word you would not escape,' he accused.

'My word, forced from me by a brigand, is meaningless. It is my duty to escape and alert the guards that there are outlaws in the district.'

'There'll be no escape for you until I say so.'

'My father will kill you for this.'

His brow lifted knowingly, infuriating her further. 'So you are the Lady Eleanor, not her hand-maiden.'

Too late she realised her error. 'If you think you can hold me to ransom, you're mistaken. I would kill myself before I allow that. My father will have your life. The only title you will win by your deeds this day is that of Sir Outlaw.'

A pulse throbbing in the side of his neck showed her that he was aware of the seriousness of his situation. His gaze travelled mockingly over her male attire. 'For you to leave the castle unescorted, and in such disguise, meant you did so against your father's orders. Take care of what you would accuse me. It is your reputation which also is at stake. . .my lady page. You have caused me considerable inconvenience.'

His nearness disturbed her. While she was angry with him, she was aware that his handsome looks had a way of undermining her fury. She had never been in such close proximity to any man—the younger guards at Highford always kept a respectful distance. He was too self-assured, his presence too commanding, and when he looked at her as he was now it brought a curling of fear unravelling through her veins. No, not fear, but something beyond her experience, something equally frightening since it was outside of her control.

Her retort was halted by the sound of horses' hoofs on the path by the waterfall. Conrad tensed and drew her further away from the entrance.

'Don't make any sound.'

She pulled back, resisting, and saw through the dense foliage of the cave entrance a splash of blue and white livery—her father's colours. The castle guard were searching for her. She opened her mouth to scream for help. The cry gurgled ineffectively in her throat, the sound stifled by the pressure of Conrad's hand clamped across her mouth. He dragged her, kicking and wriggling, further back into the cave.

'Be silent and stop fighting me!'

Eleanor continued to struggle, kicking out at his shins. He grunted with pain and, taking his palm from her mouth, pinned her arms to her side with his hands. He pushed her body against the wall, the pressure of his thighs preventing her from kicking out. As she opened her mouth to scream, his mouth came down over hers, capturing her shout so that it was no more than an outraged squeak. It was a kiss without passion, meant only to silence her. Outside was her hope of escape. She tried to twist her head away, her body writhing against him, seeking any means to be free of his hold.

Then subtly the kiss changed. The mouth covering hers gentled, moving persuasively in a way that drew the breath from her. It was her first kiss and she was unprepared for the devastating effect it had upon her senses. She should be revolted that her captor so abused her, but the warmth of his lips pervaded her mouth and, even as her body fought him, her mind whirled at the pleasure encompassing her. Her lips tingled with sensation, moving in response to his mastery. The taste of his breath was like honey and she was drunk upon its sweet nectar. Their bodies were fused from mouth to thighs, her soft curves subdued by hard masculine muscle. The heat of his body burned through the linen of her shirt as his kiss deepened with hungry possession.

Against her will, her body moved sinuously within his embrace, the delicious tingling spreading from her lips to consume her entire flesh. When his arms loosened their grip to hold her in a tender embrace, her hands no longer fought him, but played over the firm muscle of his back. the wondrous magic of this, her first kiss, robbed her of reason. The guards outside were forgotten as her mind became captivated by the intensity of her blossoming sensuality. The soft moan of surrender rising to her throat startled her back to reality.

She dragged her mouth away, her eyes rounded with shock at her wanton response. 'How dare you so abuse me?'

He stepped back from her. 'I but sought to silence your scream. The soldiers have gone now.'

His words might disparage what had passed between them, but the huskiness in his voice betrayed his desire for her.

'My lady, permit me to escort you to your quarters.' He bowed, his eyes sparkling with amusement as he made a sweeping gesture with his arm to indicate the rear of the cave.

Eleanor glowered at him. 'Just take care you keep away from me.'

'This is the second time you sought to flee so that I might catch you. I begin to think that you enjoy my embrace.' He subjected her to a mocking stare. 'Women who act as hoydens must expect to be treated as such.'

'Just as men who act as outlaws and abductors must expect to be hanged for their crimes.'

'Would you truly see me swinging from Highford's gibbet?' He put out a hand to brush his fingers along her cheek.

She jerked back from his touch, but was manoeuvred so that she was again pressed against the cave wall. She braced herself against another invasion of her senses by his kiss. Her pulses were racing. She did not believe he could allow her to live if he suspected she knew his identity. But she refused to let him see the fear she felt, and her eyes glinted with anger. But Conrad did not kiss her; instead his fingers traced the outline of her jaw and then his hand fell to his side.

'So proud and so defiant.' His gaze as he studied her upturned face was no longer mocking, but serious. 'Believe me, I mean you no harm. I am here for a reason and my duty must be done. You will go free and unharmed once the task is completed. Until then I can allow you to do nothing which will jeopardise my plans.'

Eleanor gasped as his eyes narrowed and became cold. He turned his face towards the cave entrance, listening for signs that the patrol from the castle had doubled back. His profile was hawk-like, strong, but handsomely etched. The rugged jawline showed a man of firm convictions and resolution, but his mouth held a sensitivity that made some of her fear of him dissipate. He was not a cruel man.

She stared up into his face, seeking to assess his character. At whatever cost to herself, she would thwart those plans. Why, then, as she held his stare which seemed to penetrate into the depths or her soul, did a thrill of anticipation run down her spine? Taking a deep breath, she fought the suffocating sensation caused by his nearness which threatened to steal the strength from her limbs.

'Then we are enemies.'

She pulled away from his loosened hold and walked to the back of the cave. Refusing to look at him, she sat on a boulder. The chill damp of the cave penetrated her thin linen shirt and she began to shiver.

He picked up the blanket and draped it over her huddled form. 'Yes, Lady Eleanor Twyneham, we are indeed enemies.'

CHAPTER THREE

THE morning hours crawled by on leaden feet. Every minute of them Eleanor was on her guard against any untoward move by Conrad. He made no attempt to touch her. But his vigilance as he sharpened his dagger on a small whetstone was as keen as hers. Any movement she made which could precipitate another dash for freedom was instantly halted under the glare of his watchful eyes.

The cold in the cave penetrated the blanket and Eleanor stood up to pace the floor, rubbing her hands along her arms to kindle some warmth to her body. Conrad moved to lounge against the wall and block off her retreat from the cave. She watched him with increasing hostility. Throughout the morning he tried to draw her into conversation, which she suspected was meant to glean what information he could about the castle. For his pains she had subjected him to a frosty silence.

He remained undeterred. 'Your silence speaks as loud as words,' he taunted. 'That you were out of the castle before the portcullis was raised means you used the tunnel. But where were you going? And why? The track leads to the priory. What could possibly draw you there, disguised and in so secret a manner? Yet I have heard that you visit the priory regularly.'

At her surprised gasp, he grinned. 'I know much of you, Lady Eleanor, and of the events surrounding Highford. I know that, while Sir Cedric is like a leech sucking dry Highford and its people by extortionate taxes, you are held in respect by the villagers. You saved many lives last summer when a fever struck the village. You tended the ailing, risking your own life to save theirs. I heard you sold a gold girdle to buy extra blankets to be distributed among the sick.'

Eleanor's lip curled in contempt. 'Do you think I would have let those people die and do nothing?'

'Sir Cedric would.'

'That's not true.'

Eleanor defended her father, but it galled her to admit that Conrad was right. A messenger had been sent to Sir Cedric when the fever had first struck, but they had received no reply.

'And there was the matter of the grain you dispensed to the starving last winter,' Conrad continued, his voice deepening with respect. 'Is it true that in reward for your generosity Sir Cedric made you a virtual prisoner in the castle?'

Eleanor shrugged. She had borne the punishment with her usual fortitude and, though her soul cried out for the freedom a morning on horseback would bring, her confinement was a small price to pay for the lives she had saved.

'A lady of modesty and sensitivity,' Conrad commented.

'I did my duty.' She dismissed his compliment, though the admiration in his eyes had an unnerving effect upon her senses. All morning she had been aware that he was studying her closely. He was doing so again now. There was an intensity in his expression which made her tremble and her heart pound a frenzied rhythm. Also it disturbed her that he knew so much about her life and she knew virtually nothing of him. She shivered, acutely aware that she was his prisoner, and that since he had kissed her there was a tension in him, a throbbing awareness of her as a desirable woman. He had no cause to be charitable towards her family.

She ran her tongue over her dry lips, which were still tender from the passion of his kiss. A man less honourable would not have hesitated to be avenged upon Sir Cedric by ravishing her. That he desired her yet mas-

tered the temptation to dishonour her made her feel less
vulnerable. The knowledge did not reassure her. He was
too much in command, too self-possessed and too handsome for her own peace of mind.

There was a fall of loose pebbles from the cave
entrance and Conrad drew his sword in readiness to fight
if necessary. When Ned and two other men appeared, he
lowered it.

'A word, Conrad,' Ned said, retreating several yards
out of range of Eleanor's hearing.

Other men returned from their scouting and joined in
the discussion. Several times an angry look from one of
them was directed at Eleanor. Conrad appeared to be
placating them. With a final curt command, Conrad left
them to approach Eleanor. His expression was grave.

'Gauthier and Ralph have been taken by the guards.
Gauthier is barely sixteen. The brute Le Gros had them
flogged. They told him nothing before they collapsed
unconscious. Twyneham picked Le Gros for his cruelty.
He knew the people would never love him, so he sought
to rule by terror. They will be beaten again at day-break
tomorrow and every day until they talk.'

'Then leave the district and release me.' Eleanor was
appalled at Le Gros's brutality. Without her to countermand his authority, he would inflict suffering on any
who opposed his rule. 'Only I can stop Le Gros. I
promise that your men will be set free. Bertram Le Gros
will kill them if he thinks they know where I am.'

'I cannot let you go free until my task is done.'

'You would condemn your men to die!' Eleanor was
disappointed that he was capable of such an act.

'No. I mean to release them. With your help I can do
that and achieve my aim in being here.'

Eleanor folded her arms across her chest, her eyes
narrowing with censure. 'I will not help my father's
enemy. I know you are Conrad D'Arton. I will not be
tricked into allowing you either to rob or take possession
of Highford.'

He showed no surprise that she had recognised him. His face hardened and his mouth thinned to a stern line. 'I did not come to Highford for those reasons.'

'Did you not?' She put all the contempt she could muster into her tone. 'I'm not a fool, Conrad D'Arton. Why else would you be here other than to steal back Highford, which you must still regard as your inheritance?'

The tension in the cave sparked between them. The torchlight accentuated the hard set of his features, making him look as ruthless as the brigand she had at first thought him.

'I will regain Highford. But not by force of arms, which will solve nothing while Richard still rules England. My victory would be a short one and see my head on a pike on London Bridge as a traitor.'

'Then why are you here?'

The feral light in his eyes made her take an involuntary step back. Apart from the kiss he had forced upon her, he had treated her with respect. Now there was a coldness in his eyes which unnerved her. There was a sinister hatred in his voice whenever he spoke of Sir Cedric and a softening when Highford was mentioned. He spoke of the castle as one would of an unattainable lover. Overriding that was a dark, unsettling force which drove him. It was like a shield he wielded against the world. There was a ruthlessness in him which was dangerous, but there was something else, which in itself was intriguing, and also frightening. . .

A shudder passed through his figure and he rubbed a hand across his jaw as he studied her. 'I'm here to retrieve some property which belonged to my family. A chalice and reliquary needed to perform the rites at my father's funeral.'

'There is no reliquary in our chapel.'

'Because it is hidden away. It was only used at special services.' He averted his face from her candid stare and she saw the unnatural brightness of tears in his eyes.

'Since my father could not be buried at my mother's side, his dying wish was that his heart would be placed in Highford church.'

Whatever excuses Eleanor had been expecting, it was certainly not that. She was moved by the poignancy of it. But was it the truth, or just a ruse? The pain on Conrad's face told her he was not lying.

'You will be killed if you are discovered.' She was drawn to reply. Despite her antagonism, she felt her emotions stir with admiration for this man who risked so much to honour his father's dying request.

A smile touched his lips, changing the sternness of his countenance to a rugged handsomeness which caused her heart to give an odd twist. No longer angry with him, she unfolded her arms and they rested loosely at her sides.

'Eleanor, the castle is in an uproar and the countryside is swarming with soldiers looking for you. My original plan was to enter Highford as a pedlar and during the night visit the church and honour my vow to my father. I intended to leave as soon as the portcullis was opened the next morning. Now I need you with me to gain entrance.'

She shook her head. 'I understand, even sympathise with your plight, but you ask too much. You are the last person to whom I could reveal the whereabouts of the tunnel. Let me go free and I give you my word——' she smiled with wry remembrance '—the word of one noble to another, that I will not reveal the events of this morning. I will ensure that your father's heart is buried at Highford.'

The admiration in his eyes as he studied her earnest expression increased the strange palpitation which affected her heartbeat.

'Your offer is generous, Lady Eleanor. But I must personally honour my vow. And I came also to reclaim the chalice and reliquary. As to the tunnel, I know of its existence—though my father suspected it might have caved in after so many years of neglect. Your appearance on the road before the portcullis was raised proves otherwise.'

'The knowledge will serve you ill. When I return to Highford the tunnel will be sealed against a later attack. It will be no small sacrifice. I value the freedom it allows me.'

His gaze travelled insolently over her bristling figure. 'A dangerous freedom, my lady. Had it been other than my men in the woods, fate might not have treated you so kindly.'

'You call abduction a kindness?' she retaliated. 'It is an unknightly occupation, sir.'

He bowed his head and looked sideways at her through long dark lashes in a way that made her pulse quicken. 'It was necessary, and not without its rewards.'

The reference to his kiss brought a hot flush to her cheeks. Even now her mouth tingled from the imprint of his lips, and the memory of the heavy-lidded gaze he had afterwards subjected her to sent shivers running through her.

She flinched when he put a hand on her shoulder.

'It is not fear of me which makes you start so,' he said in a soft voice for her ears alone. 'What began as my need to subdue you became a pleasure shared by us both.'

'You presume too much, sir,' she blazed, her anger rising.

'It was an experience I shall treasure always.'

'Conrad D'Arton, your flattery does not impress me,' she answered with chilling rebuke. 'And it is obvious that you seek to coerce me into helping you. Do you think I would allow my father's enemy into Highford?'

'Alone I can do nothing. And I give you my word that I have no thought at present but to honour my vow to Sir Lionel, and rescue my men.'

There was no pleading in his deep voice and she had not expected any, but it carried a note which struck right at her heart. 'It's too dangerous. Release me. When I return to Highford I promise Gauthier and Ralph will be freed after their injuries have been tended.'

He looked at her with deepening respect. 'There is still the other matter to be dealt with.'

She held out her hand. 'Give me the casket and I will ensure that your father's wishes are carried out with due deference and ceremony.'

'That I must do for myself.' His tone was implacable.

'But the risks are too great.' Inexplicably she found her antagonism wavering, and was almost willing him to succeed.

'There is a way. It requires first a truce between us. We must trust each other.' The coaxing in his voice undermined her hostility. He was regarding her in a way which bound them in a conspiracy. A private bond. She shook her head to displace the spell he was invoking.

'How can I trust my father's enemy?'

He took her hand and raised it to his lips. 'On my father's memory I swear that my only reason for entering Highford is as I have said.' He smiled, compelling her to do his bidding. 'Will you not trust me? My life is in your hands. At any time you could call the guards and have me arrested.'

'The idea is insane, Conrad,' Ned protested. 'How can you consider trusting a Twyneham?'

Conrad glared at his friend. 'I trust a woman who lost her freedom because she would spare her people from starvation. The Lady Eleanor is worthy of my trust.'

The statement filled her with a heady elation, but it was instantly tempered. Her life had been sheltered. She had been told that life at court was full of intrigue and double values. All her instincts cried out to trust this man, but she could not forget he was her enemy. Was he playing on her naïveté? He would learn that she was not so easily duped.

'You ask much. Once inside the castle you would be free to roam at will. You could wait until dark, then

overpower the gate-ward and let your men into the
castle. The advantage of this truce is all yours. Why
should I trust you?'

He tipped her chin up with his forefinger, his face
close to hers as he whispered softly, 'Because I would die
rather than dishonour a vow to so courageous a woman.'

'Fine words, pretty enough to turn many a maid's
head.'

He smiled, his eyes crinkling with laughter as he
teased, 'But not yours, my lady? You have intelligence
to match your beauty. But I spoke the truth.'

She gazed deep into his unwavering stare. His green
eyes challenged her to obey his will, but there was no
slyness in their depths; his words were honestly spoken.

'My future and life are yours to control. It was
ordained when you spied on us in the forest. A word
from you about your abduction and I would be discred-
ited as a squire and would be barred from attaining my
knighthood.'

She wavered under such smooth persuasion.

'Do I ask so much, Eleanor? The right to pay homage
at my mother's tomb and perform the dying wish of my
father. If I were fortunate enough to love my wife as Sir
Lionel loved my mother, I would never rest if our bodies
were parted in death.'

How could such a speech fail to move her young heart?
She blinked rapidly against a tear forming at the corner
of her eye. To refuse him would be unforgivable. The
magnetism of his closeness was overpowering her will.
His hand moved from her chin to rest on her shoulder
and he squeezed it gently. 'I would be forever in your
debt, sweet Eleanor.'

'We will go alone to Highford. Your men will remain
here?'

'Yes.'

'And how are we to explain my absence? When I
appear dressed like this and in your company Le Gros
could well confine me to my room to await my father's

punishment. As for yourself, you could be thrown into the dungeon. I have been missing for several hours. There is the question of my reputation and honour.'

'Your disguise will be explained by whatever reason you chose to leave Highford in such a manner.'

Eleanor set her chin stubbornly. 'You ask too much.'

'Do you then seek to protect a secret lover?' A cool reserve entered his voice.

'Indeed not!'

'Then why the need for secrecy?'

'That is my affair.'

'Is it worth risking the life of Gauthier and Ralph?' Conrad snorted in disgust.

Eleanor's eyes flashed with returning anger. 'I did not place them in danger—you did.' Even as she voiced her defiance, she knew she would not allow the two men to suffer further at her steward's hands. She could not tell Le Gros of the tunnel. She eyed Conrad disdainfully. 'I will tell the guards I had a need to escape confinement. That is all.'

'An unjust confinement. It is no wonder the people of Highford have taken you to their hearts,' he said with such conviction that the last of Eleanor's reservations crumbled.

'Sir Cedric would disagree with you.' She gave a dry laugh. 'My father saw my actions as wilful and disobedient.'

'It took courage to defy him.' The respect in his eyes was an accolade Eleanor prized.

'I trust I will never bow to injustice or fear, when the lives of others depend upon my action.' She dismissed the incident as unimportant; it was simply the code of honour she lived by. Her expression sobered as she stared at him with returning hauteur. 'You asked for my trust and I give it. Should your story prove false and your motives at Highford be dishonourable, I will denounce you. Even if you escape, I shall not rest until justice is served upon you. Do not be swayed that I am

young and a woman. However long it takes, and by
whatever means in my power, I shall see justice done.
That I most solemnly vow.'

Conrad took her dagger from his belt and held it
out to her. As her fingers closed around it, he raised
her hand to his lips. 'I will not betray your nobility
of spirit, dear lady. Rather I shall be forever in your
debt.'

The touch of his mouth upon her hand sent a spear of
sensation through her arm, and a curious ache pierced
her breast. Unsettled, she gave him a nervous smile.
'Something must be done about your appearance. If I
recognised you from the effigies on your ancestors'
tombs, so will others. They were all bearded like yourself. The older villagers who note the family resemblance
may not betray you, but the guard will.'

A light came into his eyes, the green depths flecked
with gold as he regarded her with admiration and
respect. 'You are a worthy ally, my lady.' He rubbed his
hand across his jaw and called over his shoulder. 'A
razor, someone. I will rid myself of this.'

Ned laughed. 'The wench commands you like a wife,
my friend. Why not keep her captive and compromise
her reputation? Then wed the woman and Highford will
be yours.'

Conrad rounded on him, his face white with fury.
'When I choose a bride it will be with honour. Highford
will be mine, without having to taint my heirs with
Twyneham blood.'

The insult goaded Eleanor beyond caution. She struck
out in anger and without thought of the consequences.
Her palm stung as it slapped Conrad's bearded jaw. At
the look of astonishment on his face, which transformed
instantly to rage, she blanched, but refused to give
ground.

'Conceited oaf! I would plunge a dagger in my breast
rather than wed any damned Lancastrian traitor, and
most especially a D'Arton.'

Her shoulders were gripped and from the look of fury glittering in his eyes she thought he was going to strike her. Her head went back—proud, contemptuous and defiant. The anger faded from his face, replaced by a look so profound that Eleanor's heart contracted.

'You've met your match with her, Conrad.' Ned chuckled.

Suddenly Conrad pulled her to him, crushing her mouth against his in a long, domineering embrace. Her senses reeled from the intensity of it.

There was a guffaw from several of Conrad's men and one observed, 'There's no woman alive who can get the better of Conrad.'

The words returned Eleanor to sanity and she strained away from him, outraged and furious. He held her fast, his voice a low, threatening growl. 'So shame me again before my men, and you will regret it.'

'You shamed me!' she hissed. 'So much for the gratitude of a D'Arton. You can forget about entering Highford. . .unless it is in chains.'

Abruptly, he released her, and as she stumbled away, her eyes wild with fury, she scrubbed the back of her hand across her mouth to erase the distasteful imprint of his kiss.

'Ha!' Ned slapped his thigh. 'More than a match for you, my friend. I would not like to be in a man's boots if he challenged you thus.'

Eleanor was unrepentant, but wary of Conrad's next move. To her surprise he bowed reverently to her.

'Lady Eleanor did not deserve the insult implied by my words.' He no longer sounded angry, but his stiff manner was far from conciliatory. 'My tongue played me traitor. It will take me more than a morning spent in the company of a beautiful and courageous woman to forget a lifetime of hatred towards all who bear the name Twyneham. I ask your pardon, Lady Eleanor.'

'It is given,' she responded gracefully, but remained on her guard. It would take more than sweet words and

a handsome face to wipe those heated insults from her
memory. But she conceded it took a rare man to own he
was in the wrong before his companions. His apology
did not come from weakness, but from the strength of
his own invincibility. She turned away, dismissing him,
and kept her back to the company, as Conrad shaved
himself and the men jested with him. She was not
deceived by their light-hearted banter; there was an edge
to every man's voice which told her they feared for their
leader's life. Some made no secret of trying to dissuade
him. Conrad returned the banter with like, and their
warnings with affectionate but firm repudiation.

'You will stay hidden in the cave until I return,' he
ordered. 'Except for Ned. Solomon has cast a shoe. He
will have to be taken to the next village to be shod.'

The men's voices droned on and Eleanor tried to shut
her mind to the dangers should Conrad be recognised at
Highford. Such devotion to his father's dying wishes
despite the obvious danger was estimable. Yet from what
she had come to know of his character, she would expect
no less. There was much about Conrad D'Arton which
fascinated and intrigued her.

Therein lay another danger. Was he some necroman-
cer that he so bedevilled her? One moment she hated
him, the next. . .by a look she was cast into confusion,
her heart and pulses racing. The memory of his kisses
mocked her self-imposed indifference. Her body
betrayed her by the tingling excitement his presence
roused, even in the heat of a quarrel with the man. She
must stop thinking of him as a man, remember only that
he was her family's sworn enemy. He was not and never
could be someone she could fall in love with.

'My lady, your own doublet is still wet and you will
take a chill if you wear it. You had better wear this.'
Conrad came to stand in front of her and pressed a
supple leather hunting tunic into her hands. His consideration touched her. His moods and actions were
unpredictable.

Murmuring her thanks, she pulled the leather tunic over her head. It smelt of horses and of the musky scent of the man himself, which was not unpleasant. A mare was led forward, loaded with a wicker pannier containing the pedlar's wares and also a beribboned and scuffed lute. Conrad had taken no chances with being denied entrance to Highgrove. Only rarely were pedlars not admitted, for they were carriers of news and gossip. Also the entertainment of a minstrel with new songs was seized upon.

'Come, my lady, I will escort you to Highford.'

Ned led the horse down the steep waterfall slope and Conrad took Eleanor's hand. 'Don't look down, my lady. Look at me and I will guide you.'

She put her trust in him. Whenever the dizziness from her fear of heights threatened to ovewhelm her, Conrad tightened his hold and smiled reassuringly, his voice encouraging. 'You are doing well. Your courage will not fail you.'

She forced a tremulous smile. 'It is so silly. So very foolish of me.'

'I've known stalwart men paralysed and incapable of movement as this fear gripped them. Some fell to their deaths, their hysteria was so great. Others sweated and gibbered like children, paralysed with terror. It takes a very special courage to be so affeared and to face it.'

The admiration in his voice gave her strength to master the inner quaking which threatened to turn her limbs to water. The nausea subsided beneath the compulsion of his encouraging stare. With each step she combated the dizziness and sickness. And with each step she felt her trust in him building, forging a bond which would never be entirely severed, no matter the extent of the enmity between their families. When her feet were finally upon level ground her relief was so immense that she threw her arms around him. Her shaky laugh that she had conquered her fear won an answering response from him.

His arms closed around her and his breath was warm against her cold cheek. 'You are a remarkable woman, Lady Eleanor.'

She leaned back in his arms and looked up at him. In the full sunlight she was struck afresh by his arresting face. Without the beard which had given it a stern severity, his handsome looks stole beneath her reserve, captivating, his touch causing a thrill of pleasure to heat her body. He looked younger and, despite the danger he was soon to face, carefree. She touched his clean-shaven jaw. 'That's so much nicer. The beard made you look formidable and much older.'

Self-consciously he rubbed his chin. 'I shall remember that whenever I need to impress someone with my ancient and venerable wisdom.'

They laughed together and as Conrad stared down at her he was aware that with laughter replacing the usual anger in her face she was breathstealingly beautiful. Her courage stirred him and he was startled at the intensity with which he desired her. Her lips parted as she recovered her breath, which her fear of heights had stripped from her. They beckoned, inviting to be kissed, and he was sorely tempted. He checked the impulse. The memory of her response to his first kiss was too recent. The magnitude of her passion had fired his blood. He had not thought it possible for a woman to rouse him as this one did. She was a diversion he could not afford. Her Twyneham blood was a barrier too great to be surmounted. For that he could neither forget, nor forgive.

He moved away and as he lifted her on to the mare's saddle he saw the puzzlement and disappointment in her eyes. It was madness that even for a moment he had allowed her beauty and feminine charms to slide beneath his guard. She was the enemy. The old resentment flared that he must steal like a thief into Highford to pay reverence at his mother's tomb. He forgot Eleanor's benevolence and regarded her solely in the light of an adversary. Often he had envisaged himself entering Highford as its master, proudly at the head of his followers. Always in his mind he had seen his people lining the roadside to cheer him for rescuing them from Twyneham's tyranny. Now the bitterness of reality tightened his throat. He walked at the side of Twyneham's daughter, dressed as a pedlar, his safety dependent upon her goodwill.

The change in Conrad was so stark that Eleanor rode in silence. They were within sight of Highford when a troop of soldiers rode them down and surrounded them. Beneath his domed helmet, Le Gros's heavy face was red with outrage; his small, cruel eyes under thick prickly brows roamed disparagingly over Eleanor's figure.

'Well, at least you are safe,' he thundered. 'What is the meaning of your scandalous attire?'

Eleanor's face burned with humiliation that Conrad had witnessed the disrespect shown her by Le Gros.

'You forget yourself, Le Gros. In my father's absence I am mistress of Highford. I'm not answerable to you.'

'We shall see what Sir Cedric has to say about that!' There was a lecherous leer in his eyes as he threatened. 'You were placed in my charge.'

'A duty you failed to perform.' The steward disgusted her, but she knew better than to antagonise him unnecessarily. He was capable of turning his wrath upon an innocent victim. 'Sir Cedric will hold you responsible for my misconduct. Your punishment will be greater than mine.' With a conscious effort she sweetened her tone. 'The incident could however be forgotten. I have come to no harm. There is no need for Sir Cedric to learn that you were careless in your duties.'

Le Gros glowered at Eleanor. 'Why did you leave the castle in such disguise? Answer me that, my lady.' Le Gros spoke her title with heavy sarcasm.

'I was tired of being treated like a prisoner in my own home. Is it so surprising I felt the need to walk free for an hour? I lost my bearings in the fog and fell down a steep bank. It left me shaken. Then, realising how foolish I had been to leave the castle without an escort, I began to panic. I lost my way. Fortunately this pedlar came upon me in my distress and said he knew the way to Highford.'

Le Gros fixed Conrad with an accusing glare. 'If you have laid a finger upon the Lady Eleanor. . .'

'The man treated me with the respect and courtesy due my rank,' Eleanor declared. 'Unlike yourself, Le Gros. I believe an apology is in order, unless you would rather Sir Cedric learned of the disrespect to which I am subjected.'

Le Gros looked about to burst a blood-vessel. But her threat to report his insolence to Sir Cedric took some of the belligerence from his voice. 'Your pardon, my lady. It was concern that you had been harmed which made me speak so hastily. How was it you were not discovered sooner?'

'I wondered that myself,' Eleanor bluffed. 'It is past midday. I had expected to be found before this.'

Le Gros's eyes glinted savagely. 'How did you get out?'

He reached forward and grabbed Eleanor's wrist in a bruising hold. She saw Conrad tense. Fearful lest he was about to destroy his disguise as a humble pedlar by defending her from the steward's brutality, she reacted before Conrad betrayed himself. 'Every castle has its secret exit. I discovered one some weeks ago. It is impossible for me to tell you where it is.' She spoke with a cool hauteur, putting him firmly in his place as a servant and she the mistress. 'That is information only the Lord of Highford can be party to. . .not his lapdog. If you have finished proving your superior strength upon my wrist, I would like to have it released.'

From the corner of her eyes she saw Conrad bow his head to hide the amusement tugging at his mouth. The steward had paled considerably at her rebuff. Though she had won this round, she knew she had made a dangerous enemy. Once released, she kicked the mare forward, dismissing Le Gros. She called back over her shoulder, 'The pedlar is to be rewarded. He has many tales that I would hear. He will attend me in the solar.'

Leaving Conrad to follow on foot, she urged the mare to a canter. Briefly acknowledging the chorus of greetings and cries of concern from the castle attendants upon her arrival, she ran straight to her room. There she called for a bath to be prepared.

'What possessed you to sneak out of the castle like a thief, my lady?' Griselda set her fleshy jowls wobbling as she shook her head. Her vast bulk was being heaved around the chamber as she set out the gown and head-dress Eleanor had chosen to wear. 'Le Gros whipped two strangers, thinking they'd done you harm, and had them thrown in the dungeon.'

'They must be taken to the infirmary. Ask Eadgyth the wise-woman to tend them. I will go to them as soon as I am dressed.'

'There's no need for that, my lady. It will not be a pretty sight. Eadgyth can tend them well enough.'

Eleanor was no stranger to the infirmary and had long ago learnt all that Eadgyth could teach her in the ways of healing. She felt responsible for Gauthier's welfare. The boy had been kind to her, and she felt guilty that the events set in motion by her escaping the castle had led to him being whipped. But had she been dutiful and remained confined within Highford's walls she would never have met Conrad.

The thought brought a soft sigh to her lips and she nestled lower into the bath. An image of Conrad formed in her mind and she found herself smiling for no apparent reason. At the thrill of excitement which her memory aroused, she sat up with a jolt, splashing the jasmine-scented water over the floor. Conrad had told her she was beautiful. Was she? she wondered. She had never given the matter any thought before. She turned

to Griselda to ask her maid's opinion and realised the
vanity behind such a request. What did it matter what
he thought of her? He was her enemy. It was perilous,
even for an instant, to forget that the truce between them
was only temporary.

Fearing that if Conrad was left alone for long he would
take too much interest in the castle's defences, she
stepped out of the water and wrapped the towel Griselda
held out to her around her body.

'The pedlar is to entertain us with stories and songs. I
will receive him in the solar. It is months since I have
been so diverted.'

Griselda rubbed the towel across Eleanor's back. 'I
warrant today is not the first time you've escaped the
castle,' she announced. 'There was always a glow of
mischief about you when I returned from visiting my
sister. And today, there is something more.' Griselda's
expression was disapproving. 'This pedlar-cum-minstrel
would not be young and handsome, would he, my lady?
You are looking too pleased with yourself. It's time Sir
Cedric found you a husband. A strong man in both mind
and body to curb your wildness. But not so young — he
will be charmed around your scheming finger.'

'I suppose the minstrel is young and for his humble
origins not uncomely,' Eleanor said as she pulled her silk
chemise over her head. 'Dress me quickly, Griselda. I
must first visit the infirmary before the pedlar attends
me.'

She fidgeted while Griselda worked at her usual pon-
derous gait. Any exertion shortened the maid's breath.
In the last five years, after her husband had been killed
by a wild boar, the maid had taken solace in food. At
forty, folds of fat had overtaken her beauty. Her once
cheerful nature had become soured and the only time
her eyes lost their antagonism towards the world was
when she gazed upon her mistress. Even then her tongue
could still hold its bitter sting.

'The pedlar must be handsome indeed, if you intend

to wear your best gown.' Griselda snorted as she laced
the front of the lilac brocade bodice, its low neck
trimmed by a wide band of purple velvet. 'I would have
thought the elegance of this head-dress was out of place
for the infirmary.'

Griselda held up the pearl-encrusted cylindrical head-
dress and fixed it over Eleanor's braided hair. 'Looks to
me like you intend to impress this lowly pedlar. All
women like to test their charms and beauty on a handsome man, but no good will come of it, my lady.'

'Who am I supposed to try my wiles upon?' Eleanor
quipped. 'Ranulf the deer-hound?'

Eleanor went to the infirmary before attending Conrad
in the solar. At the door, the tiny grey-haired figure of
Eadgyth put out a bony, chapped hand to stop her
entering. 'My lady, 'tis not a sight for you. Le Gros
made pulp of the young lad's back.'

'I am to blame for their beating and I will see to their
welfare,' Eleanor replied.

She stood at the foot of the first bed and stared down
at Gauthier, who was lying on his stomach. A light gauze
covered with balm was laid over his back. In several
places long red lines showed the whip cuts which still
oozed blood. The boy was unconscious. She put a hand
to her mouth and swallowed against her disgust at the
cruelty done in her father's name.

'These men say they are pilgrims on their way to
Glastonbury,' Eadgyth said heavily. 'Good men. Le Gros
should look to his back. There's many with cause to see
that monster dead.'

Eleanor moved to the second bed, where Ralph lay on
his side. She recognised him from the cave. He was a
year or two younger than his leader, his hair bright
blond where Conrad's resembled a lion's mane. His
brown eyes were sunken with pain and a fair beard
covered cheeks pitted by the smallpox.

'Damn the name of Twyneham and all who bear it,'

he rasped through lips he had bitten through to stop his cries of pain.

'I'm sorry you were beaten,' she answered, her voice choked with compassion.

'I don't want your pity.' He glared at her with loathing.

Eleanor bent closer to whisper, 'It's not pity. Your bravery in withstanding Le Gros's brutality is commendable. Your silence has given Conrad the chance to fulfil his vow.' She straightened and said in a louder voice, 'The hours will pass slowly for you. There is a pedlar come to the castle. Later I will send him to you; his tales will hearten you.'

Eleanor turned away. 'One day Le Gros will pay the penalty for his brutality.'

Eadgyth looked at her with understanding as Eleanor stared into her wrinkled face.

'Both men received thirty lashes,' the wise-woman said with a sigh. 'The older one will be fit to rise on the morrow, but young Gauthier is becoming feverish.'

'Stay with him all night.' Eleanor put her hand on the old woman's skinny arm. 'If his condition worsens I wish to be told, no matter what the hour. See the other gets the best food and wine. And if the pedlar comes he can stay with them for as long as he wishes. I shall return later to see how they fare.'

She confronted Le Gros on her return to the keep. 'You exceeded your duty in having those men whipped. They were pilgrims under holy vows.'

'Then perhaps you will remember their fate, should you again try to escape my guards,' Le Gros growled insolently. 'How was I to know that they had not been part of an abduction attempt? They don't look much like pilgrims.'

'How would you know, Le Gros? You serve but one master — the Devil. Get out of my sight. You disgust me.'

He gave a cruel laugh and sauntered away, kicking a

dog which did not get out of his path fast enough. If there was a way of getting Le Gros dismissed she would find it.

Aware that Conrad had been left too long alone and was capable of outwitting an unsuspecting guard, she hurried up the stairway to the solar above. She halted in the doorway, her face flushed from her rapid pace.

Conrad was staring out of the window across the expanse of inner and outer baileys to the gatehouse and cluster of thatched village cottages beyond. One leg was bent and rested on the window-seat, his elbow resting negligently upon it, the hawk-like profile of his face bleak and forbidding. It was not hard to imagine the bitterness of his thoughts.

Highford was stately and beautiful, set in a magnificent landscape on the curve of the river. The land surrounding it was lush and green, the livestock fattened and multiplied with ease, and the yearly harvest was always abundant. It was a rich and magnificent prize and Eleanor loved both her home and the people who served it. It was criminal that Sir Cedric saw it as no more than an isolated outpost, its merits counted only by the amount of silver earnt from its crops, livestock and the hard labour of its people.

Conrad turned absently at the sound of her approach.

His expression altered to one of delighted astonishment at the sight of her changed appearance. He quickly recovered himself, but Eleanor felt a moment's exultation that he had shown his admiration. She glided gracefully into the room, enjoying the effect she was having upon him.

'My lady.' He put his hand to his heart and bowed low with all the reverence he would bestow upon a queen. 'You honour me.'

Griselda, who had followed Eleanor into the room, gave a loud sniff of disapproval and muttered to herself in her usual blunt manner. 'Ha! I said he'd be young and handsome. The knave has a silvery tongue to match. No good will come of it.'

Eleanor moved to the window and followed the direction of Conrad's gaze. The longing in his eyes as he surveyed Highford had been unmistakable. She understood what he felt and it added to the complexity of the emotions this man aroused in her. 'I can understand why you hate my father. Highford can weave a spell over you. I'm sorry you had to lose it.'

He looked at her steadily, questioning the absurdity of her statement. The gaze in his green eyes was enigmatic, showing her nothing of his thougths, and yet it held her entranced. It was true her words were ridiculous, but in a strange way she had meant them.

Griselda coughed and Eleanor saw to her alarm that the maid's short-sighted eyes were studying Conrad intently. Griselda had been born in the village. Had she recognised Conrad? The maid was too embittered to feel loyalty to her past masters. During Sir Lionel's time, her son, a boy of six, had wandered unattended into the stables. He had been trampled to death by Sir Lionel's destrier. The shock of the boy's death had caused Griselda to miscarry her second child and left her barren. In her grief and bitterness the maid blamed the D'Artons and over the years her sour and vengeful disposition had turned the bitterness into hatred. If Griselda recognised Conrad she could well betray him.

Eleanor glanced anxiously at the maid, who had resumed her sewing. It did not appear that Griselda had recognised Conrad, but the scare was enough to make Eleanor draw away from him and make her voice impersonal. 'Later I would inspect your wares. But as you claimed you are a minstrel, first I would like to hear you sing for me.'

'There I may have misled you, my lady. I'm no minstrel, but sing occasionally in a tavern to pay for my board and meal.'

He picked up the lute and, after tuning it, struck a

chord. His fingers moved nimbly across the strings. An occasional discord, followed by his grin, showed his lack of practice. A glitter in his eyes warned her he did not like playing the subservient role which circumstances forced upon him. There was devilment also in that challenging stare. When he began to sing, Eleanor bit her lips to halt her laughter. His voice had as much melody as corn being ground. And she suspected he was deliberately singing off-key.

She put her hands to her ears to stop him. 'I should guess that patrons at any inn where you sing would pay for your silence. Have you not tales to tell me. . .of London or other fair cities. . .of feats of chivalry?'

'My wanderings have taken me to the Continent. Would you hear of the latest fashions worn in Paris?'

'No, I would hear of the sights, of the people you met on your travels.'

That her request surprised him he quickly concealed, and the shadows grew long outside as he told her of the distant places he had visited. Eleanor sat enraptured by the world he created, which was so far removed from anything she had experienced. At last, as Griselda lit a candle against the gathering gloom, she sighed, saying, 'I envy you your travels. You have seen so much.'

He looked away from her to the view outside the window and as his mouth set into a line of pain she realised the callousness of her words. *He* envied *her*, her life at Highford. She leaned forward and placed a hand over his and said in a low voice to make amends, 'The church will be deserted at this hour. I usually spend an hour with Father Hubert before we dine. No one should disturb you while you fulfil your vow to your father.'

There was such compelling gravity in his green- and gold-flecked eyes that Eleanor felt her heart steal out to him in her need to ease his pain. Throughout the afternoon she had found herself staring at his lean countenance, watching the sensual lines of his mouth, instead of giving her full attention to his words. It was happening again now, and with a start she saw from the teasing way his lips twisted that he was aware of her close scrutiny. A flush heightened her colour and to her consternation his lips twitched into a taunting smile.

'I'll not forget your kindness, Lady Eleanor.'

For the benefit of Griselda, she said more loudly, 'There are two men in the infirmary. I believe their discomfort would be greatly eased if you could visit them. Your tales are very entertaining.'

There was a light so profound in his eyes as he bowed to her that Eleanor felt a quiver of response tighten her stomach. It was as though an unspoken promise had been sealed between them. As she watched him leave the solar, it seemed all the warmth and vitality had left the chamber. He moved with an easy, fluid grace; his broad shoulders, carried proudly, betrayed no sign of the torment, or anger he felt that he must stalk these corridors in disguise — and not stride purposefully through them in his rightful role of master.

She put a hand over her mouth and turned her face towards the sunset. It had turned the limestone walls to rose and gold. She had come to love Highford. If Conrad were to rule here she would be banished.

The sound of Father Hubert's soft tread on the stairs made her seek a composure she was far from feeling. Throughout their hour-long conversation her mind was constantly on Conrad D'Arton in the church.

Suddenly the horn blew, announcing that the villagers should return to their homes for the portcullis would shortly be lowered for the night. There was an answering note from the road, followed by several shorts blasts. Eleanor jumped to her feet. It was the herald proclaiming the arrival of Sir Cedric. Conrad must be warned. If her father discovered him, it would mean his death.

CHAPTER FOUR

'GRISELDA, see that Father's rooms are prepared and the kitchens told that Sir Cedric approaches.'

The maid-servant's tasks would keep Griselda too busy to notice what her mistress was doing. When Griselda left the room, Eleanor hurried to the church. She hoped Conrad was still there. If someone had disturbed him he could be anywhere in the castle, and there was little time to spare.

The vaulted roof echoed the sound of her running footsteps. It looked deserted. She pivoted around, peering into the corners — still nothing. Fearful for Conrad's safety, she crossed to the D'Arton tombs. They were behind a painted hanging in the lady chapel, partitioned off from the main aisle on the orders of Sir Cedric, who said they offended his eye. Eleanor drew back the hanging. The scent of the fresh flowers she had decorated the church with yesterday mingled with the smell of burning tallow in the enclosed space. Her heart contracted with dread at seeing the two candles burning beneath the Madonna's statue. Of Conrad there was no sign.

She knelt before the Madonna, offering a swift prayer for his safety. She rose and surveyed the chapel. She often prayed here and decorated it twice weekly, as she did the main church. Apart from the burning candles there was no other sign of disturbance. Had Conrad been able to fulfil his vow?

She studied the tombs of his ancestors with renewed interest. Three were of stone: Conrad's grandparents and that of his mother. The earlier ones bore painted wooden effigies. In the dim, flickering candlelight, the painted faces of his ancesters mocked her with their wooden, unseeing eyes. They were all blond and Conrad had inherited the same hawk-like profile. Any of the servants or villagers who had known the D'Artons could not fail to recognise Conrad, even though he was now clean-shaven. But would they betray him?

Eleanor hoped not. Had there been time for Conrad to get out of the castle? The fears ground through her. If he was caught they would discover the chalice and reliquary on him, and, whether they recognised him as her father's enemy or not, they would hang him as a thief.

Raised voices penetrated the peace of the chapel. Sir Cedric had arrived and she must attend him. If Conrad was still in the castle, and was captured, there might yet be a chance she could plead for him.

She entered the great hall to discover her father shouting for food and wine to be brought for his guests. Though Sir Cedric had appropriated all the tapestries within Highford for his other residences, the fresco she had ordered to be painted last winter brightened the austerity of the hall. Fresh rushes had been laid two days ago and at the heavy tread of the men on them the bruised fragrance of lavender and rosemary rose up to fill the air. Several servants were busy erecting trestle-tables and laying out the best pewterware for the feast. Sir Cedric had taken all the silver on his last visit. Some of which, she recalled with a guilty twinge, had borne the D'Arton coat of arms. At least he had left the painted leather hangings to decorate the walls and keep the draughts out. These had been carefully cleaned and rehung during her confinement over the winter months.

Every candle in the two large wooden chandeliers overhead had been lit, throwing their light over the colourful and noisy gathering of men. Most wore long gowns with wide sleeves, to add dignity to their ample girths. The swish of her trailing gown over the rushes drew several of the guests' gazes to her. She smiled absently at them as she curtsied to her father.

'Why, daughter, you have become a young woman.'
Sir Cedric sounded surprised. 'How old are you, child?'

Eleanor felt a flush creep up her cheeks that her father
had to ask her age. 'I am seventeen, sir.'

'And a beauty too, Sir Cedric,' a man at his side
commented. 'You'll be beating off offers for her hand
from the look on the faces of some of your guests.'

Sir Cedric grunted. His florid face had coarsened since
last Eleanor had seen him, but the man's words had
pleased him. Aware of the appraisal of several of the
men, Eleanor was disheartened. She had no wish to be
bartered over like a prize horse. Her impression of her
father's guests was that they were all middle-aged, many
with their faces hardened by excesses. One, however,
was looking at her with particular intensity. The first
threads of grey touched the temples of his dark hair and
narrow clipped beard, but, though she surmised he was
about forty, his face and trim figure were those of a man
a decade younger.

Uncomfortable beneath his close scrutiny, Eleanor
turned away, but she could feel his stare upon her as she
moved across the room to take her place by the fireplace.
She picked up the cover of a footstool she was embroi-
dering. The voices of the men droned in the background
as she sewed. Outwardly she looked serene, but she was
worried whether or not Conrad had managed to leave the
castle.

She looked up as Griselda offered her a goblet of wine.
Her maid smiled. 'You have caught the eye of Sir
Richard Norton. Now that would be a man worthy of
you, my lady.'

Eleanor followed Griselda's gaze and saw the dark-
haired knight watching her. She shifted uncomfortably.
'He's old enough to be my father. I cannot say there is
any man among Sir Cedric's guests whom I would want
as my husband.'

'Age is not everything, my lady.' Griselda's brown
eyes sparkled beneath her fleshy lids. 'An older man will

appreciate your beauty and spirit, whereas a young handsome one may well play you false with every strumpet who looks sidelong at him. Sir Richard is a man of refinement. You could do a great deal worse than marry him.'

'Griselda, I've no wish to discuss my marriage.'

'You can put all thoughts of that pedlar out of your mind.' Griselda folded her podgy hands under her vast bosom. 'Handsome he most certainly was, and there was no harm in a little flirtation. But when you marry, it will be to a man of rank and position. A man chosen by your father.'

Eleanor was relieved that Griselda had not guessed Conrad's identity. 'I am aware of a daughter's duty,' she answered without enthusiasm. 'But I refuse to worry about it until my suitor is chosen.'

'That may be sooner than you think,' Griselda simpered, her chins a-quiver as she waggled her head in satisfaction. 'Sir Richard has been speaking to your father and is now coming to escort you to dine.'

Griselda disappeared from Eleanor's side. As the knight bowed, she saw that he had taken the trouble to change his travel-stained clothing. None of the others had bothered.

'Lady Eleanor, I am Sir Richard Norton. Your father has given me the honour of escorting you to the dais.'

She stood up and accepted his proffered arm. His slender body was elegantly attired in a short tunic of black velvet embroidered with silver and his hose were also black. She did not like the way the knight had singled her out, but she had no wish to be discourteous to a guest.

Her misgivings rose at discovering that Sir Richard was to sit next to her at the high table and that throughout the meal, as custom demanded, they would be forced to share a platter and drinking cup. Not that Eleanor believed herself capable of eating. There was a constriction in her throat, and her stomach was tightly knotted as she continued to worry about Conrda's presence in the castle.

'You must forgive my staring at you, Lady Eleanor,' Sir Richard broke through her thoughts. 'But you are the image of the Lady Isobel, your mother. I knew her when she was lady-in-waiting to the Queen. That was before her marriage.'

'What was the Lady Isobel like?' There was a kindness in the knights's voice which drew her to explain, 'I saw so little of her—and of course she died so tragically young.'

He twirled the goblet they shared for a long moment before he lifted it to drink from. Lowering it from his mouth, he offered it to Eleanor. 'Lady Isobel was beautiful like you, graceful and sweet-tempered. She was greatly missed by many when Sir Cedric took her away from Court.'

A harsh note entered his voice when he mentioned her father and Eleanor had the impression that Sir Richard did not particularly like his host. She also resented the note of censure upon her parents' marriage. 'Perhaps Lady Isobel was not so enamoured of the fawning life at Court as you believed.'

He looked surprised at her words. 'You have an unflattering opinion of courtiers. Yet you have never attended Court. I would have thought that all young noblewomen were eager to enjoy the entertainments there. Your father is remiss that you do not attend.'

She considered her answer with unusual gravity. 'It would be pleasant to visit Court for a short time. But I have heard it is a place of intrigue and false friendships. That people say one thing yet mean another. I do not think I would like a world where dishonesty and deceit are supreme.'

Clearly, from Sir Richard's astonished expression, he was not used to such openness. Eleanor looked past him to see her father watching them. Sir Cedric nodded his approval at the interest Sir Richard was showing in his daughter.

'Richard, is not Eleanor as sweet and beautiful a creature as ever her mother was? She will make some man a fine wife.'

Eleanor blushed and dropped her fork with a clatter. 'Father, I dislike being spoken of as though I were not present. Sir Richard is being very kind, but——'

'No buts about it.' Sir Cedric winked. 'The wench is no mouse. Needs a firm hand. I'd not be adverse to a match, Richard. Think on it.'

'Father! How could you?' Eleanor leapt to her feet with such haste that her stool toppled over. Her eyes were bright with anger and mortification. 'Forgive me, Sir Richard.'

She walked from the dais.

'Eleanor!' Sir Cedric shouted. 'Get back here!'

She ignored his summons, too angry to consider that her punishment would be severe. She felt stifled and, seeking fresh air, went outside to stand on the top step of the keep entrance. Taking a deep breath to regain her composure, she stared across the castleyard, which was lit by burning flambeaux, sentries' fires and silvery moonlight.

'Lady Eleanor.' Her heart plummeted as she recognised Sir Richard's voice behind her. 'You are upset. Your father was wrong to embarrass you like that.'

Keeping her head bowed, she turned towards him. 'He put you in a difficult position. Please pay no heed to his words.'

'You are angry, but it must take much courage to stand up to his wrath.'

She glared at him, suspicious that he was mocking her. 'Some would see it as disobedience. I will not be treated like a child.'

There was no mockery, only admiration in his answering smile. 'Would a match between us be so distressing to you?'

Her head shot up in shock. The knight was serious. 'I have known you for less than an hour. How can I answer that?'

'Often marriages are arranged without those involved meeting beforehand.' The mellow torchlight made him look much younger, and he was a prepossessing figure. 'But perhaps there is a younger man to whom you have given your heart?'

The image of Conrad filled her mind. Such a knight as he would easily win her love. But her father would never agree to a marriage between them, and Conrad had made his own feelings upon the subject painfully clear. It was absurd that she was even considering the possibility. That it had occupied her thoughts was unsettling.

'How could there be?' she evaded, pushing the lingering image of Conrad from her mind. 'Highford is isolated. I meet no one of my age and rank. But age should not matter. It is the manner of the man which counts.'

Sir Richard smiled. 'You have wisdom as well as honesty. Dare I hope that upon further acquaintance you may look upon me with favour?'

The intimation behind his words filled Eleanor with alarm. 'You honour me, Sir Richard, but. . .'

He raised a taunting brow. 'I am almost a grey-beard and you would wed a younger swain.'

The gentle teasing in his voice made her look at him more closely. Since her father's arrival, her thoughts had been all for Conrad and the danger to him. It annoyed her that she had wasted so much energy upon an enemy. She had paid little attention to Sir Richard, but throughout the meal he had patiently drawn her into conversation. Now she looked at him with fresh interest. He was more than twice her age, though he did not look it. His unlined face was handsome and his figure was slender and straight. There was a confident ease about his manner which she warmed to. What little she knew of Sir Richard Norton she liked, but marriage was another prospect altogether.

'As we both know, Sir Richard, I will wed whom my father commands. I trust that it will be a man who has many qualities I can respect. Also who would honour me as a woman and his equal, not a mere chattel.' She regarded him levelly, knowing her next words could earn his censure. 'Few men would want a wife who has an unwomanly interest in theology, astronomy and the history of peoples and their languages.'

'Sir Cedric did not mention that you were an educated woman, though he was lavish in his praise of your beauty and biddable nature.'

She saw that his expression was both amused and intrigued. It rankled. What did Sir Cedric know of her education or sweet nature — which at this moment was certainly souring by the moment? Her eyes sparked with rising anger. 'I will not be mocked, Sir Richard. In Sir Cedric's haste to barter me to the highest bidder, he has misinformed you. I was educated not at my father's command, but because I wished it. I warn you my nature is not so sweet to those who cross me. I made Father Hubert's life a misery until he agreed to take me as a pupil. Unknown to Sir Cedric, I dismissed the bailiff last winter because the man was robbing him blind, and have since kept the estate records myself. I expect at any moment to be severely called to account for both tasks. As for biddable. . .' She gave a dry laugh. 'You will shortly hear my father's wrath shake the foundations of this castle, when he is informed of my misadventure this morning.'

To her astonishment Sir Richard laughed.

'I am glad you find it amusing, sir,' she replied coldly as she began to move past him.

He put a hand on her arm to stop her. 'I meant no insult by my laughter.' His eyes crinkled at the corners with kindly humour. 'After the deceit and false flattery at Court, your honesty is refreshing.'

She remained suspicious. 'Do you now mock my naïveté, Sir Richard? I do not like being humoured like a child. Now if you will kindly release me, I have duties to perform.'

'Eleanor, you are no child, but a treasure beyond compare. Am I forgiven?'

There was something about the knight which she found disarming. In other circumstances it would have been pleasant to cultivate his company as a friend. 'It is I who should ask your pardon for my rudeness to a guest in my father's house.'

'Then we are friends, Lady Eleanor.'

'We are not enemies, Sir Richard,' she parried.

'You have the wit and beauty of your mother. But she never had your spirit. It is an irresistible combination. I have long cherished my bachelor status, but it is time I provided an heir for my estates. I want no empty-headed vessel for a wife.' He smiled with accomplished charm. 'Sir Cedric intends to stay here for a week to enjoy the hunting. Time enough for us to become better acquainted.' Placing his hand over his heart, he bowed and, as he straightened, took her hand to raise it to his lips. 'Will you not rejoin us in the hall? Your company will be sorely missed.'

'Tonight I ask your indulgence, Sir Richard. I have had a tiring day and it is not yet over. We had no warning of Sir Cedric's arrival. I must check with the chamberlain that all the rooms have been made ready for our guests and adequate provisions and entertainments will be provided for your stay.'

'Until the morrow, dear lady.' Sir Richard left her to return to the hall.

Eleanor sighed. Her heart and mind were in turmoil. So much had happened today that her world seemed to have spun off its axis. At the forefront of her mind was her concern for Conrad. Yet why should the safety of her enemy so concern her? She had kept her part of the bargain, though perhaps foolishly. If he truly came not

as a spy, but to honour his father's dying wish, then
Conrad did not deserve to be caught and punished by
her father.

Thoughts of retribution reminded her that she would
not escape punishment once Sir Cedric learned of the
day's escapade. Then there was the knowledge that he
obviously favoured a match between herself and Sir
Richard Norton. And the knight had made his interest
in her plain. She touched her temple to ease a dull
headache. Also she must confront her father as to
Daniel's plight. In many ways Sir Cedric's arrival at
Highford looked to make the next few days stormy ones,
and she would be at the centre of his fury.

So absorbed had she become in her thoughts that she
started violently when a hand upon her shoulder spun
her round. Her cry of protest was stopped by a rush of
relief as she recognised Conrad. It was instantly replaced
by fear for him to be in so public a place. She was pulled
roughly into the deserted master of the rolls' room.

'It was a neat ruse of yours to lure me to Highford,
knowing Sir Cedric would arrive today.' A shaft of
moonlight from a window above thier heads showed the
contempt in his eyes.

'I swear I did not know. The moment I heard the
herald I came to warn you. But you had left the church.'

'Fortunately the new custodians of Highford have not
learned all its secret places.' A muscle pulsated near
Conrad's mouth and his tone was scathing. 'So much for
your word, my lady.'

Conrad stared down into her beautiful, proud and
treacherous face. His anger was as much directed at
himself for trusting her as at her betrayal. He should
have expected as much from a Twyneham. Her treachery
had released him from his word to her. He had used the
hours since Sir Cedric's arrival to learn the castle's
defences. He had not been recognised by any of the
villagers working in the castle as he explored its precincts. His information gained, he'd decided against

leaving by the secret tunnel. Sir Lionel had told him of its entrance in the armoury tower. But by remaining, Conrad now hoped to learn something of Sir Cedric's plans.

An inexplicable rage had seized him at overhearing Sir Richard Norton's conversation with Eleanor. The knight made no secret of his wish to marry her. From where Conrad stood, it had sounded as if she had appeared willing to accept the match. And Highford would be her dowry—he had learned that from overheard gossip in the castle. His hatred and fury towards the Twyneham family possessed his mind. Highford was his.

He could feel a tremor gripping her body as he continued to hold her arms, but her eyes were clear and without fear. Her courage was remarkable, but it was unwise—he had been goaded to the limits of his restraint.

'Why did you not escape?' she challenged.

'Because no one betrays me without paying for their treachery.' His anger was eating into him.

Eleanor was shaken by the glacial fury glittering in his eyes. She shrank away from him, her hand flying to her throat as she realised he meant to exact that vengeance upon herself. He believed she had betrayed him. All the hatred and prejudice against her family was there in the menace of his uncompromising glare. It had unleashed a savagery within him which was beyond rational thought.

'Let me go,' she croaked, the colour draining from her face. 'Don't make me call the guard.'

'You do well to fear me.' His hands jerked her hard against his body. 'Were you a man I would kill you for your treachery. I was so blinded by your witch's smile that I trusted you.'

Eleanor held herself rigid in his grasp. His hand circled her throat. For a terrifying moment she thought he intended to throttle her, but the pressure did not increase. 'Conrad, it is your hatred which blinds you. Are you so bitter that you can trust no one? Had I betrayed you, would not every guard at Highford be searching for you?'

His fingers spread across her neck in a light caress. 'What cause have I to trust a Twyneham?' His voice rasped with pain as the admission was wrenched from him.

'None,' she whispered. 'But I would never betray you.'

Her need to convince him brought a huskiness to her voice. She could feel the warmth of his breath on her face. In the dim moonlight she could see the tension ease from his face, the fierce light in his eyes gentling as he studied her. She was held captive by that compelling gaze, driven by a fierce need for him to believe her. He lifted a brow, his fingers stroking the line of her jaw as he drew her closer.

'Who put the flowers in the lady chapel?' he confounded her by asking.

'It is the task of the mistress of Highford. In my stepmother's absence it is my duty.'

'I doubt your stepmother would trouble herself to decorate the lady chapel. Especially since it has been curtained off. That would be on your father's orders. Does he fear the tombs of my ancestors mock his fragile tenure?'

'We fear neither the dead nor living D'Artons.' Bristling, she pushed against his chest to free herself.

'You would do well to fear us,' he taunted.

Guessing his intent, she twisted her head away to avoid his kiss. He had anticipated her move; his hands moved to the sides of her head-dress, gently turning her face back to meet his mouth. He meant to punish her. She would not give him the satisfaction of fighting him and being subdued by his strength. This time she intended to turn his knavery back upon himself. It would be he who would be taught a lesson.

Eleanor wound her arms around his neck, her body moving sinuously against his. Naïvely she believed her action would prove he could not frighten her, that since she was the instigator of the kiss she would remain in control. Nothing in her experience had prepared her for his response.

She was pulled against him in a passionate embrace, his hands pressing her to the sinewed contours of his body in a way that both shocked her and excited her senses. The scent of him assailed her—musky, fresh, but, above all, threateningly male. His supple mouth played over hers, stimulating her response as his tongue teased the softness of her lips, probing, entering to steal the breath from her body, until she clung to him, weak and light-headed. His mouth became a mobile flame as it skimmed across her jaw and travelled to the hollow of her throat. She moaned softly, her head rolling back as the heat of his lips continued its masterly onslaught. Her entire body took fire as though time and again a lightning bolt sizzled through her.

Another soft moan was drawn from her as his hand covered her breast and stroked it gently through the thickness of her gown. Her mind warned her that this was her enemy, but her dormant sensuality was skilfully roused to an all-devouring fever. The low neck of her bodice was eased from her shoulders and his kisses continued their enticing trail. When his hand slipped beneath her bodice to take her high, firm breast, his fingers teasing its hardened peak, she gasped, engulfed by a bitter-sweet pain of almost unbearable pleasure.

Sanity fled beneath searing kisses. Lips demanded and burning flesh responded. Hands played expertly over her body, loosening laces without her being aware of it, running along her tingling spine, stroking the fullness of her breasts.

'Conrad, my love,' she sighed softly against his ear.

She was abruptly released. 'Conrad, what's wrong?'

'Cover yourself, my lady,' he ground out derisively. Her false words of love had returned him to sanity, yet his body still ached with his frustrated need for her.

Eleanor was shocked to feel the cool night air on her breasts and when she looked down she was horrified to find that her bodice was open to her waist. She held it together. He must despise her as a wanton. No more so than she despised herself for abandoning herself so shockingly to his lovemaking. Her fingers shook as she fastened her gown.

'What trickery are you up to now?' he accused. 'Damn you for a conniving bitch.'

Humiliation washed over her. Her body had played her false. Somehow her wayward senses had become embroiled by this man who saw her only as his enemy. What madness had possessed her to play him at his own game? He was a master and she a novice. He had callously used her and made her feel degraded. For that she would never forgive him.

'I want you out of Highford immediately,' she ordered. 'Unchivalrous knave, you have abused my trust. I should have expected as much from a D'Arton.'

The coldness of her tone brought a frown to his brow. Only his will-power stopped him taking her back into his arms to savour again the sweet joy of her surrender to his touch. It had been a shock to discover how easily she had stripped him of control. It was that realisation which had made him put her from him. The woman was the Devil's handmaiden. She had almost succeeded in making him forget she was his avowed enemy. Her false words of love had returned him to sanity, yet his body still ached with his need for her.

'What new deceit were you weaving with your wiles?' In the dim light his sneering eyes glared at her cruelly.

Everything in Eleanor rebelled. She had been abused, insulted, threatened and finally ridiculed when her body had betrayed her into yielding. 'I learned how a D'Arton pays his debts — by seeking to shame me!'

'You were a willing enough accomplice,' he jeered.

'Never again,' she retorted. 'Go, before I forget I gave my word that you would be safe here. Since you know

of the existence of the tunnel—use it. I will watch from
the battlements. When you emerge on the bridge you
will startle the swans nesting there. If they do not take
flight telling me you are outside, I shall raise the cry that
we have an intruder within the castle. It will not be just
your life which will be at stake, but Gauthier's and
Ralph's as well. They will be linked with you.'

'The next time I enter Highford it will be in triumph
and the Twynehams will be vanquished.' The ferocity of
his tone lashed her.

'You will find the tunnel sealed as from tomorrow,'
she retaliated with all the contempt she could muster.
'So don't think you can sneak in like a thief to breach
our defences and let your men invade my home.'

Eleanor pronounced the words 'my home' with such
pride that Conrad's hands clenched. He left her before
his rage overcame what was left of his restraint. The fury
stayed with Conrad as he proceeded to the armoury.
Satan must be rocking with laughter this day. Who but
Lucifer would take such delight in bedevilling the holy
vow Conrad had made to his father? To have walked
within the walls of Highford strengthened his resolve to
regain it. Then Eleanor would not be proud. Soon Henry
Tudor would face Richard Plantagenet in battle over the
throne of England. When Henry won, as Conrad was
confident that he would, Highford would be returned to
Conrad.

Yet today he had learned that Sir Richard Norton was
considering Eleanor as his bride. Norton was a wily
diplomat and had been in secret negotiation with Henry
Tudor. He was opposed to the more excessive measures
taken by some of King Richard's counsellors. Highford
was Eleanor's dowry, and if Norton gave his allegiance
to Henry it would be unlikely that Henry would alienate
one of his followers to appease another. There was a
possibility he would lose Highford. Possession often
carried more weight than justice. Conrad's thoughts were
bleak. Henry would be generous and reward Conrad

with an even larger castle and estate. But it was Highford he wanted.

Conrad stepped out on to the bridge and, as Eleanor had predicted, several swans flapped into flight. He looked back at his birthright. Highford's turrets were outlined blackly against the moon-bright sky. A fierce yearning possessed him. It was in his blood; it was part of him. Until he was Lord of Highford, he would take whatever steps were necessary to prevent the Lady Eleanor's marriage to another Lancastrian.

CHAPTER FIVE

'DAUGHTER, where is the minstrel who came to the castle yesterday?' Sir Cedric Twyneham bellowed when Eleanor answered his early morning summons. He was alone in the solar. 'I would have him entertain our guests.'

She was not deceived by the falseness of the last remark. From his flushed expression he was working himself into a fury. The page who had come to her had been shaking with fear and begged her to come at once — a sign that her father had already vented some of his rage upon him.

Eleanor had been seated at her toilette with Griselda brushing her hair. She had thought it expedient to dispense with the lengthy procedure of having her hair braided and an elaborate head-dress pinned in place. Sir Cedric's temper would not improve by being kept waiting. With a veil secured by a gold fillet covering her thigh-length hair, she had hurried to the solar.

'He was no talented singer, Father. Just a pedlar. I have not seen him since your arrival,' she evaded. 'He must have left as soon as the gates were opened this morning.'

'No. I've asked. He did not pass the sentries.'

'Then I have no idea where he is. Yesterday I was too busy ensuring the comfort of our guests to worry about a chance pedlar. I have already sent a man to town. He should return before nightfall with musicians, minstrels, mummers and tumblers enough to entertain your guests.'

'Yet you showed interest enough in this pedlar yesterday. He spent two hours with you in the solar. Unfitting conduct for my daughter.' His anger broke over her like a thunderclap and his florid face became mottled with purple spots of rage. 'I've heard from a dozen sources of your disappearance yesterday. That you were found in the pedlar's company. And that you were dressed as a page. Have you no shame?'

An inner trembling seized Eleanor, all her childhood terror of his violent rages threatening to return. She fought it. He could beat her for disobedience, but he would hear her out. She owed it to Daniel. Her stance was proud and unflinching. 'I stole out of the castle in disguise so that I could visit Daniel. It was cruel for you to part us. He is my brother and I love him dearly.'

'You went to the priory?' Spittle flecked his mouth. 'The prioress was instructed that no one was to see the boy.'

'That's inhuman!' Eleanor's sense of justice rebelled. 'He's a lonely small boy. If he's frail and a little backward for his years, his unnatural existence must be to blame. Eadgyth told me that after a difficult birth some children are slower to learn. How can being shut away from others of his age help him?' Loyalty to her brother and outrage swept her along in the face of the gathering storm which darkened her father's eyes. 'Daniel is your heir. Yet you treat him as though——'

The force of his slap sent her reeling back against the wall. Eleanor put a hand out to stop herself falling as her senses swirled. Her ears rang from the force of the blow and her cheek bled where it had been cut by his ring.

'Do you think I will acknowledge a half-wit as my heir?' Sir Cedric snarled at her. 'I forbade his name to be mentioned. Daniel is dead to me. The boy's sickly and will never reach manhood. God grant that the Lady Clemence will bear me a healthy son. You will not visit the boy again.'

Eleanor straightened to glare at her father. A vein stood out on each side of his now crimson temple, his eyes were wild and bulging in their sockets, and his beard was speckled with his saliva. His anger was terrifying to behold, but Eleanor stood her ground. 'I'll not abandon my brother. My mother gave her life for Daniel. It's an insult to her memory that he is shut away like a creature to be ashamed of.'

'I forbid his name to be mentioned.'

Sir Cedric's second blow knocked her to her knees. The shock of its brutality brought a cry to her lips. At the third and fourth blows she remained stoically silent. Her hair was grabbed and viciously tugged, sending red-hot needles of pain through her scalp and forcing her to bite her lips against the agony. 'I'll kill the boy before I allow word of his existence to reach the outside world. Understand?'

'Let me at least continue to vist him,' she gasped out through her pain.

'I'll teach you not to defy me!' Her head snapped from side to side as he struck her hard across both cheeks.

There was an angry shout from the doorway and suddenly Eleanor found herself released as someone dragged her father away from her.

'Good God, man, have you lost your senses?' Through a haze of slowly receding pain, Eleanor recognised the voice of Sir Richard Norton. 'Guest though I am in your house, I will not stand by and see a woman mistreated.'

'The girl was insolent and disobeyed me,' Sir Cedric grunted. 'It's not your affair, Norton.'

'Then perhaps I should make it my affair.'

Turning his back on her father, Sir Robert took Eleanor's elbows and, raising her gently to her feet, led her to the window-seat. She could not stop trembling, and tears of pain and humiliation blurred her vision as she tried to thank him. His face paled as he saw the bruises and the cut on her cheek.

'My lady, you are safe now. I will not allow Sir Cedric to hurt you while I remain at Highford.'

The violence of her father's attack had shaken Eleanor more than she cared to admit. She was still furious with him for his cruel treatment of Daniel, but was powerless to sway him. The knowledge sapped her strength. Sir Richard sat beside her, placing a comforting arm around her shoulders. There was no passion in his embrace, just reassurance, and his consideration after her father's cruelty eased her humiliation. Summoning an embarrassed smile, she eased back from his arms, though she was too aware of the bruises on her face to lift her gaze to him.

'If you are feeling stronger I shall escort you to your room, Lady Eleanor. Your maid will tend you.'

Sir Robert stood up and helped her to rise. There was no need for the steadying arm he placed about her waist, but Eleanor felt that after his kindness it would be churlish to push it away. At the door she looked back at her father. It had surprised her that he had given way to Sir Robert's intervention. Now he was looking at her almost fondly, his good humour restored. Not out of love for herself, she admitted wryly, but because he regarded Sir Richard as her suitor.

Eleanor examined her face in the mirror after Griselda had completed her toilette. An application of rice powder hid the shadows of the bruising, and all that remained visible after a stiffened veil had been pinned so as to cast a shadow on her features was the crescent-shaped cut on her cheek from her father's ring. Eleanor had no intention of hiding away in her rooms to conceal her bruised face. She had promised Conrad that Gauthier and Ralph would be tended to. Despite her antagonism towards their master, she would not allow it to compromise his men. When she entered the infirmary she found Father Hubert and Ralph kneeling in prayer before the plain wooden cross on the room wall. The priest rose stiffly, rubbing his arthrithic knees with a knobbled hand.

'How are our patients, Father?'

'Progressing, my lady.'

Ralph glowered at Eleanor and was slow to rise. He was still pale and his mouth was clenched against his pain, but it was resentment and not his wound which

made him slow to pay her the respect due her rank. He
was recovering from his beating, but Gauthier was not
so fortunate. He lay very still and Eleanor bent over the
boy, who lay on his stomach. She lifted the gauze which
covered his back. Four of the deeper weals were still
inflamed, but the other cuts were beginning to heal. She
picked up the horn cup which contained the pain-killing
posset prepared by Eadgyth. It was empty. When she
placed her hand on his brow she found that, though it
burned, his fever had lessened. Gauthier opened his
eyes.

'My lady.' He grimaced as he tried to turn and sit up.

'Do not move, Gauthier.' She smiled down at him.
'The fever has weakened you. It will be another two days
before you can leave your bed.'

She held the cup out for Father Hubert. 'Would you
have Eadgyth refill this?'

Once the priest left, Eleanor turned to Ralph. 'Have
you been questioned further?'

Ralph's lips twisted into a sour line. 'Ay, but that
swine Le Gros now seems to accept we are pilgrims.
That's why the priest was here praying with us. He's
been chanting his prayers by the hour. He's convinced
our punishment will ease our penance and that we are
blessed with the Lord's grace.'

Eleanor controlled a smile. 'Father Hubert is very
devout. And well intentioned.' She went on at a faster
pace to have her say before the priest returned. 'Ralph,
I want your word that you will stay here with Gauthier
without the need to place a guard on the door. Conrad
D'Arton got safely away last night. You must be aware
that unexpected guests arrived at the castle. If there is
any suspicion that you are D'Arton's men I fear for your
lives.'

'Why haven't you handed us over to your father?'
Ralph eyed her warily. 'You've no loyalty to us.'

'Because I gave Conrad my word that you would be
safe. You paid a high price for your loyalty to him. By

beating you Le Gros exceeded his duty. Had you spoken out there would a man-hunt out for Conrad.'

Ralph thrust his thumbs into his belt, his expression less belligerent as he noted the bruises and cut on her cheek. 'Not that you appear to have escaped unscathed.'

'No. I paid for my disobedience in leaving Highford against my father's orders. Should Sir Cedric learn that Conrad was here I would be beaten as viciously as you were.'

'We'll not talk, my lady,' Gauthier vowed.

Eleanor smiled at him. 'Get well quickly, young man. I shall always remember your kindness and loyalty. Some day you will be a gallant knight. I will come again tomorrow. Eadgyth will tend to your needs. The best food and wine will be sent to you to speed your recovery.'

She paused at the door to address Ralph. 'I'm ashamed you were beaten in such a savage manner.'

'Ay, if the Good Lord is merciful he will grant Le Gros pays dearly for his brutality,' Ralph grunted. 'And you have treated us more kindly than we deserve. Conrad did abduct you when all's said and done.'

She nodded, accepting his surly words as a form of truce.

Outside in the courtyard she saw Sir Richard waiting for her. 'You visit the infirmary every morning, so Father Hubert tells me. A caring gesture which will be much appreciated by your people. Will we be favoured by your company when we ride to the hunt later this morning?'

'If my father permits, I would very much like to ride.'

Sir Richard smiled. 'I am sure Sir Cedric will not deny us any opportunity to further our acquaintance.'

Eleanor hid her misgivings that Sir Richard seemed intent upon pursuing his suit. She should be flattered by his attention. He was a powerful and distinguished knight and an estimable match; she could not fault either his appearance or his manner. It was obvious he enjoyed the company of women, and there was a charisma about him which was impossible not to respond to with warm

affection. It was reflected in good humour, which sparkled so readily in his eyes. There was much about Sir
Richard to commend him. His face was that of a man
with a strong sense of purpose, but there was something
in the way his lips curled upwards and his eyes softened
when he spoke to her that showed a rare sensitivity. He
would be a husband she could admire and respect, and
with time feel a true affection towards. But she knew she
did not love him. It was not he who had plagued her
dreams last night, but another. A man she convinced
herself that she hated, and who as a squire was beneath
her in rank.

Her anger returned at the treatment she had received
from Conrad. She must forget the flames of passion the
squire had kindled. He had made his loathing for her
obvious, his lust preying upon her innocence. The
humiliating manner in which he had scorned her proved
he was unworthy of her consideration. She would not
waste her thoughts on him.

It was months since she had been allowed to ride and
she decided she would enjoy Sir Richard's company.
The knight had shown her kindness, and the admiration
in his eyes soothed her lacerated pride after the callousness of Conrad's rejection.

'I shall look forward to our ride, Sir Richard. But first
I have duties to attend to.' She walked across the
courtyard, intending to visit the armoury tower and have
the stores rearranged to seal the entrance of the tunnel.
She was not about to risk Conrad using it to re-enter the
castle.

As she passed the bakehouse she returned the greetings of the village women who waited in line to bake
their day's bread in the great domed castle oven. The
men raked the wood-ash from the oven, their faces red
and running with sweat from the fierceness of the heat.
Eleanor walked on and smiled at the sleepy-eyed scullion
turning the oxen which had been spitted over the glowing
fire pit.

An hour later she emerged from the armoury tower assured that if Conrad attempted to regain admittance to the castle by that means the barrels of malmsey wine would stop the trapdoor being opened. As she entered the courtyard Eleanor heard her father's angry tones coming from the stables. His raised voice was making a bay horse prance nervously. The groom was white-faced at bearing the brunt of Sir Cedric's rage.

To Eleanor's alarm she recognised the bay as the one she had ridden from the cave. At her approach Sir Cedric rounded on Eleanor.

'Is this the pedlar's horse?'

Eleanor looked it over with apparent disinterest. 'It could be, Father. I remember it was a bay.'

'Then why is there no sign of the pedlar himself? The castle has been searched.'

'What is your interest in the man? Is not Highford a refuge to all travellers? If that is his horse, then the pedlar is still in the castle. He must have drunk too much and gone to sleep it off in a corner somewhere. Has his pack been found? No pedlar would leave here without it.'

She knew the wicker pannier was safely hidden away because she had emptied it and carefully dispersed the contents, but she resented having to lie to protect Conrad. She did it to save Gauthier and Ralph from suspicion.

Sir Cedric grunted in disgust. 'Everywhere has been searched. Something is not right here.' The mottled spots of rage drained from Sir Cedric's face as he noticed Sir Richard advancing towards them. Eleanor felt a rush of gratitude towards the knight for deflecting her father's anger.

Sir Cedric leaned closer to Eleanor, his tone ominous. 'A match between you would please me. Your conduct yesterday proves you need a husband to control you. You are of marriageable age. Sir Richard holds a high position at Court. He has shown his interest in you.' A menacing light entered his pale eyes. 'Should he not offer for you I will know where the fault lies, and you will pay for it.'

Eleanor grew cold as she saw the calculation in her father's face. He was set upon this marriage. But at least Sir Richard's arrival had taken her father's thoughts away from the search for Conrad. She knew better than to antagonise her father. If a marriage was decided between the two men, her wishes or feelings would not concern them. She might not love Sir Richard, but he had many qualities she admired. All noblewomen were brought up to accept that they must be pawns to secure the advancement of their family. From the respect in which she held Sir Richard it would not be hard for affection to grow. Insight told her that the comfortable companionship she felt with the knight was rare between a man and woman. Why should her marriage to him not be a contented one?

The huntsmen were already mounted and the hounds ran excitedly about the courtyard. Sir Richard waved aside the groom who held the scarlet-tasselled reins of her dappled mare. 'My lady, permit me to assist you to mount.'

He lifted her easily into the saddle, and with a dexterity many men half his age would have envied he vaulted on to his mount. Laughing, he turned to her. 'I've not done that in years. You make me feel young again, my lady.'

'You put every other knight here to shame,' she responded, delighted that such an important and accomplished knight still retained his boyish exuberance.

The huntsman blew his horn, and the hounds, baying loudly, ran through the gatehouse, over the drawbridge, and straight for the woods, their noses to the ground in search of wild boar.

Conrad D'Arton pulled his hood low over his face before emerging from the hut set apart from the others in

Highford village. Sir Lionel had vouched for the loyalty
of his old servants, Oswald the falconer and Eadgyth the
wise-crone. Conrad had sought out Oswald and had not
been disappointed at the old man's response. Oswald
assured him that the people who had lived at Highford
when Sir Lionel was their lord had little loyalty towards
Sir Cedric, though he was adamant that none would
countenance any harm befalling the Lady Eleanor.

Eadgyth confirmed that, though Gauthier would be
better left abed for two days, as the need of Conrad to
leave the district was urgent the lad would sustain no
great harm if he travelled on the morrow. Assured that
Oswald and his son William would prove worthy
accomplices within the castle, Conrad prepared to return
to the cave. He could afford to await another day to
ensure that Ralph and Gauthier travelled with them. It
irritated Conrad that the falconer and woman were loud
in their praise of their mistress. To hear them talk one
would think she was a paragon of innocence and virtue.
He knew Eleanor for the troublesome vixen she was.

At the doorway of her hut Eadgyth touched his arm.
'A new master will shortly own Highford. The runes tell
it clearly.'

'So does gossip,' Conrad said with returning anger.
'Highford is the Lady Eleanor's dowry — the bait to win
an influential alliance in Sir Cedric's thirst for power.'

'Mock me not, young master.' Eadgyth thrust her
wrinkled face towards him. Her eyes glazed as she spoke
her prophecy. 'There's a portent in the heavens which
speaks of a change which will soon come to England.
First blood must run. Then the old conflicts will be laid
to rest. The runes speak true. The next man to call
Highford his own will not be deposed from it. His family
will hold it for many generations.'

'Then I will take pains to ensure that the next owner
of Highford is myself.'

Eadgyth eyed him sombrely. 'Beware the long talons
of the cockerel. They can sink deep.'

Conrad laughed. 'The cockerel in the Twyneham coat of arms will be no match against the D'Arton wolf.'

'I would not be so sure,' Eadgyth cackled.

From the shelter of the covering trees Conrad watched the hunting party from the castle canter past. Eleanor rode by the side of Sir Richard Norton. Her face was flushed with the excitement of the chase, her expression rapt as she turned her face to the knight, who was speaking. They laughed in mutual pleasure, but it was the triumphant note in Sir Richard's laughter which goaded Conrad to follow the hunt.

The gossip and speculation of Eleanor's marriage to Norton had been the talk of the village. When the huntsman's horn sounded, proclaiming a boar had been found, he saw Sir Richard and Eleanor slow their pace to a walk, allowing the rest of the party to overtake them. A cornered boar was a dangerous beast and Sir Richard was prudent to keep Eleanor out of danger lest the boar turned and charged.

Conrad's eyes narrowed as the two horses drew to a halt in a clearing. Eleanor laughed at something the knight said and, as she did so, looked in Conrad's direction. He drew Solomon further back into the trees, but from the tilt of her chin he was certain that she had seen him.

After her shock at discovering Conrad still in the district, Eleanor was overtaken by a desire to teach the squire a lesson. His kiss had unwittingly drawn an avowal of love from her, which of course was absurd. The sooner he was disabused of the idea that she cared for him, the better she would feel. She still burned with humiliation at the way he had degraded her. All at once Sir Richard seemed the ideal husband. She turned to the knight and smiled radiantly.

'It's a lovely morning, Sir Richard. Shall we await the return of the huntsmen by that willow? From there we will have a spectacular view of the valley and castle.'

Sir Richard leapt nimbly from his destrier and raised his hands to close upon Eleanor's waist. 'There is much about Highford to commend its beauty. Not least of all yourself, my dear. By the hour I fall more deeply beneath its spell.'

She put her hands on to his shoulders and when he lowered her to the ground kept them there, her smile enticing as she stared up into his handsome face. 'Sir Richard, you are shamelessly taking advantage of our being alone.'

'How else are we to become better acquainted?' The tenderness mixed with merriment in his eyes was a combination Eleanor found hard to resist. It made it easier to teach Conrad the lesson he deserved. Removing her hands from Sir Richard's shoulders, she walked to a tree which was in full view of Conrad's vision, and, leaning back against it, watched the knight as he tethered their mounts before joining her.

'The hunt has brought the colour back to your cheeks, Lady Eleanor.' Sir Richard placed a hand on the tree-trunk at the side of her head and smiled down at her. 'You are a very beautiful and delightful companion.'

'It is long since I was in such enjoyable company.' It was exciting to spar verbally with him, but his nearness did not stir her senses as another had done. She suppressed the comparison. This was the man she intended to marry.

'Lady Eleanor, I had hoped we would have longer together, but a messenger arrived at Highford an hour past. Your father and I have been recalled by King Richard. I leave tomorrow.'

'You are leaving so soon?' She was surprised at how much the news disappointed her.

'Your words give me heart.' He took her hand and raised it part way to his lips. His expression became serious. 'Before I formally speak with your father, I would know whether you would look favourably upon our marriage. I have been too long unwed to wish for an unwilling bride. And I will do all in my power to make you happy, my dear.'

The sincerity of his words moved Eleanor and cast aside the last of her doubts. 'I would be honoured to become your wife.'

The joy in his eyes reassured her she had made the right decision. Few women of her rank were fortunate enough to marry for love. He bowed his head to press his lips to her fingers, but, seeing she still wore her riding gloves, he laughed softly. Taking her into his arms, he kissed her mouth tenderly. The touch of his lips was pleasant, but that was all. It increased her confusion. She could not understand why she did not feel desire for the knight, when in so many other ways he roused such feelings of warmth and friendship. Dismayed, she prayed that she would make him a good wife. The distant sound of a horse pushing through the undergrowth brought her eyes open. Conrad's figure was disappearing through the thick foliage.

Sir Richard drew back, his smile undiminished. He would see her reticence as maidenly modesty.

'I shall speak with Sir Cedric when we return. Our betrothal will be announced tonight. There's no reason why King Richard will not approve our match. We will have a late summer wedding.' His gaze was ardent as he kissed her once more before he released her. 'My people at Belrise will decorate their houses and the village streets in your honour. There is no finer place in England in September than Belrise, but none of its beauty will equal that of its new Lady.'

Eleanor blushed at the extravagance of his compliment. September was weeks away, time enough, she hoped, for the raw edge of panic she now felt at her impending marriage to ebb into stoical acceptance.

The great hall at Highford blazed with light. The mummers and musicians had arrived in time for the celebration. Sir Cedric had ordered the wine to flow freely throughout the evening, and the villagers had been invited to dine at trestles set out in the courtyard. When Eleanor and Sir Richard presented themselves to the gathering, they were met with rousing cheers. But Eleanor was aware of the restrained note in many of their voices. Some of the older inhabitants of Highford still regarded her family as the intruder here. Her marriage to Sir Richard was another link in the chain which took them further away from the old ties with the past.

'Sir Richard, will we visit Highford often?' Her distress entered her voice. She had not realised how much she cared for Highford and its people. They were a part of her life which she had taken for granted. This was the only home she really remembered and she regarded its people as an extension of her family. Sir Richard might own grander castles, but she knew none would hold the same place as Highford in her heart. 'I would not like to see Highford relegated to an accounting house to fill your coffers.'

He considered the matter, giving her question the serious thought it deserved. 'It is far from my estates on the Welsh border, but clearly it is a place you cherish. We will come here as often as possible. Three or four times a year.' On seeing her crestfallen expression, he smiled. 'If you are truly homesick we will come more often. I doubt I will be able to deny you anything. But I promise you will not be disappointed in Belrise or Westchester castles when we visit them. There is also the town house along the banks of the Thames in London, for when I must attend my duties at Court.'

'So much travelling, Sir Richard.' She was excited at the prospect of visiting so many new places, but knew that Highford would never be far from her thoughts. In the future would come a time when Conrad would lay siege to the castle. Would the people welcome him with open arms? She suspected that they would. He would be no absentee lord. It was a matter she must discuss with Sir Richard, but time enough for that once they were

married. She dragged her mind back to the compliment
Sir Richard was paying her.

'You will be the most beautiful and fêted lady at
Court. My people will adore you.' His expression sobered as he smiled into her eyes. 'As I already adore you,
dearest Eleanor.'

Before she could collect her thoughts, he took her arm
and led her into the space cleared for the dancing. The
musicians struck up a stately dance and she was surprised
at the lightness of his step. Was there nothing this man
was not accomplished at? With each passing hour in his
company, the prospect of marriage to him became less
daunting. Throughout the banquet he was kind and
solicitous to all her needs. His conversation was entertaining, interspersed with amusing anecdotes of his life
at Court. It was impossible not to be relaxed and
comfortable in his company, but, as the evening progressed, a nagging unease pressed on her mind. Too
often for her comfort, the image of Conrad D'Arton
haunted her.

Determined to ignore it, she gave her full attention to
her betrothed. In repose, his face was youthful and that
of a man at peace with himself. Laughter was never far
from his eyes, or lips, as he exchanged quips with his
men. Yet there remained a commanding authority about
him. It was there when he entered a room, present in the
deference shown him by her father and his vassals. It
was a combination she had sensed in Conrad, but Sir
Richard had honed it to a more subtle, mature quality.

Eleanor turned her most ravishing smile upon Sir
Richard as he raised his goblet in salute to her. She was
angry at allowing her thoughts to return to her enemy
during this special evening. To her surprise she saw that
the candles had burned low, casting giantic shadows of
their guests up on to the walls. The hour must be late.
Many of Sir Cedric's and Sir Richard's retainers had
fallen asleep over the table, and the heads of several
others were nodding down on to their chests. 'I would

bid you goodnight, Sir Richard. You will be wanting an early start in the morning and, from the looks of your men, many will have thick heads.'

He stood up to take her hand and escort her from the dais. 'Your loveliness tempts me to dance with you until dawn. I have held you so briefly in my arms. The weeks ahead will be desolate until our marriage.' He placed a hand over his heart. 'I will have only my dreams to remember you by.'

She laughed aside his outrageous flattery. 'I will see you again before you depart. I shall miss you too, Sir Richard.'

It was the truth, and the knowledge pleasantly startled her. Yet a cynical voice reasoned that she would not miss him as a lover, but as a close and trusted friend. None of her doubts showed in her face as she took her leave, though her thoughts remained dark and forbidding throughout the night.

Unable to sleep, Eleanor tossed and turned in her bed as the castle gradually stilled in slumber. From the antechamber where Griselda slept she could hear her maid's resonant snores. Griselda had enthusiastically celebrated her mistress's betrothal and it was unlikely that even a violent thunderstorm would disturb the maid's stupor this night.

Eleanor sat up and gave her pillow a hard thump. She glanced at the unshuttered window which let in a wide beam of moonlight. Perhaps if she closed the shutter sleep would come more quickly in a dark room. The warmth of the bed made her hesitant to leave it. Then her attention was caught by a movement from the hanging on the curved wall which abutted a turret. She tensed and stared harder into the corner. The white unicorn on the tapestry was picked out by the moonlight. It appeared to leap forward, then jump back. The far corner was in dark shadow and Eleanor could discern nothing, but a sixth sense warned her that she was no longer alone.

'Who's there?'

She sat up, her hand seeking the heavy bronze candlestick at her bedside. Her fingers brushed against it as the figure materialised out of the gloom. 'Guar——!'

Her cry for help was smothered by a hand. Instinctively, her fingers gripped the candlestick and, using all her strength, she swung it up towards the intruder's head. Her wrist jarred as the improvised weapon contacted with a body. The man's weight slumped across her into the beam of moonlight splashed across her bed. His hand remained clamped across her mouth, but in the fall his hood had fallen back to reveal a mane of tawny hair.

'Of all the rooms that passage had to open into, it would be yours.' Conrad lifted his head to glare at her.

Eleanor tried to speak, but words were impossible beneath the pressure of his hand. The furious glitter in her eyes as she began to fight to free herself brought a chuckle from him.

'You cannot fight me and win. Be still.'

Eleanor's answer was to struggle harder, desperate now to free her mouth and scream for the guards.

CHAPTER SIX

'WILL you be still, Eleanor?' Conrad ground out.

He could not believe his ill fortune that the passage came out into her room, and that she was still awake. The struggling virago, whose eyes spewed venom up at him, bore little resemblance to the seductive sorceress who had swooned in his arms yesterday. What game had she been playing then? Did she think him such a slave to his senses that her submission and soft words of love would turn him from his vow to reclaim his birthright? Exasperated by her defiance, he mounted the bed and straddled her to stop her wriggling from his hold and giving the alarm.

He had been right to distrust her. He had seen her for the liar and wanton she was. After her avowal that Gauthier and Ralph would be cared for then set free, Oswald had sent him word that Sir Cedric had ordered the two men imprisoned in a cell at the top of the keep. He had returned to free them.

On his return to Highford, Conrad had discovered the guard had been doubled and that Sir Cedric was to ride north on the morrow to rejoin King Richard at Nottingham castle. Word had it that Henry Tudor had left his exile in Rouen to sail from Harfleur and had already landed at Milford Haven in Wales. Conrad would ride at first light with all the men he could muster to serve Henry.

The second secret passage he had learned of from Sir Lionel went no higher than this room. By misfortune it now belonged to Eleanor. His anger returned as he stared down at her struggling figure. Treachery was in her blood. It had not taken her long to throw herself at Sir Richard Norton. He had thought the bachelor knight too experienced to be taken in by such false innocence. Several times the knight's name had been romantically linked with a high-ranking noblewoman. None of his mistresses had he taken to wife. Yet Norton had soon become enmeshed in Eleanor's scheming web. Were it not that Highford was the wench's dowry, he would think the couple well suited.

Now, as she threshed beneath him, the covers slid down from her writhing figure, and he was acutely aware of the feel of her breasts and hips trapped beneath him. It brought the inevitable response from his virile body. In their struggles her hair had spilled from its loose braids and spread its tendrils of purest gold over the pillow. She was his enemy, a liar, and, from her responses to his kisses, probably a wanton. Yet he could not stop his senses from becoming throbbingly aware of the tantalising pressure of her firm breasts and soft feminine body. She was beautiful and alluring. Her skin was as translucent as mother-of-pearl and the smell of its perfumed freshness fed his desire. He had never in his life taken a woman by force, and he had no intention of doing so now, but the insidious ache in his loins, if not suppressed, would soon drive him beyond coherent reason.

He eased back. Instantly she increased her attack. Something in that continued defiance, in the way her eyes sparked their fury, touched a chord within in him. His anger was tempered by tenderness, by an irrational need to protect her. He almost laughed aloud at the nonsense of that impulse. It took all his strength to subdue the writhing hell-vixen without hurting her. She had no need of protection.

'Eleanor, give me your word you will not cry out and I will release you.'

She nodded, though her eyes continued to glitter dangerously. He removed his hand from her mouth, but reamined poised ready to silence her should she attempt to scream.

'How did you get back into the castle? The trapdoor to the tunnel was blocked.'

He grinned. 'I left instructions with those loyal to me to ensure that any alterations of the armoury stores were to be returned to their original places. I met with no obstacle.'

'Where does that second passage lead?' Her curiosity overcame her anger at his treatment.

He raised a mocking brow. 'The true owner of Highford knows all its secrets.'

As her mouth opened to protest, he placed his hand lightly upon it. 'Protest all you will, lovely Eleanor. Highford will be mine. And all who live here will be my vassals.'

Her answer was muffled behind his hand and he lifted it to permit her to speak, but his expression warned her of the folly of crying out.

'You live in dreams of past glory, sir squire.' The words were not louder than a whisper. 'My husband will be Lord of Highford, not you.' She stopped struggling, but the fury remained brilliant in her indigo eyes. 'Why are you here? It's madness. Sir Cedric will hang you if you are caught.'

'As he intends to hang Gauthier and Ralph. So much for your promise they would be safe.'

'They are. They will leave the infirmary tomorrow and——'

'They are in chains. Just two floors above this room in the prison cell. I returned to rescue them.'

Her shocked expression was too real to be feigned. At seeing her eyes flaring with outrage, Conrad inwardly sighed. Her beauty affected him deeply and at that moment he regretted that the force he had exerted to subdue her had provoked her anger against him.

She stopped fighting him. 'Father was suspicious when he found your horse in the stables. I should have taken more care that your men were not harmed. I thought their story that they were pilgrims had been believed.

I'm sorry, Conrad.' The admission was sincere. Then her eyes narrowed. 'But how did you learn of this? Have you spies in the castle?'

'Not spies — loyal vassals to their rightful overlord. They know that I will take my rightful place at Highford.' His gaze travelled over her figure. She slept naked and only a sheet protected her from his eyes. 'Admit it. Admit also that you can never fight me and win.'

'I will die before I submit to your lechery. I will be mistress of my own life.'

'You are first the King's, then your father's pawn in the marriage stakes,' he said with fearsome honesty. 'As to controlling your passionate nature. . . Ah, there, sweet Eleanor, you will be a slave to the man who masters it.'

He kissed her with deliberate intent to rouse the passion in her blood. At her gasp he drew back triumphant to stare into her eyes. They still blazed with defiance, but there was a subtle change in their luminous depths: indigo had turned to violet, betraying her submission to his will, though pride kept the blue sparks of anger alive. It was then as his own anger cooled that he noticed the bruises on her face.

'Who did that to you?' He lightly touched the purple shadow. Shamed, she turned her head away, but his fingers were insistent and she was forced to meet his outraged stare. His face was tight with torment. 'Sir Cedric did this. The man is a brute. He should be called to account.'

Eleanor lay still, outwardly vanquished while her eyes defied him to force his will upon her. When he continued his bold appraisal of her figure, outlined clearly beneath the sheet, she knew the battle lost. From the instant he had lain across her, she had felt her body tingle and play her traitor.

During the hours she had been unable to sleep, she had imagined him beside her, felt again the touch of his

lips and the response of her body. It had shocked her
that her body craved his touch, yearning to be carried
beyond the first smoulderings of passion to the promise
offered by a forbidden mystery still to unfold. No matter
how hard she fought her longing, her mind betrayed her.
The remembered flames, all-consuming, all-replenish-
ing, fanned her body, branding Conrad's image into her
mind. Then like a conjured demon he had appeared.
Reality had been brutally cruel. The gentle lover of last
night was gone, replaced by an avenging tormentor. So
why did his nearness inflame her soul, causing her heart
to beat wildly in a way that Sir Richard's never could?

She glared at him, conscious of the wicked coercion of
his grin. His smile transformed his rugged countenance.
That smile was a blatant assault upon any woman's
heart. Her own fluttered alarmingly. When his gaze
returned to her breasts, she felt their crests hardening.
She heard him draw in his breath, desire hardening the
handsome lines of his face, his eyes dark as they burned
into her, commanding her submission.

'Never will I admit you are my master.'

The husky challenge broke through Conrad's resolve.
Impulse conquered reason. He saw her swallow. The tip
of her tongue flicked nervously over her lips, and her
mouth parted, tremulous, beckoning. With a tortured
groan he lowered his lips to hers. It was a savage kiss
meant to punish her. As her lips moulded to his, her
body pliant beneath his weight, he savoured the pulsating heat that emanated between them. He forgot everything but the sensuality they provoked. His kiss became
tender, his hand sliding beneath her slender body.

Eleanor moaned softly as he kissed her eyelids. It was
happening again. The magic he created upon her senses
made her powerless to resist. His lips caressed the
corners of her mouth and travelled with infinite slowness
to the hollow of her neck. She moved languorously,
closing her eyes to experience more fully the ecstatic
sensations washing over her. Her head rolled back, her

body moving with an unfamiliar restlessness aroused by his touch. His hands moved over her shoulders and slipped beneath the sheet to capture her breast. The touch of his palm, calloused from hours of sword practice, was excitingly abrasive against her soft flesh. When his mouth travelled the same path to tease and fasten over its crest, she sighed low in her throat, a deep and devouring ache taking her in its thrall.

Her arms went about him, her murmurs muffled against his hair as her kisses became wilder. Her hand felt the clamouring urgency of his heart, which matched the rapid pounding of her own. Every touch and kiss was causing sensations to spiral through her which set her emotions into discord. The trail of lips blazoned across her ribcage to the taut flatness of her stomach. Her body was moving in a slow gyration, her will was no longer her own. It was in harmony to the fine attunement of his commanding touch.

'Eleanor.' Her name was a husky throb as his hand slid over her thighs to touch the core of her womanhood and slide into its moist heat.

The shocking intimacy of that touch jolted her back to reality. She yelped and pushed against his shoulder. 'No!'

He looked at her as though she had gone insane. His face was taut with the savagery of his desire.

'Please—no!' Her eyes were wide with the terror only a virgin would convey.

'By all that's holy, woman! Do you think I am cast from bronze to stop now?'

'Stop you must. I beseech you. I'm a maid.' Her voice broke on a sob. 'What manner of devil are you that would make a wanton of me? Make me forget that today I was betrothed to an honourable man?'

A look of pain contorted his face and with a shudder Conrad drew back. He took several deep breaths and Eleanor seized the advantage to pull the sheet to her chin. She was shaking from reaction and her face felt on fire with embarrassment at the liberties she had permitted. After a moment he turned to regard her, his expression masked of emotion.

He lifted a curling lock of her hair, his voice gruff. 'I believe the Devil mocks us both.'

Releasing her hair, he rolled from the bed and crossed the room to the door. 'I go to release my men. I spared your virtue. Have you the grace to spare their lives?' He swept her a mocking bow and was gone from the chamber.

Eleanor flopped down on to the mattress and stared unseeing at the canopy above her head. She knew she would not rouse the guard. She did not want to see Gauthier and Ralph hang. She wanted Conrad to free them. And that was the only reason that she remained silent, she convinced herself.

Eleanor was awoken the next morning by the clatter of heavy feet running through the castle and a great deal of shouting. Griselda came into Eleanor's room, her plump face pale from the excesses of the previous night.

'Such goings-on, my lady. Those two pilgrims — who apparently were not pilgrims at all — had been locked up. Last night their guard was knocked unconscious and they escaped. The portcullis had not been raised, but there's no sign of them within the castle. They disappeared without trace, just like that pedlar did.'

'A puzzle indeed, Griselda.' Eleanor yawned and stretched her arms above her head. 'Sir Cedric will solve the mystery. It is impossible for two men to vanish without trace.'

She avoided Griselda's watchful stare, afraid that her face would show her guilty secret that, instead of raising the guard to arrest her enemy, she had allowed Conrad to make love to her. 'Now I must dress. From the noise in the courtyard the horses are being assembled. Sir Cedric and Sir Richard leave as soon as they have broken their fast.'

Eleanor was glad that Conrad and his men had escaped but could not shake off the guilt she felt at the abandoned way her body had reacted to Conrad's lovemaking. Sir Richard did not deserve such disloyalty. From this moment she would be an exemplary affianced bride. She was determined to forget Conrad. D'Arton had more conceit in his own self-importance than an earl, yet the man was no better than a lowly squire. Furthermore his manners were atrocious and he had no concept of chivalry. She chose to blot from her mind that he had not ravished her against her will. From this day she would be all Sir Richard desired in his future wife, loving and dutiful.

When she entered the great hall, the admiration and tenderness in Sir Richard's eyes made it so easy to respond to his kindness. She summoned her brightest smile, loath that he should suspect that her heart was in turmoil. He was the most worthy of knights, and she would be deserving of him.

Their fast broken and Mass attended in the church, Sir Richard took her aside as Sir Cedric and his followers left the room. 'You look pale, Eleanor. Dare I hope it is because I am leaving?'

After the callousness of Conrad's treatment, Sir Richard's concern was reassuring. She had a true fondness for her betrothed. 'I think you know the answer to that. Do you not ride now to join our King? It is rumoured that soon a battle must be met with Henry Tudor.' She reached out, her affection for him making her take his hand in hers. 'I fear for you. A woman's foolish fears, I know, for the reputation of your prowess in the lists goes before you.'

Pleasure at her words lit his face. The years had not taken their toll upon his handsome looks; rather they had added a serenity which came from a refined power and confidence in his own ability.

She unpinned the pale blue veil from the point of her low hennin head-dress and pressed it into his hands.

'Will you ride into battle wearing my favour, Sir Richard?'

'I would be honoured, my lady.' He took it and placed it within his tunic, then stooped to press a kiss to her lips. She returned it with what she hoped was warmth, but it had roused no passion within her.

He linked her arm possessively through his as they walked from the church to the courtyard. Sir Cedric and their two small armies of retainers were already gathered. When both knights were mounted, Eleanor took the stirrup cup from a page and offered it first to her father. He drank from it and handed it back. 'I regret I must take your betrothed from you so soon, Eleanor. Send to town for a seamstress and materials for several gowns to be made. There's little time before your wedding to prepare.' He leaned closer, his tone menacing. 'There will be no more visits to the priory either.'

Eleanor stepped back, her eyes lowered so Sir Cedric did not see the rebellion which sparked there. After years of neglect he was prepared to be generous now that she was to be married to a rich and powerful baron. But she would not forget her brother. She intended to visit Daniel as soon as her father left Highford.

Nothing of her rebellion showed in the sweet expression she bestowed upon Sir Richard. He had been watching her father and for a moment his mouth had curled with intense dislike. It shocked Eleanor. She had realised that during their stay Sir Richard did not seek her father's company. It was strange then that Sir Richard was so eager for a marriage which would unite their two families.

'Why do you wish to marry me?' she asked bluntly. 'You have little regard for my father.'

Their hands touched as he took the stirrup cup from her. Her words had surprised him and he stared down at the cup, considering her words. Then with a gallant gesture he leaned forward in the saddle and raised her fingers to his lips in loving salute. 'My dear, I'm not marrying Sir Cedric, but his lovely and vivacious daughter. When next we meet, it will be when I come to claim you as my bride.'

He had skilfully parried her question by pleasantry, and from his expression he would at this moment elaborate no further.

'God protect and keep you, my lord.'

As the cavalcade rode out, there were a few weak cheers from the villagers. Eleanor frowned as she saw the sullen expressions on the faces of her people. Only a few of the villagers had ridden to swell her father's ranks. Yet there were few young men of fighting age present today in the castle. These were conspicuous by their absence.

She noticed the same when an hour later she rode through the village accompanied by an escort of three grooms. Her excuse of visiting the priory was a simple one. She went to give alms to be dispensed to the poor, as part of her betrothal celebrations. The men would wait outside while she visited her brother.

However the absence of the men of Highford worried her. She suspected they had joined Conrad. He had made no secret that many families at Highford remained loyal to the D'Artons. The villagers had little love of Sir Cedric, but until now Eleanor believed they had accepted her. It was disquieting to have that faith shaken. Who at Highford could she now trust?

Conrad was on the road to Wales an hour before dawn brightened the horizon. When word had got around the village that he was in the district, a score of men led by Oswald's son, William, had come to the waterfall. When confronted by Conrad's guards they had demanded to see the rightful Lord of Highford. To a man they had sworn fealty to him. Deeply moved, Conrad had accepted their homage and their demands to fight for the Lancastrian cause. That only one of the men possessed a horse had not deterred his followers. They rode doubled up to the outlying villages sequestering in Conrad's name enough mounts for his men, with promises of repayment when Conrad returned as Lord of Highford.

He had not expected to carry away with him from Highford a sense of regret which with each mile became a deeper part of him. It tore through his body, consuming his thoughts. Anger, distrust, betrayal, thwarted desire, even loss, all raged through him. And the loss was not all for the castle and lands, but for the woman who had brought a madness to his blood. Repossessing Highford had become an obsession as important to him as winning his knighthood. The woman had become entangled in his schemes. Weeks of tension, deprivation and exhaustion had taken their toll upon him. The male within him had responded to her courage and beauty. Knowing that a battle was imminent, he had reacted to the basic need of all warriors to seek succour in physical pleasure and forgetfulness in the arms of woman.

The spell of Highford lingered, fuelling his obsession. That the image of the woman refused to be banished and became irrevocably intermeshed with the fulfilment of his desires he was not prepared to acknowledge.

Eleanor reined in her horse at the priory gates and ordered the escort to take their ease and await her. On entering the priory, she was presented to Mother Benedicta, who was taking her exercise in the cloisters. The prioress's long, thin face, wrinkled by thirty years of austerity, regarded her with unusual severity.

'Sir Cedric has commanded that you are not to see Daniel.'

'But he is my brother!' Eleanor protested.

Mother Benedicta closed the bible she had been reading and held it close to her chest. 'We must do what is best for Daniel. Sir Cedric visited him yesterday. Daniel behaved badly.' She shrugged in a gesture of sadness and defeat. 'You know how Daniel is with strangers. He threw one of his fits—it was terrible to see. Sir Cedric was distraught. Daniel is to leave us. He is to go to Arnwood Abbey. Apparently the monks there have dealt with such cases of brain fever before.'

Eleanor refused to believe that Daniel was mentally unstable. 'Daniel was frightened. It will make him worse to take him away from the people he knows. He has no brain fever. He's just——'

'My child, calm yourself,' Mother Benedicta instructed. 'In this Sir Cedric knows best.' She regarded Eleanor, seeking the right words of comfort. 'We all love Daniel dearly. None of us wanted to believe there was more to his tantrums than childish frustration. Since Sir Cedric left he has been uncontrollable.' She bit her lip and the creases in her face deepened with sorrow. 'We have had to tie the boy to his bed to stop him from injuring himself.'

Eleanor was appalled at such treatment. Her shock must have showed in her face for Mother Benedicta's eyes were tearful in understanding. 'Lady Eleanor, we had no choice. Daniel has lost his reason. He became demented.'

Eleanor shook her head. 'It's love Daniel needs. Not being shut away. It's time he led a normal life.'

'Sir Cedric must be obeyed.' The prioress's expression softened. 'But perhaps you should see Daniel. Then you will understand that he is beyond our help. Perhaps your voice will calm him. He trusts you. Try and explain to him what is happening.' Mother Benedicta shook her head sadly. 'My dear, there can be no normal life for Daniel.'

She led the way to Daniel's cell, which overlooked the gardens. The door was shut. The prioress motioned Eleanor to be silent. She drew back a peep-hole in the cell door and looked through it. 'He is quiet for the moment.'

Eleanor put her eye to the opening. Daniel lay on his bed with several ropes binding his body to the structure. He lay still, his mouth dropped open into a silent scream, a red hole in his pinched elfin face. His eyes were round and staring fixedly at the ceiling, his brown hair was tousled, his fingernails were bloodied and his fingers twitched. He was locked into some inner horror.

'You cannot leave him like that,' Eleanor said, aghast. 'He needs the comfort of loving arms around him.'

She pulled at the door to open it and it rattled in the aperture. It was locked. The noise brought a high-pitched scream from within, followed by animal grunts. Eleanor looked through the peep-hole, and was sickened at what she now saw. Daniel was unrecognisable. His face was twisted into a demonic mask, foam and spittle spraying from his mouth, his eyes large and bulging from their sockets, while all the time he grunted and made guttural animal sounds.

'Sweet Mary, Mother of God, what ails the child?' Eleanor turned on the prioress.

There were tears in Mother Benedicta's eyes. 'He is mad. That is why he must go to Arnwood Abbey. The monks there know how to treat him. He will be well looked after.'

'I will not permit it.' Eleanor remained firm. 'He is not mad. He needs love and I can give him that.'

The prioress sighed. 'Sir Cedric should have spoken to you of this. Lady Eleanor, you must accept it is for the best. I fear that Daniel is not the first Twyneham to spend his life in the care of the monks.'

At Elanor's stricken expression, Mother Benedicta went on with evident reluctance. 'Several men in your family have been similarly afflicted. Your grandfather ended his days there and also Sir Cedric's younger brother.'

Eleanor put her hand to her mouth to stem a rush of nausea. 'Are you saying that madness runs in our family?'

'It is not for me to say. Sir Cedric must speak of it.'

'He will not.' Eleanor lifted an imploring hand towards

the prioress. 'I must know the truth. Tell me all you
know.'

Mother Benedicta faced a small figure of the Madonna
set into a niche in the wall. After a pause she turned to
Eleanor and spoke in a troubled voice. 'The sickness
strikes your family only in the male line. When Sir
Cedric first saw the signs in Daniel he had the boy
confined here. Several boys so afflicted have died in
infancy.'

'How do you know all this, when I have been told
nothing?'

'Sir Cedric broke down when he saw Daniel.' Mother
Benedicta tucked her hands into her wide sleeves as she
continued to hold Eleanor's forthright stare. 'He con-
fided in me. Then swore me to tell no outsiders of his
family shame. I tell you because you are his daughter.
But you have no need to fear for yourself.'

'Of course it affects me.' Eleanor reeled against the
wall. 'Sweet Jesu. My father has just betrothed me to Sir
Richard. Any son I bear him could be equally affected.
How can I marry anyone and risk that?'

'It is your duty to marry, Lady Eleanor,' the prioress
said sternly. 'The fate of your children is in God's hands.'

'No. It is in mine.' She began to pace the narrow
corridor, her hands clenched hard against her sides to
prevent the impulse to strike out at the wall. She wanted
to hit out at the world which had just dealt her so cruel
and bitter a blow. The future of marriage and children
she had always believed would be hers was now in ashes.
'I will bear no man a child. Do you think I would risk
giving birth to a child who could live his life in an insane
hell?'

'My dear, the shock has made you distraught. Sir
Cedric assures me that not all the male line are affected.
Is not your father sane enough? And your uncle Godfrey?
There are your cousins, Edward and Thomas.'

'And endless miscarried sons and dead infants,'
Eleanor responded darkly. And her father had the

Devil's own temper, which bordered perilously close to the edge of insanity. When she again found the strength to speak, her voice was a jagged thread of its former vibrancy. 'And how many children were shut away and forgotten to hide the Twyneham shame?'

She put a trembling hand to her brow and her throat cramped in a spasm of agonised misery. She stared at the figure of the Madonna, its serene face blurring as tears spilled on to her cheeks. Her voice crackled with pain as she made her vow. 'I will never marry. Sir Richard Norton does not deserve that I should taint his line. I will never bear a child lest I condemn it to Daniel's fate.'

CHAPTER SEVEN

ON AUGUST the twenty-second, 1485, two armies faced each other across Bosworth Field. Except for the differing badges showing the supporters of York or Lancaster, the men of both armies looked much the same. Conrad felt the sweat dampening his palms beneath his steel gauntlets and the blood pumped harder through his heart. The anticipation of battle heightened all his senses. Somewhere in the pre-charge stillness a skylark hovered high above, trilling out its song.

The air crackled with tension and Conrad adjusted the weight of his shield on his arm. As he looked down at the gold background with the black wolf of D'Arton emblazoned upon it, he felt a fresh glow of pride. The shield was his father's, but his was now the right to bear the noble arms of D'Arton in battle. Two days ago Henry Tudor had knighted him.

Conrad stared along the line of knights, their weapons and armour glinting in the sunlight. With surcoats, shields, pennons and the horses' caparisons all bearing the colourful heraldic devices, the knights were a riot of colour against the greys and browns of the soldiers.

Conrad studied both armies through the restricted vision of his raised visor. Pikemen guarded the ranks of musketmen and archers. The common soldiers wore padded tunics and were less encumbered than the gentry in their breastplates, or the noblemen encased in full armour. Everywhere coloured pennons and standards fluttered in the breeze. The field was as brilliant as any pageant or tourney, but Conrad knew that today there would be no quarter given. It was kill or be killed, for there would be no prisoners.

Opposite them across the field, the short figure of

King Richard, his crown gleaming in the sunlight, rode along his ranks, rousing his men. To the right of Conrad, beneath his standard bearing the Welsh dragon, Henry Tudor addressed his troops. There was no doubt in Conrad's mind that throughout the years of the Wars of the Roses it had been the Lancastrian cause which was the just one. By upholding his belief, his father Sir Lionel had lost everything. From the battle this day Conrad hoped to reclaim his family's estates and fortune.

Henry Tudor raised his mailed fist as his voice rose to a fervent pitch. 'In the name of God and St George, ride forth.'

Conrad snapped down his visor. His sword was poised ready to strike down the enemy as his destrier trotted forward, then beiefly cantered, before the ground vibrated from the thunder of galloping hoofs as the two armies charged each other.

A cloud of arrows and crossbow bolts from the Plantagenet bowmen hailed down upon them, killing a squire on Conrad's left. A musket shot wounded a knight's horse directly ahead. Conrad manoeuvred his destrier around the falling horses and men, his arm jarring as his sword skewered his first opponent. He saw limbs hacked off, skulls split open, blood and gore obliterating a knight's heraldic device as he lay trampled on the ground beneath the stamping hoofs. In the thick of the battle when it had begun to turn in their favour, Conrad caught sight of the bull device of Sir Richard Norton.

The heat in his blood intensified as he regarded Eleanor's betrothed. He had turned his destrier towards Norton before he realised that the knight was locked in combat against two others, both bearing the white rose of York on their sleeves. Norton had changed his allegiance to support Henry Tudor. No easy matter now to wrest Highford from his clutches should he marry Eleanor Twyneham. The thought was mercurial in its swiftness. There was no time for reflection upon a battlefield — he needed all his wits just to stay alive.

Conrad threshed his way through a dozen knights and squires, his sword arm aching from wielding his sword. Ahead of him he glimpsed the cockerel device of Sir Cedric Twyneham. His enemy was in the thick of the fighting, and as Conrad hacked and sliced his way towards him he saw Twyneham's tunic ripped apart, exposing the dented armour beneath. The thought that the traitor who had stolen Highford must die rang through Conrad's brain, muting the screams of dying men and horses. His sword locked with that of Sir Cedric and the older man reeled in the saddle from the force of its blow. A glint of steel from Conrad's right forced him to parry a mace blow from another Yorkist knight, which would have sent him sprawling to the ground. His reaction and counter blow was swift. He lunged, feeling the resistance of shattering bones as his sword point entered the armoured knight's body at his most vulnerable spot, beneath the armpit. Breathing heavily from his exertions, Conrad wrenched it free. The knight keeled sideways in his saddle and veered out of Conrad's limited range of sight.

Partially blinded by the sweat dripping over his eyes, Conrad again whirled to face Sir Cedric. Too late he saw Twyneham's blade slicing across to behead him. Conrad ducked, at the same time deflecting the lethal thrust with his shield. There was a flame of fire along his thigh, then his mind shut out the pain as he concentrated on fighting for survival. He blinked aside the sweat which blurred his vision, fighting by instinct, needing to cover all sides at once to avoid a chance blow from behind unseating him.

Another horse had pushed its way between him and Sir Cedric. Sir Richard Norton was to the right of Twyneham and Conrad glimpsed a sword arcing downwards into the mêlée of riders. Then Twyneham was no longer visible. His enemy had fallen and Norton was engaged in deadly combat with another knight. Too hard-pressed to pursue a single vendetta, Conrad found himself carried forward in the momentum of the battle.

Time became a haze of forcing tired limbs beyond their limits. His brain dulled to the cries of the dying. A white charger jostled his destrier as the rider charged towards the Tudor standard. There was a flash of sunlight upon the golden crown, circling the domed helmet. Conrad gave pursuit as Richard Plantagenet bore down upon Henry Tudor. Loyalty to save Henry drove Conrad to defend his suzerain, but he was too accomplished a soldier not to mark the bravery of the Plantagenet's attack. Richard was alone. The battle was going against him. It was a last desperate bid to wrest glory out of failure — to kill and reign supreme, or die in the fight.

Conrad slowed his pace. Richard Plantagenet's prowess as a soldier was legion. In single combat he would undoubtedly have triumphed over Henry Tudor. But Henry was well defended by his knights. King Richard's sword struck down the standard bearer, but, as it was raised towards Henry, the King was surrounded by the Lancastrians. He went down under their attack. The brutality of their butchery as they continued to stab and hack at the fallen body of Richard sickened Conrad.

A cry went up. 'The King is dead — long live the King!'

It spread through the battleground. Men lowered their swords. The defeated hung their heads, while the supporters of Henry raised their triumpant voices. 'A Henry! A Henry!'

Conrad watched as a knight lifted Richard's crown from a thorn bush. He handed it to Thomas Stanley, who knelt before Henry Tudor. All the knights dismounted to kneel in homage, and, to rousing acclaim, Stanley placed the crown on the head of King Henry VII. As the new King moved on to take his place at the head of his army, Conrad became aware of the pain stabbing through his thigh. He looked down at it and was surprised to discover that the steel plate had been smashed, and it hung down from a broken leather strap. Beneath it blood seeped through the broken links of his chain-mail. He dimly recalled a blow from Twyneham, but since then the battle had numbed him to everything except vanquish or perish. He bit back a wince as he straightened. The life was returning to his leg with a vengeance and he limped stiffly to his horse.

He joined the triumphant procession on its journey to Leicester. Henry Tudor, wearing his crown, ordered the trumpeters to precede him. As they picked their way across the fallen bodies on the battlefield, Conrad saw an aged squire bent over the dead body of Sir Cedric Twyneham. At first he thought the man was weeping, but as he came closer he saw that the squire was struggling to pull a gold ring from Twyneham's finger. It was stuck fast and the man drew his dagger to hack off the member.

'Hold!' Conrad commanded, incensed at the desecration of the dead. For all the hatred he bore Twyneham, the knight had fought bravely and deserved more respect. 'Return Twyneham's body to Arnwood in Kent for a proper burial and his widow will richly reward you beyond the value of that ring. I've noted your face. You are Twyneham's squire. If the deed is not done I will see you hung for theft from your master.'

Conrad took his place in the middle of the cavalcade. Ahead of him rode the proud figure of Sir Richard Norton. Had it been his sword which had killed Twyneham? He could not say for certain, but the look he had seen on the knight's face as he fought him had been filled with the same hatred that scoured his own heart. If Norton so hated Twyneham why had he become betrothed to Eleanor and thus aligned himself with Sir Cedric? It was a thought which was to trouble Conrad for some days, but each time the answer which came to him was that Eleanor was beautiful enough to attract any man, and, as Twyneham's heir, she was now an immensely wealthy woman.

The triumphant army progressed slowly to Leicester. Conrad could hear the shouts of derision as they passed through villages and the people beheld the naked body of Richard III, which was strapped to a horse at the rear of the riders. Each mile of that heinous abuse became more intolerable to stomach. This was the unacceptable side of victory. In the years the last Plantagenet had reigned, Richard had broken the hold of the Woodvilles over England. He had ruled wisely, but his enemies were many. Conrad had never believed the tales that Richard had had his two nephews murdered in the Tower. Yet it was true that it was several months since they had last been sighted. Murdering a child was not Richard's way. It was to fight in gallant combat, as that last valiant charge had signified. For that valour alone, his body did not deserve the desecration to which it was now subjected.

Such was war. No one emerged from it unsullied — even the triumphant. Henry was the undisputed King of England. At the next crossroads Conrad turned his horse away from the procession. He had won his knighthood, and had vowed not to rest until he was the Lord of Highford.

'It is wrong for me to marry!' Eleanor pitted her will against Father Hubert. 'Better I dedicate my life to God. I want to enter the priory at Highford.'

'You life is for this world, my lady, not the cloisters. Put your faith in God. He alone will decide whether your children will be touched by the misfortune which smites your family.'

'I cannot risk it.'

'You would put yourself above God's will?' Father Hubert remonstrated with gathering heat.

'Don't say that, Father. Don't twist my resolve.' Eleanor gripped her hands together in her distress, but she was convinced that in this she was right and the priest wrong.

Father Hubert's thick brows ran together as he frowned in accusation. 'To question God's will is heresy. Each of us has been put on this earth to serve God's purpose. Yours is to marry.'

Eleanor shook her head. His arguments were powerful and carried the weight of the church behind them. 'I cannot.'

'Then you doubt in God!' the priest yelled with rage. 'These dark thoughts must be cast from your mind. They are sent by the Devil. You are guilty of the sins of obstinacy and pride, my lady. Sink not into the pit of heresy. Repent! Accept your duty. Only then will you receive absolution.'

Father Hubert turned from her to walk to the altar and kneel in prayer. The anger had left him and his narrow shoulders drooped in sadness. His prayers were for her and Eleanor felt crushed beneath the burden of his piety. He believed that all life was in God's hands. Was it heresy to question that? Undoubtedly it was. And Eleanor was wrong to question the foundation of her faith. But in this her faith did not ease her conscience. She could not banish from her mind the image of Daniel's dementia.

Needing to be alone to pray, Eleanor drew aside the hangings of the lady chapel. She turned her back on the tombs of the D'Artons to kneel before the statue of the Madonna. With her head bowed in prayer, she sought to reconcile conscience and faith while the shadows grew longer and the chapel became dark.

She was jolted from her devotions by the sound of the tocsin bell sounding in alarm. As she rose stiffly upon legs cramped from the long hours of her prayers, her concern was for the safety of her people. They had received no news of the outcome of any confrontation between Tudor and Plantagenet. Was the castle under attack?

Eleanor hurried to the courtyard. Several men armed with crossbows were running towards the battlements. Seeing Le Gros shouting orders, she went to him.

'Why has the alarm been sounded?' She looked up at the battlements and saw that the score of men left to guard Highford each held aloft a burning torch to pierce the darkness beyond the moat. A trumpet sounded from without. The indistinct shout of a herald announced his lord's arrival. There was the grating of the portcullis being raised and the drawbridge slowly lowered.

Alarmed, Eleanor ran to the gatehouse, demanding from the guard, 'Who asks for admittance at so ungodly an hour?'

''Tis the Lord of Highford.' His reply was terse.

'Sir Cedric is here? Back so soon!' With a start Eleanor remembered that her father never went by that title. 'Stop! Raise the drawbridge. It's not Sir Cedric.'

To her horror her orders were ignored. The drawbridge continued to lower. From the light of the flickering torches she saw a small army of riders amassed by cheering villagers. Only one person would be greeted with such acclaim.

In desperation Eleanor commanded, 'Raise the drawbridge. Or I'll have you put in irons. Our enemy is without.'

Le Gros repeated her orders, wielding a whip to emphasise his words. His voice was cut off by a choking gurgle. Eleanor spun round and saw his stocky figure crumple to the ground, an arrow piercing his throat. An arrow from the bow of one of her own guards. Wide-eyed with horror, she stared along the battlements. The soldiers' bows were trained upon any of their companions who showed signs of resisting the entrance of the men outside. All around Eleanor the servants were leaving their duties in the castle to fill the courtyard.

A cheer ran through the excited murmurings. 'Lord D'Arton has come home.'

Eleanor's blood simmered with impotent fury. She had been betrayed. She lifted her head proudly. 'I order the drawbridge raised. I am mistress here. Obey me!'

Any guard brave enough to face her enraged glare

soon looked away shamefaced. All were deaf to her commands. The people of Highford cast aside the new loyalty to herself in the face of the ancient fealty to the D'Artons. Pride and anger stiffened her spine. She would not surrender.

When the drawbridge thudded on to the ground and the raised portcullis creaked to a halt, she ran to Le Gros's body. Snatching his heavy sword from its sheath, she gripped it in both hands and wielded its great weight in front of her. Thus she faced the chestnut destrier, caparisoned in black and gold and emblazoned with the wolf of the D'Arton crest.

She scowled up at Conrad, who was bareheaded. His armour gleamed golden in the torchlight, and behind him the D'Arton standard streamed out over the cheering crowd. She was alone, friendless, with only her defiance to protect her.

'Put down the sword, Lady Eleanor,' Conrad ordered.

Her blue eyes were wild and her face devoid of colour as she defied him. 'More noble that I should die by it. My people have betrayed me.'

'Not you, just the regime you represent.' His voice held no animosity. His victory had been swift — the defection of her people total. 'The D'Artons have been Lords of Highford since it was built. One woman cannot change centuries of loyalty. I have no fight with you, my lady.'

The arrogance and self-assurance in his handsome face spurred her fury beyond reason. 'I will not surrender.' She brought up the sword, her arms already aching from its weight.

Conrad drew his own blade, but Eleanor felt no fear. Marriage and children were barred from her. So was a cloistered life, according to Father Hubert. And the priest had scolded her for the sin of pride. That pride now was all she possessed. In the absence of Sir Cedric she must defend Highford against his enemy. 'I hold

Highford in the name of Sir Cedric Twyneham and King Richard.'

'Richard is no more. Neither is Twyneham,' Conrad announced, then added more gently, 'Put up your sword, Lady Eleanor. Henry VII now rules England. Highford is mine.'

'The King and my father are dead!' She staggered under the news, but quickly recovered herself. Her chin tilted with defiance, the feral light in her eyes clearly revealed in the torchlight. 'I will not surrender. Better I die than live with the knowledge that my people loved me so little.'

There was an angry murmuring from the villagers.

'That's not true, my lady,' a gruff voice shouted.

'My lady, you've always treated us well.' Another sounded upset. 'But our Lord has returned. . .'

'And I have been rewarded by betrayal.' She stared round at the people she loved, her heart wretched. Every one of them hung their heads rather than encounter her glittering stare.

Oswald the falconer stepped forward. 'My lady, forgive us. We cannot discount that older loyalty. Sir Conrad's father was driven from Highford when Edward took the throne. 'Tis Sir Conrad's by right. That don't mean we haven't come to love you, Lady Eleanor.'

Beneath such honest logic, she acknowledged defeat. She threw down the sword. 'Then I bid you all farewell.'

Keeping her gaze fixed on the drawbridge, she began to walk past the line of mounted riders.

'Halt!' Sir Conrad commanded. She turned to face him, her stance and expression imperious as she waited for him to continue. 'Where are you going?'

'To the priory. This has ceased to be my home.'

She walked on.

'I have not given you permission to leave.' Conrad's voice was rough with irritation.

Eleanor ignored him. She kept her back stiff and mustered a calm dignity as she continued her passage

through the crowd. All emotion had for the moment
frozen within her, and her expression was set as she
looked straight ahead to the path beyond the drawbridge.
From the corner of her eye she saw a woman curtsy to
her as she passed.

'My lady, you cannot go like this,' the woman wailed.

Others knelt as she passed. The homage melted the
ice which had encased her emotions. The gateway
became an indistinct blur as the tears formed but were
held in rigid check. Still she walked on. At each side her
people knelt in homage, many of the women openly
sobbing. There was an irritated oath from behind her
and the clatter of hoofs on the cobbles as a horse
advanced. She refused to turn.

'My lady, I will not allow you to leave,' Conrad
ordered.

'I am not your vassal,' she retorted, her step
unfaltering.

Suddenly an arm was about her waist, scooping her
up into the air. It was the final humiliation. She beat her
hands against his breastplate as he set her down across
his knees.

'Curse you!' Her rage exploded. 'Will you leave me
nothing, not even my pride?'

'I will not turn a woman out on to the road at night.'
Conrad's green eyes were dark with anger. 'When you
leave it will be with due ceremony as befits your rank.'

'Then give me an escort now,' she demanded as the
horse retraced its steps towards the keep. 'I will not
remain here a single night under your protection. My
reputation will be in shreds. You will answer to Sir
Richard Norton for this outrage.' Her eyes widened with
fear. 'He was not killed?'

Conrad set her down on the stone steps of the keep
and dismounted to stand beside her. 'At last you show
concern for your betrothed,' he mocked. 'Somewhat
tardily, Lady Eleanor. Norton is safe. He fought for
King Henry in the battle.'

Eleanor hid her shock that Sir Richard had changed his allegiance. She was aware that Conrad despised him for it. The knowledge stirred her loyalty to her betrothed. 'Sir Richard is an astute diplomat. Clearly he saw that the future of England lay with Henry Tudor.'

Conrad's lips drew back into a sneer. 'He will be amply rewarded when he takes you as his bride. As your father's heir, you will bring him Arnwood and two other estates. I doubt he will miss Highford.'

Her eyes narrowed. 'From your words, I gather the King has not restored your land.'

'He will. They were promised long ago.'

Eleanor sensed the first sign of uncertainty in Conrad's voice and seized upon it. 'Sir Richard has influence. He will demand justice for the infamy of this night. Highford is not as large as Arnwood, but it is my property by law — not yours.'

'You forget that it is now held in my name,' Conrad warned.

She bristled at his manner. 'You are no better than a brigand. Am I to be your hostage?'

'I had not thought upon it.' He laughed, but its sound held little humour. 'But now you have suggested it, I may well accept your generous offer.'

'Then I promise you will regret it.'

She knew she could not beat Conrad D'Arton in strength, but she could ensure that he took little pleasure in his reclaimed booty. She had faith that Sir Richard would not allow her to remain Conrad's hostage. This upstart young knight would learn that she was not without her champions. She began to precede him up the stairs into the keep, then remembered that as the professed Lord of Highford he should enter first. It galled her to have to show him deference, but she was wise enough to concede on this point. At any show of defiance before his people, Conrad would be forced to retaliate or lose face. She stood back against the wall to allow him to pass, her eyes firing with her hatred.

His stare was enigmatic as he regarded her in silence before ascending the stairs. Eleanor saw that he favoured his right leg as though it pained him, but to other less discerning eyes the limp would be barely perceptible.

In the great hall he turned to her. 'Show me to the Lord's chamber. And I would have food prepared for my men. It has been a hard ride and they have not eaten all day.'

'It is for you to command the servants, not I. A page will show you to your room.'

'No, Lady Eleanor, you will.' There was something in his eyes which warned her his patience was wearing thin and that it would be foolhardy, if not dangerous, to goad him too far.

She inclined her head. 'Follow me.'

The Lord's chamber was on the same floor as her own, but was much larger and one exit led through to the solar. The bed had been stripped after her father's departure and the mattress was bare of sheets. She paused in the doorway as he strode inside to inspect the room. When he turned back to her, she unfastened the keys which hung from an enamelled belt at her waist. 'If a meal is to be prepared for so many, the cook will need provisions from the store-chests.' She held the keys out to him.

He raised an arched brow. 'You still regard yourself as mistress of Highford; keep them and perform your duties well.'

'I will not serve brigands.'

'You will do as you are told. My men are tired and need to be fed. I will not have them served inferior scraps.'

'They can starve for all I care.' She stood her ground. 'I will not serve thieves.'

'You will do as I command.'

'I think not.'

He eyed her stonily and there was something in that condemning glare which made Eleanor's heart quake.

'Your stubbornness will serve you ill. I will be obeyed.'

'I am no man's vassal—no man's slave.'

There was a dangerous glitter in his green eyes which warned Eleanor that she had gone too far.

'I have asked nothing that as mistress of Highford you would not give graciously,' he said with deceptive softness.

Eleanor could not back down even though she knew her obstinacy was folly. Her defiance was her only protection. She would not let him see her vulnerability or fear. 'The mistress of Highford does not attend upon brigands.'

'I have treated you fairly and with respect—yet you continue to name me brigand. It displeases me, my lady.'

'The truth rankles, does it?' she retaliated. 'You are all I call you and more. . .'

'Then I must not disappoint you.'

He advanced purposefully towards her and Eleanor retreated several paces, but was brought up short against the corner of the bed. She was trapped.

He answered her defiance with a grin. 'Perhaps I should act the part. . .'

Conrad clamped his hands on her shoulders, jerking her to him and crushing her against him in a powerful embrace.

Eleanor's lips parted in a shocked gasp, her protest abruptly silenced as his mouth fastened over hers. His hands moved behind Eleanor's head, preventing her twisting her face away from him. His lips plundered her mouth, twisting, bruising, demanding. She felt the savage dig of his armour against her side, and was aware of the threatening strength of his body which could so easily dominate her slender form. She began to struggle. It was futile. Somewhere within the darkest and most secret recesses of her being, the spark of the passion he had once so easily roused kindled and flared. It flickered through her body, freeing her mind from its fragile barricade of loathing, singeing and scalding, searing her whole consciousness. Her nerves awakened with the warm excitement only he could elicit and she stopped resisting. She had no will but his.

The ice of her hatred melted to a fiery heat, taken and possessed by him as his kiss gentled to a sweetness which left her trembling. It no longer mattered that he was her enemy; he had the power to bedevil her senses and she yielded helplessly to a greater will than her own, returning his kiss with a passion which she had not believed she possessed.

Conrad released her abruptly. There was no sign on his face that the experience for him had been other than the need to teach her a lesson. No amount of force could have subdued her to his will, but a single kiss had rendered her weak and yielding. Her face burned with shame as she realised that her weakness had put her into his power.

'Take care how often you force me to prove that I am your master. I may forget you are bound to another and take what is so temptingly offered.'

Her clenched fist thudded against his breastplate as her fury returned at his arrogance. Conrad laughed and took her hand in his. 'When will you learn you cannot fight me without harming yourself? Now behave and help me unbuckle my armour.'

Her eyes flashed their defiance. It was answered by an amused glint in his own. 'Do you need a further lesson in obedience, Eleanor? I shall be happy to oblige.'

She glowered at him as she began to unbuckle his breastplate and worked quickly, more to be free of his presence than for any wish to please him. The armour was dented in several places and he rolled back his shoulders to ease the stiffness in them. With a casual ease which infuriated her he sat in an x-shaped chair and extended his legs towards her for the buckles of the cuisses which covered his thighs to be unfastened. In her anger her fingers became less gentle and she all but

wrenched off the cuisse. He flinched and his face
blanched at her heavy-handedness. It was then she
noticed the torn and blooded mail beneath. Immediately
she was contrite. He was wounded. A grimy bloodstained
bandage was wrapped around his thigh and from it came
a sickly odour which told her the wound was infected.

She removed the rest of his armour before going to the
door and calling for a servant. Griselda answered her
summons. The maid was white-faced with fear.

'My lady, has he harmed you? You've been closeted a
long time alone with that. . .that brigand.'

Eleanor smiled at her maid's vehemence and at the
sentiments which echoed her own. 'I am unharmed. But
Sir Conrad has an injury which must be tended.'

'Have you forgotten he is your enemy?' Griselda
scolded. 'Or are you allowing your heart to rule your
head? You knew all along that the pedlar was D'Arton.
From your manner that day I suspected there was an
attraction between you. Why else should D'Arton stop
you leaving?'

'I have no such insight into his mind. Please fetch my
tray of unguents from my chamber. Sir Conrad was
wounded in the battle.'

'And you tend him as lovingly as a wife.' Griselda
studied her sharply. 'No good will come of this. I told
you before. You are pledged to Sir Richard. A man any
woman would be proud to call master. I'll send Eadgyth
to tend D'Arton.'

Eleanor was angered by the maid's censure. 'I will
tend Sir Conrad and you will remember your place,
Griselda.'

Griselda shuffled away and Eleanor dismissed the
maid's ill humour. Unlike most of the old retainers at
Highford, Griselda had no love for the D'Artons. She
still blamed them for the accidental deaths of her children. Griselda had always been overprotective of
Eleanor's welfare and at times it was stifling.

When she re-entered Conrad's room she saw that he

had shed his chain-mail and was frowning over the
wound on his thigh. He paled as he tried to peel the
bandage from it. Impatiently, she slapped his hand away
as she would a child's.

'Let me see it.' The bandage had stuck fast. 'You'll
have to soak in a bath to remove the bandage and a
thorough cleansing will help the wound. Once you have
bathed I will return to tend the wound.'

'No. You will stay.' His hand shot out to grip her
wrist. 'I want no one to see that I am injured.'

'Surely I am the last one who should know of your
weakness,' she responded coldly.

'Must I teach you another lesson in humility?' he
goaded.

Eleanor's eyes blazed as she glared at him. He would
learn that she would not be insulted without reparation.
Every insult he levied upon her would be repaid fourfold,
she vowed.

'You alone will tend me, Eleanor. Besides, your father
dealt me this blow in the thick of the battle.'

'So it amuses you to make me tend the man who slew
my father,' she flared at him, anger and bitterness rising
like bile in her throat.

His jaw tightened. 'Sir Cedric did not die by my
hand.'

There was anger in his voice.

'But you wish he had?'

His green stare hardened with brutal honesty. 'Yes, as
reward for his treachery.'

It was the honesty which disarmed her. She respected
it, though it confirmed the enmity between them. But a
contrary part of her was at variance with her loathing for
this knight. She did not want to see him crippled by her
father's hand. 'Once you have bathed I will return to
tend your wound.'

He gazed searchingly into her eyes for a moment, his
expression enigmatic. Unexpectedly he smiled, and it
seemed to curl around her, wrapping her in its warmth.

All signs of anger, hostility, even arrogance had left his features. What remained left her oddly breathless.

He grinned. 'Is it not the custom for women of the household to honour their guests by tending to their bath?'

Her eyes rounded with shock and affront. The knave was making fun of her. She made her voice deliberately cold. 'Once it was so, but it is a custom which I now believe is rarely followed.'

From the way his grin broadened as he turned away from her, she realised he had been deliberately provoking her. Eleanor resented the quick-fire changes in his manner. They had a disconcerting way of burrowing beneath her guard.

He stood up and pulled off the padded gambeson which cushioned the weight of his mail and armour. He stood half naked, clad only in a shirt which covered him to mid-thigh. His hips were slender and long, well-shaped legs were disturbingly male with their dusting of dark blond hair. She looked away from the sheer masculinity of his figure, his limbs honed to a sculptured perfection from hard riding and hours spent practising with weapons in the tiltyard. It was obvious he was a man who did not indulge in excesses or spend much time at leisure.

Small wonder that when he chose to exert his will upon her it had been impossible to evade him. She knew too well the strength in that muscular body and the sensuality it could so disastrously arouse in her.

'It will take a while for the water to be heated and carried to your chamber. In the meantime I will give instructions to the cooks.' She replaced the keys at her waist and went out.

Conrad eyed her warily. She had been too compliant too easily. What was she up to? He shrugged. It would be nothing he could not handle. He felt his blood heat at the challenge of taming her. When he had ridden into Highford he had fully intended that Eleanor be housed at the priory until Sir Richard Norton sent an escort to collect her. Her defiance had provoked him. The sight of her dignified figure walking so proudly across the courtyard had impelled him to act without thought of the consequences.

Since that moment, her every word and deed had driven him. One minute she was ice, the next a searing flame. She had been unpredictable since the first moment he met her. The wench had got into his blood and he would know no peace until he proved that she was but a woman, like any other.

CHAPTER EIGHT

ELEANOR waited until Conrad had had time to bathe and dress before returning to his room. She had removed her hennin head-dress and replaced it with a simple fillet and veil which would not impede her tending of his wound. He had donned a clean shirt, but his legs remained bare as he bent over his wound, poking it tentatively with his finger.

In the flickering candle-light he looked tired and haggard, and Eleanor sensed the exhaustion which sapped his strength and drooped his frame. He was driving himself by force of will. The castle was full of news of the battle. The ride from Bosworth had been long, and to be covered in so short a time he must have gone without sleep. Even though he was her foe, she reluctantly admired the bold determination which had driven Conrad to reclaim his lands.

A thread of compassion caught her unawares. In all honesty, he, more than herself, had the right to regard Highford as his inheritance. There was something about Highford which none of her father's other castles possessed. It was impossible to name what it was that made it so special. It just crept into your heart, making you aware that, though you might call yourself its master, or mistress, you were merely its custodian, and were privileged to be so.

As Conrad straightened and stretched his weary muscles, she saw the exposed wound for the first time. It looked viciously painful. To cover the feeling of misplaced compassion he aroused, she remonstrated, 'Was nothing done to heal your wound? Men! Neglect is a sure way of losing a limb.'

'I had more pressing matters upon my mind.'

125

'And little good winning Highford would have done you had the poison from this reached your heart. Or had you ended up a one-legged cripple,' she snapped, exasperated by his short-sightedness. 'You'd give attention enough to a lame horse. Sit down and let me tend it.'

'Such tender concern, Lady Eleanor. I am flattered.'

She lifted the tall iron candlestick and brought it closer to the chair. The light from the flame fell upon him as she fixed him with a wrathful glare. 'Don't be. I don't like to see any creature suffer. I would give a wounded dog or hawk the same attention.'

He put a hand across his mouth as though hiding his amusement at her peevishness. Would nothing stem the knight's conceit? She had never met a man who could so easily provoke her antagonism. She decided to ignore him and concentrate solely upon his wound. Kneeling at his side, she placed the tray of herbs and unguents on the floor. 'The bath has cleansed it well, but not enough.'

She had brought with her a small cauldron of boiling water. Into this she spinkled some dried herbs and then dipped a length of cloth into the pot, lifting it out with her dagger. Allowing it to cool for some moments and the surplus water run from it, she said without looking at him, 'This must be as hot as you can bear, to draw the poison.'

Eleanor placed the cloth over the wound and saw his knuckles whiten as they gripped the chair arm. She looked up and saw the tight set of his jaw, his upper lip stippled with sweat, and a shudder pass through his body. She lifted the cloth away with a loud tut of vexation. 'I said as hot as you can bear, Sir Conrad. You may deserve to suffer more, but I would not inflict pain unnecessarily.'

He eyed her sourly, unconvinced she had not deliberately meant him to suffer.

Once the cloth had cooled further Eleanor replaced it over his thigh. When she removed it, she bent her head to inspect the wound. There were several pieces of broken chain-mail embedded into the flesh which were causing a red line of poison to run upwards along his thigh. Sitting back on her heels, she picked up the flagon of wine from the table at his side, filled a goblet and offered it to him. 'The metal must come out or it will cause the flesh to rot and the poison will eventually kill you. You would do well to drink all that and more. It will help to ease the pain while I work.'

'I prefer to keep all my senses about me while you hover over me with a dagger in your hand,' he quipped.

She looked up at him for the first time since working on his wound. To her surprise he gave a tight-lipped grin.

'You are wise, Sir Conrad.' She could not resist nettling him while he was at a disadvantage. 'Why should I not end what my father began? Yet I would need no dagger. Any one of the herbs I put into the water could contain a lethal poison.'

She had the satisfaction of seeing his pallor increase, and his green eyes narrowed. 'Do you hate me that much?'

The question caught her off guard, and she blushed. The censure in his eyes faded to an enticing look of speculation, and he said softly, 'That is not your way, sweet Eleanor.'

That he understood her so well was galling. 'The temptation was great, Sir Conrad,' she returned, refusing to pander to his conceit. 'But I resisted. The King will judge you innocent, or guilty, of first abduction, then unlawful seizure of my lands, and finally holding me hostage.'

It was meant to put him in his place, but to her annoyance he took neither offence nor warning. Instead his lips curved into his most disarming smile, and, despite all her antagonism, she was disturbed by its potent lure. Giving herself a mental shake, she returned her attention to his wound. She worked quickly, knowing that every pluck of the tweezers would be torture.

Not once did he flinch or utter a sound. When she had extracted several broken links she took up a salve pot to smear the healing balm over the jagged edges and keep them free from further infection. He put a hand over hers, stopping her.

'You have a good knowledge of healing, Lady Eleanor, but this I learned from a Moorish doctor when I was on the Continent.' He picked up her discarded dagger. 'Heat the blade and when it glows red-hot draw it quickly across the wound to seal it.'

Eleanor shuddered.

'It will not heal otherwise.' Pressing the weapon into her hand, he raised a taunting brow. 'Again I must trust you that you do not the run the blade through my heart, or leave me maimed for life.'

'Perhaps you should give me one good reason why I shouldn't do just that,' she returned, puzzled that he could jest over so grave a matter. After the way he had treated her, she would be justified in doing either.

'Because you have your own code of chivalry.' Conrad laid his hand on her shoulder. 'I could pay you a no higher compliment.' His hand slid along her arm in a light caress, then he snatched it back to lay across his lap. He nodded towards the candle flame. 'Do it quickly, Eleanor.'

The quiet command and his trust touched her in a way no amount of force could. She held the blade over the flame, conscious that his gaze was studying her profile. It brought a flush to her cheeks and a tingling of awareness to her body. She fidgeted, but kept her gaze averted. What power within that appraising green stare could reach into the depths of her soul and leave her breathless and trembling?

When the tip of the blade glowed red she drew it from the flame and braced her body between his thighs. Her hand shook as she held the dagger towards the wound. She inhaled deeply to steady it and rapidly laid the blade along the length of his wound. The poisoned flesh sizzled as it was burnt away and the two edges were sealed together.

Conrad drew in a sharp breath as the sickening stench of scorched flesh filled the air, but otherwise made no sound. She closed her eyes, appalled at the pain she had inflicted.

'You did well, Eleanor.' His voice was gentle and he put his hand under her chin to lift her face to meet his gaze.

She refused to look at him, fearing the tenderness she would find in his eyes. She could not fight that. She must not fall beneath the spell he so effortlessly wove around her senses. At all times she must remember that he was her enemy. Jerking her head away from his touch, she dipped her fingers into the salve. Expertly she smoothed the herbs mixed with goose grease over the wound and fixed a clean bandage over his thigh. The task completed, she picked up her tray and stood up, and, without looking at him, said, 'The bandage must be changed twice a day and you would be wise to rest your leg for the next day or so — to allow the poison to drain.'

'Rest is for old women. The pain eases already. You have done well.'

He stood up with a stiffness which spoke of other bruises from the battle which beleaguered his body. She held out a second pot of balm. 'From the dents in your armour, you will need this for your bruises.'

His fingers closed over hers as he took the pot. 'Such concern, Eleanor. Dare I hope that you no longer see me as the Devil incarnate?'

Her gaze was lowered to the floor, which was splashed with droplets of water from his bath. 'You are my enemy. Nothing can change that.'

'Do you dispute that my claim to Highford is just?'

'I have lived here only a few years, your family for generations.' She lifted her gaze, her eyes challenging. 'It is the only home I know.'

The warmth of his hands over hers began to seep through her entire body. There was command and a subtle note of seduction in his husky voice. 'Yet you put flowers in my family's chapel, and allowed me to take the chalice and reliquary.'

'Many would see that as weakness.' She tried to pull her hands away, but found them held too firmly. Her anger at the way he would rule her returned. With deliberate insult she widened her eyes as she held his glittering green stare. 'It is one thing to wish to honour your dead as tradition dictates. And another to enter my home like a brigand.'

'I will never relinquish what is mine by right. Now that Henry is King he will see justice is done. As for the flowers, that was an unselfish gesture of respect.'

He smiled in a way which made her heart turn over. Eleanor clenched her fist to combat the treachery of her wayward emotions. He was being deliberately provocative. To feed her rage, she recalled the humiliation of the night he had rescued Gauthier and Ralph. 'Which was repaid by you sneaking into my room and attempting to ravish and dishonour me.'

'A memorable night, sweet Eleanor. And one that has given me no peace.' He pulled her closer so that their bodies touched. 'How could I allow you to leave Highford? I wanted you that night. . .and I want you now.'

Eleanor fought to resist the tingling pleasure flooding through her at his touch. She pushed back from him. Again he was seeking to manipulate her to his will.

'You took Highford by trickery and betrayal. I will never yield to a tyrant.'

'Your eyes do not speak the same as your words.' He laughed triumphantly. 'Highford. . .you and me. . .we are irrevocably bound. To the conqueror go the spoils. And you are willing despite your venom.'

'You conceited knave!' Eleanor flew at him, her fingers curled into claws to scratch at his face. 'I hate you!'

Conrad grabbed her arms and pinned them behind

her, crushing her against him. Her words of fury were muffled against his chest as she tried to gain her release by scraping her foot along his shin. He side-stepped, avoiding her feet, but his expression changed. The look in his eyes made her blood run cold. She read in them that his patience had come to an end. The fear which flooded through her was too great to know caution. With a screech of rage she wrenched herself free of his hold and her outraged gaze noted a bucket of water still unused from filling his bath. She ran towards it. Heaving it up, she spun round as Conrad advanced on her. The cold water caught him full in the face.

'Let that cool your lechery!' she cried.

For a second his dripping features registered shock, then ungovernable fury. If he caught her his punishment would be dire indeed. Frightened, Eleanor ran for the door. She heard a sloshing of water and the thud of the wooden bucket against the side of the tub. As her hand reached for the latch a lukewarm deluge soaked her to the skin.

'It's time you were taught a lesson,' Conrad grated.

'Oh!' she spluttered with rage. She had not expected him to retaliate in kind. One look at his expression told her that was just the beginning of the lesson he intended to teach her. He was furious.

Eleanor opened the door, and, with her feet slipping precariously on the wet floor, she fled his wrath. Her heart pounded as she ran to her chamber, convinced that her virtue depended on reaching it before Conrad caught her. Behind her, she heard his bare feet slithering on the wet floor of his room as he gave chase. There was a loud thud, followed by a grunt of pain and an unsavoury curse. Risking a look back over her shoulder, she saw Conrad skidding along the soapy floor on his back to career into the doorpost of his room. He rolled to a stop. A thunderous fury darkened his face as he attempted to rise, only to fall back down.

Seeing him sprawled there in such an undignified state

pricked her sense of humour. Laughter burst from her.
The glare he shot her was so incensed that her laughter
increased. At last she had got the better of him. She
laughed so hard that she was forced to hold her side to
get her breath. 'Not so proud now, my conquering
knight.'

He raised his head and attempted to rise, but he fell
back, his face contorted with agony as he cradled his
injured thigh. The bandage was soaked. Instantly,
Eleanor sobered. He had grievously injured himself. She
edged warily forward. 'Are you hurt, Sir Conrad?'

He groaned loudly and answered with an uncharitable
grunt. 'Go away, you've caused enough damage.'

'It was your own lechery which brought you to this
end,' she persisted. 'I trust it has taught you a lesson.'

He turned his back on her and, visibly in pain, tried
again to stand. When he appeared unable to put any
weight on his injured leg, Eleanor's compassion overrode
her anger.

'Come let me help you rise, Sir Conrad.'

She put her arm through his and braced herself to take
his weight. The next moment his arms closed about her,
and with a twist of his body he flipped her over on to the
floor. Before she could recover from the shock, he rolled
them both back into his chamber. With Eleanor firmly
trapped beneath his body, he kicked the door shut with
his foot.

'Curse you,' she fumed. 'That was a despicable and
underhand trick. I thought you were hurt.'

'And came running to my aid. No enemy would have
done that.' He was grinning at her. 'When I gave you a
taste of your own medicine your face was a picture of
outraged propriety.' He gave a throaty laugh.

'And yours was of furious disbelief that I had the
temerity to take such action.' She refused to apologise
for her conduct. 'It was no more than you deserved.'

His grin broadened. 'No one has dared treat me with
such disrespect. What form should your punishment

take? For I cannot allow you to make a fool of me and escape unscathed.'

'I but defended my virtue.' She was aware of every muscle of his body which pressed down upon her. To her chagrin her vision blurred with angry tears she refused to shed. 'You have turned my people against me, taken control of my home. What have I left, but my virtue and honour? Please, Conrad, leave me something. You are bound by your vows of chivalry. Forget not that — though I am your captive — I am a noblewoman.'

His dark lashes hid the expression in his eyes. He eased back from her, but did not release her. 'We roll about the wet floor like humble peasants and laugh at the absurdity of our false dignity.' His tone was coercing. 'Would that for a night we were those carefree peasants. Free from restraints. Free to love as we would. . . without dishonour.'

He touched her cheek. 'How foolish are our pretensions. Beneath our fine clothes and manners runs the primeval blood of our ancestors. What they wanted they took. No less than theirs does our blood clamour for ease from this torment.'

The tone was soft and beguiling — so beguiling that the taunting mockery it held pricked her temper. 'That may be so for yourself. I do not have the instincts of a rutting stag. Now let me up or I will scream for the guards.'

'No, you won't. You lie only to yourself, sweet Eleanor.' His eyes simmered to a dangerous black. 'Not once have I forced you. You have responded willingly, unable to deny a mutual attraction — a mutual need.'

As he spoke in a low entrancing voice, he removed her fillet and veil; his eyes caressed her in a way which held her spellbound in its intimacy as he removed the pins from her hair and it tumbled down about her shoulders.

'It is a crime to hide such glory from the world,' he murmured.

Then before she could even deny his arrogance, his

warm lips were upon hers, moving slowly and kindling fires which had lain smouldering since the night he came to her chamber. Through the clinging wetness of her gown, where his hands touched her flesh seemed to burn and waves of pleasure sizzled through every sinew. When his mouth nuzzled the nape of her neck, his warm breath caressing her skin, Eleanor sighed, closing her eyes as her senses swirled in rapture. Her hand came up to caress his neck below the fall of his hair. She could feel herself being drawn into the vortex of a whirlpool as her passionate nature was overwhelmed by his mastery. This time she fought it.

They were not the peasants Conrad had spoken of, but nobly born. They must live by the code their rank inflicted, or suffer dishonour. With a strangled sob, she pushed him away. 'No. I am not part of your plunder.' Her voice strengthened, the contempt in it as much for herself as him. 'I belong to another. Sir Richard is an honourable knight. I will not bring shame to his name.'

Conrad rolled on to his side and sat up. Drawing up his knees, he rested his elbows on them, his fingers interlocked between them. Eleanor levered herself on to one elbow, watching him as he frowned into the candle flame. She felt bereft at his withdrawal, not relieved.

'Go,' he said sharply.

She could not move. Her heart refused to slow its frantic beat and she clenched her hands to stop them from beckoning him back into her arms. He whirled to face her, desire stark in his handsome face. It was too late now for retreat. What she saw in his eyes mirrored the hunger in her own.

Conrad was at the end of his restraint. Why had she not gone as he ordered? What was there about this maid that could drive him beyond the bounds of his control? He opened his mouth to shout at her to leave. Instead, he found her back in his arms, his voice low and throbbing with desire as he breathed her name against her ear. He was deaf to her words as his lips hungrily took hers. Whether they were the smothered moans of despair or the soft cry of ecstasy, they were filled with the promise her lovely body had for so long held for him.

Eleanor cried out in a feeble attempt to stave off his passion and to stifle her own inflamed desire. It was suffocated in her throat as her senses filled with the coercion of his voice, her body pliant to the will of his hands, which moved with demanding urgency over her. Their passion was wrong, but she had no power left to fight the inevitable. She had known this would happen from the first contact of their bodies in the wood. The silk of her gown was a fragile barrier to his ardour. There was a competent tugging at her back and her bodice fell loose. The exquisite joy of his touch as his hand found her breast drew a soft gasp from deep in her throat. Her senses exploded in a fiery blaze as his fingers touching her so familiarly caused ripples of sensations to undulate through her body.

Their lips remained melded together as he drew her gently to her feet. There was a brush of silk against her hip as her gown and chemise slid to the floor, then his hand was beneath her knees as he carried her to the bed. Their lips remained fastened in a ravening kiss. Her hands spread across his shoulders and her fingers wove through the tawny locks of his hair. Briefly her body tensed with anticipation at the feel of the mattress along her back. Her fear was overwhelmed by the expertise of his caresses and the passion he evoked. His parted lips slanted across hers, savouring their sweetness with a fierceness born from his long-suppressed need. The kiss was ruthless in its demand, stirring her response until she was trembling with pleasure. Every flick of his tongue set her whole being aflame in a torrent of sensual enslavement. His shirt was discarded and they lay entwined, flesh against flesh, satin breasts taut against the teasing contours of a strong hair-roughened chest.

'Oh, Conrad,' she murmured softly as she buried her head into the hollow of his throat.

He eased back to look down at her, his mouth swooping to nuzzle her earlobe as he whispered, 'Sweet love.'

She stared up at him, trying to dampen the flames which consumed her, but she was helpless, caught in the maelstrom of her own desire. She clasped him close. Their mouths joined in heavenly communion, tasting, fusing in tempestuous possession. Passions flared, fuelling the ecstatic melody laying seige to their senses. His hand stroked the sensitive smoothness of her thighs, trailing between them, boldly claiming the softness of her, where no other had touched. A quiver expanded through her at the intimacy of a caress which brought pleasure beyond her wildest imaginings. The green eyes above her own glimmered with intensity as his caresses sought the heat of her inner warmth. Softly, she cried out as the rhythm of his hand caused her hips to writhe, no longer in control of the aching need for fulfilment demanded by her body. A shimmering heat spread through her, pulsing in waves of increasing magnitude until an explosion of sensation left her spent, her moans of pleasure captured deep in his mouth.

Sighing, she curled against him, and heard her name hoarsely whispered. It was impossible to conceive of a greater ecstasy, but there was more, as her body discovered when Conrad continued to caress her. She arched against him, deliciously relaxed and dreamily sensitive to a new and more insistent ache growing deep within her. Through lids heavy with languor, she stared up at him, her arms reaching up to bind him close as he adjusted his weight beneath her thighs.

A battering on the chamber door made them start. Conrad voiced a frustrated expletive as the door burst open. With a cry of alarm Eleanor dived beneath the covers.

'Conrad!' Ned's voice showed his own surprise at the scene he had interrupted. 'I had not realised——'

'Get out, damn you!' Conrad raged.

'Your pardon, my friend, but this will not wait. The stables are on fire.'

Conrad leapt from the bed and snatched up his hose and shirt. 'Then don't just stand there gaping, man. Every hand is needed if the fire will not destroy all the outbuildings. Any idea who started it?'

'Someone saw Lady Eleanor's maid near the stables before the fire broke out. It could have been the old crone.'

Ned craned his head to get a glimpse over Conrad's shoulder as to which wench his friend had taken such a fancy to. He saw only an indeterminate bundle in the centre of the bed.

'Ned, stop gawping and go and fight the fire,' Conrad snapped. 'I'll be down directly.'

Conrad glowered at his friend and, following his glance, was relieved that Eleanor was well hidden. Ned retreated as Conrad was pulling on his boots, but he saw his friend's gaze fall upon Eleanor's gown, which was easily recognisable.

Ned gave a low whistle of appreciation. Conrad crossed the space between them, his hand placed in warning upon his shoulder. 'It's just a wench, Ned. No one important that you should concern yourself with.'

'Taking Highford was just and right. But its mistress belonged to another.' Ned voiced his concern. 'My friend, only marriage will atone for the wrong you have perpetrated this night. Though even that will not stop the repercussions your actions will bring. I hope she was worth it.'

As Ned's footsteps faded into the distance, Eleanor emerged from her hiding place. Her hair was tousled and in golden disarray about her shoulders. 'Just a wench, am I? Unimportant?'

She hurled the pillow at his head. He ducked it easily,

but the second landed with a thump in the centre of his chest. She snatched up the third as he advanced on her and with all her might slammed it over his head.

'I must have been addle-witted to fall beneath your spell. Lecher!' She landed another hit and the pillow burst over his head, smothering them both with feathers. She spat out the clinging tufts from her mouth. 'I hate you.'

'We shall discuss this later.' He brushed the feathers from his tunic and glared at her. 'You are a sore trial, Eleanor. The stables are afire. I'll not argue with you now. But I meant none of those words to Ned. They were just to stop his suspicions.'

'Lies come easily to you. Especially soft words of love to seduce an innocent maid to your bed.'

Conrad eyed her suspiciously. Had he spoken words of love? He stared at her lovely body rising up out of a cloud of white feathers. Most women would have looked ridiculous. Eleanor looked even more seductive. He felt a smile tugging at the corners of his mouth at the havoc her temper had wreaked upon his room, and bent his head to hide his amusement from her.

'By the grace of an ill-meant fire you may still be a maid. Innocent, my lady—you are not!'

'Because of you!'

The words touched a chord of disquiet within his heart. However he chose to interpret her responses, he knew she was still a virgin. Only just! From their first meeting he had been bewitched by her courage and beauty. The wench had the ability to make him lose control. He could not change what had happened between them, neither did he regret it. Her beauty had left its brand upon him, more so now as she drew her hair about her to cover herself from his gaze like tattered remnants of shredded pride and innocence.

'Everyone is fighting the fire. No one will see you leave my room.' He bowed to her and ran out.

Eleanor stared after him aghast. Again he had made

her forget honour and decency. Though she remained a virgin, she would still go sullied to Sir Richard Norton's bed. A deeper fear clutched at her heart and throat. In the throes of the passion Conrad roused, he had obliterated her most recent vow: the refusal to bear a child.

She began to tremble. How could she have allowed the risk of conceiving a child like Daniel? That shocked her more than permitting Conrad to make love to her. How could she have been so stupid, so selfish? Worldly love was forever denied her. Her penance would be to live a barren life, a passionate body trapped into a confinement of perpetual frustration and enforced sterility.

Pulling the covers around her, she went to the window and stared down at the burning stables. Sparks were already falling on to the thatched roofs of the buttery and across the yard to the falcon mews. Guards, servants and villagers formed two lines, passing along buckets which were hauled from the well, the water hissing as it was thrown over the leaping flames. It was fast getting out of control. Chaos was everywhere. The freed horses milled about in the courtyard as grooms and pages tried to lead the frightened mounts to safety. Men ran, stooped over by the weight of heavy food sacks rescued from the smouldering storehouses. Someone had loosed the ducks and chickens before their pens had been destroyed by flames and the poultry were getting under the feet of the fire-fighters.

It was an ill-fated fire indeed which had saved her virtue. Or had Griselda started it? The old maidservant must surely have noted Eleanor's long absence. Had her suspicions concerning Conrad's motives towards her mistress led the maid to start the fire? Eleanor hoped not. Whoever was responsible must be punished. Arson was a serious crime.

Eleanor was appalled by the destruction and the speed with which the fire was spreading. She loved Highford too well to see it wantonly destroyed. Time enough had been wasted—everyone was needed to combat the blaze, including herself.

She peered out in to the passage to ensure no one would see her leaving Conrad's room in so dishevelled a state. The corridor was deserted. She ran into her room and pulled from the clothes-press her oldest gown. Moments later, plaiting her hair into a braid as she ran, she headed for the falcon mews to help the falconers save the birds. Even hooded, the hawks sensed the fear communicated by the less experienced handlers. They rose up, setting the bells on their jesses ringing and beating their wings, making their rescue difficult. Eleanor ordered them to be taken to a turret room far from the fire. Back in the courtyard she saw the horses were being led to the tiltyard at the far side of the castle.

Next she turned her attention to the spreading fire. All the outbuildings along the west walls were in flames. She shouted at some villagers who were trying to shoo the ducks out of the way. 'Leave those. Get some more buckets.'

'There's none left, my lady.' Father Hubert shook his head sadly as he crossed the courtyard.

The cobbles were awash with puddles from the spilled water and these reflected the flames from the fire consuming several thatched roofs. The castle courtyard had become a scene likened to hell's inferno. On the far side Conrad was waving his arms and directing the firefighters.

'Then fetch pitchforks!' Eleanor ordered the villagers. 'Use scythes, anything you can to tear off the thatch from the buildings next to those alight. We must stop the flames spreading. Use blankets to beat out any new fires starting.'

A bright orange flame soared skywards.

'My God, the haystacks!' Eleanor shouted. 'They must be saved. There's a year's hay from the harvest brought in last week.' Her voice rose in alarm. 'Here, give me that.'

She took a horse blanket from a sweating page and began to beat one of the patches of ignited straw that was scattered around the base of the three fresh haystacks. Others joined her. The heat from the flames was intense, scorching her hands and face. She worked until her back ached, then drew upon her reserves of strength to continue her beating. No one spared themselves as they fought to save the harvest. Her hair became flattened to her scalp with sweat, her arms blackened from the smoke. Exhaustion threatened to overcome her, but she worked on through the agony, ignoring the pain of aching muscles. All around her were shouts and cries, the roar of flames, the crack and thud of falling blazing timber.

Several times she heard Conrad shouting orders and once she raised her face to see him risking his life as he climbed a ladder to rake a burning thatch from the bakehouse roof. She screamed out as a gust of wind turned the flames upon him. Then to her relief she saw him jump to safety from the top of the ladder. He rolled and came nimbly to his feet, but his limp was pronounced and the fall must have been agony to his injured leg. A woman near Conrad ventured too close to the fire and her skirt suddenly went up in flames. The woman screamed and began to run. Conrad tore after her and grappled the terrified woman to the ground, rolling her in a puddle until the flames were doused. He limped tiredly away from the wailing woman, leaving her to the ministrations of a friend.

She marvelled at the strength Conrad found to go on. She had seen how near to exhaustion he had been earlier—though he had recovered sufficiently to make love to her. Unwilling to dwell upon her complex feelings for the knight, Eleanor worked on. The fire had taken hold and as the haystacks went up in three pillars of flames she screwed her eyes shut to combat the pain of anguish and frustration. Her failure to save the harvest struck her hard and she wearily dragged herself away from the devastation.

Even with the battle to save the haystacks lost there was still no respite. The fire seemed inexhaustible, seeking new fuel as its tentacles sped further along the roofs of the outbuildings built against the curtain wall. There was a huddle of children crying in a corner, their hands burnt from their efforts to stop the fire. Lying around them were people injured by falling timbers. Eleanor sent a page to collect her medicine tray and, examining each of the wounded in turn, ordered the most serious cases to be taken to the infirmary, which was well away from the fire. For a further two hours she tended the injured until the last of them was cared for and left in the charge of Eadgyth.

Everywhere stank of smoke. It clawed at Eleanor's lungs and stung her eyes. She looked down at her hands and saw her nails were broken and the skin raw with blisters. Her gown was singed and torn in several places. Everyone looked in the same sorry state, but they had won. The fire was almost out.

Wiping a hand across her brow, Eleanor sank down on an upturned barrel and rested her head in her hands, overcome with exhaustion. At the touch of a hand upon her shoulder, she look up into Conrad's soot-blackened face.

'Come, my lady. We have done all we can. A watch has been mounted to ensure none of the fires flares up again.'

She rose wearily to her feet, just curbing in time the impulse to rest her hand upon his chest. He saw the movement and frowned. He took her arm to help her back to the keep.

'I need no help from you.' She tried to shrug off his unwelcome hold and failed.

'Pax, Eleanor. You spared yourself nothing to save Highford.'

'I did it so that the people would not starve this winter. But the haystacks were destroyed.'

'Eleanor, you are a remarkable woman.' The respect she saw in his eyes lifted her flagging spirits. 'Did you not believe those people betrayed you? They did not deserve such loyalty.'

She shrugged. 'Their welfare has been my concern for some years now. Some habits cannot be broken overnight.'

She felt him stumble and knew he was calling on the last reserves of his strength on this walk back to the keep. It no longer mattered who was the lord here, or who the mistress. They had fought together to save Highford. It had woven another bond between them. Neither of them would forget this night. Highford would bear the scars of the fire for months, but it would eventually be returned to its former glory. Whereas she wondered if she would ever be the same. . .

At the top of the stairs leading to their chambers, Conrad paused. He smiled, the pearly luminance of his teeth and glittering eyes all that was visible in his blackened face.

She gave a shaky laugh. 'You look like a chimney-sweep.'

'Then that makes two chimney-sweeps.' He lifted one blackened and singed golden curl which lay upon her breast. His voice sobered. 'I wronged you, Eleanor. Ned spoke true. Only marriage will right the dishonour I have brought to you.'

She reeled back from him. It was not what she expected, or could accept. 'You forget I am contracted to Sir Richard.'

'You and Highford are bound together. Nothing would please our people more than that you should remain their mistress.'

A long curling pillow feather he had taken from her hair clung tenaciously to his finger as his smile became devilish. She snatched it from his nail and crushed it in her hand.

'I will not be shamed into marriage with you. Whatever madness possessed me in your chamber earlier will never be repeated. I will not humiliate Sir Richard, who has shown me nothing but kindness, by even considering your offer.'

He gave a lop-sided smile. 'You spoke of kindness and I know well your loyalty. But what of love, Eleanor?' He stepped closer. 'If you loved Norton you would not have responded so ardently to my lovemaking. Must I make you see reason?'

She backstepped. 'No. Never. I am no man's plunder.'

'You could never be that. You must know by now that——'

'I know you would shame me. That is enough.'

He eyed her for a long moment, the amusement gone from his face. After considering his words, he pronounced, 'Both you and Highford will be mine. The matter is settled.'

It was a command. She shuddered. He would have no mercy on her. What frightened her most was that she knew her own limitations. She had vowed there would be no child from her body. Yet a single touch from him and her whole being burned with passion. A kiss or a caress would be all it needed for her downfall. He was too persuasive for her to withstand his ardour. She would inevitably succumb, as her pride had succumbed to his deliberate attack upon her senses. He had exposed the depths of her sensuality, shown her the sweet promise of rapture—an ecstasy forbidden to her—leaving her bereft with the knowledge that she would forever yearn for, yet must find the strength to deny, the temptation of such devastating pleasure. She could not fight him with her body, for her body would always betray her. She must combat him with the power of words. In this he would not triumph.

'You can lead a beast to the slaughter, but you cannot

expect it to slit its own throat. I will not be used. The fire was started as a protest against your rule. Not everyone here is as loyal to you as you would believe. By marrying me you think to secure your tenure. I'd die first.'

She went into her chamber and slammed the door so hard that it rocked on its hinges. Seconds later there was the sound of another angrily slammed door from the direction of Conrad's room.

CHAPTER NINE

A TORMENTED sob escaped Eleanor, and she thrust herself away from the door. This new dilemma chased the exhaustion from her mind and body. She pressed her knuckles to her breast, and, too restless to settle, paced the room. What had possessed her to allow Conrad to take such liberties? She was bound to Sir Richard. A betrothal was as binding as any marraige. Her teeth bit into her lower lip as she felt a snare closing about her. Had she not vowed never to wed? Now there was not one marriage she had to evade, but two.

A violent trembling took hold of her. Her emotions were in turmoil, and she could find no solution, though her mind explored countless paths. Her panic grew. She was trapped. How could she escape either marriage? If she told Conrad the truth about Daniel, he would not marry her. But he had no cause to respect the Twyneham name; he could use that information as a weapon to ensure he did not lose Highford.

And what of Sir Richard? She was bound in honour to a man she did not love, but felt great affection and respect for. In the circumstances, to ease the humiliation Sir Richard would feel when she refused to wed him, would it be right to tell him of Daniel? Sir Richard deserved the truth. But the situation was more complex than that. While Daniel lived, he was the true heir to Sir Cedric's lands. As such he would be given to the care of one of her Twyneham uncles. His guardian would then administer the properties, could appropriate whatever money he saw fit. Eleanor did not trust any of them. Until now Daniel's existence had been kept secret. It was even likely that the Lady Clemence, her father's widow, believed him dead. Mother Benedicta and the monks would be bound by holy vows not to disclose his infirmity.

With Daniel locked away the uncles could seize all Sir Cedric's lands for their own. If she remained unmarried she would never be safe from their manipulations. They would become her guardians as well. She would be their pawn to use as they willed. Never would she countenance that. She knew enough about the Twyneham men to realise that those not touched by insanity were brutal in their greed. At least if she inherited Arnwood and Highford the people would live prosperously during her lifetime. But she could give them no heir.

Her stride lengthened as her agitation mounted. Was there no escaping this tangle? Only by marrying a powerful knight would she find a man to fight for her rights—to fight for Daniel's rights.

Eleanor continued her pacing. The situation was intolerable. Loathing deceit, she admitted that Sir Richard deserved to learn the truth. But could she trust him? What did she know of the knight to judge his reactions by? A man setting out to win a bride was likely very different from that same man bent upon retribution for a slight upon his honour. And refusing to marry Sir Richard would be a grave insult.

As for Conrad, she knew the depths to which he would stoop to get Highford. He did not love her. She was a means to an end. How could she tell him of Daniel? He would use it against her family to claim Highford as his own.

So her thoughts revolved upon a ceaseless turning wheel.

There was a knock on the door and Eleanor whirled, fearful lest Conrad had returned to taunt her. It was Griselda. 'My lady, I thought you would welcome a bath.' She stepped aside as four manservants entered carrying the tub and several buckets of hot water.

'Thank you, that was most thoughtful. But I would

not have the servants work so late. They must all be exhausted from fighting the fire.'

'My lady.' One of the older men, known as Spindle because of his exceptional height of over six feet and skinny body, went down on his knee before her. 'We would work all night to ease your comfort, gracious lady. You put us all to shame this night. In our joy at welcoming the return of Sir Conrad D'Arton as Lord of Highford, we forgot the kindness you have always shown us. I speak for everyone.'

'Ay,' the other men affirmed, shifting their weight self-consciously from one foot to the other.

A knot of emotion formed in Eleanor's throat. 'Old loyalties die hard. Why should you be loyal to Sir Cedric? He regarded Highford only as a source of revenue to fill his coffers.'

'But you were different, my lady.' Spindle's face was haggard with remorse. 'You took care of us. You have shown your love for Highford. Sir Conrad is regarded by many to be the true heir. But he is a stranger. My lady, forgive us for the wrong done you this day.'

'I forgive you all, Spindle,' she said. 'It is for our new King to decide who is the true heir to Highford.'

Spindle stood up, linking his fingers in distress. 'My lady, I ask a boon of you. Will you show yourself to the people? Let them see you have forgiven them. They have refused to leave the castle, their shame is so great.'

'I will go to the keep entrance in a short while.'

Eleanor dismissed the men. She quickly washed her face and hands and put a clean veil over her singed and sooty hair. She would not keep the people waiting longer. When she appeared in the open doorway a roar of, 'Eleanor! Eleanor!' filled the packed courtyard.

Overcome with emotion, Eleanor swallowed and looked down into their upturned faces. Looks of guilt at their betrayal were clear on many of their faces.

'I bear no grudge against any here,' she addressed them. 'Go to your beds and be at peace. The hay and food-stores lost in the fire will be replaced by provisions sent from Arnwood. No one will go hungry this winter. I promise you.'

'God bless you, my lady,' Oswald the falconer shouted, and the cry was taken up by everyone.

As Eleanor turned to go back into the castle she looked up at the lighted window of the Lord's chamber. The candles within illuminated Conrad's hair to a golden halo as he stood staring down at her. She could not see his expression, but the people's show of loyalty to her must have displeased him. She could not resist a triumphant smile up at the window. Conrad disappeared back into the room and from behind Eleanor the people of Highford continued to chant her name.

When she entered the hall she was overtaken by Oswald and Spindle, who seemed to have appointed themselves the spokesmen of the people.

Oswald cleared his throat. 'My lady, the people love you. But they are torn by the old loyalty to the D'Artons. Nothing could please us more than if a match was possible between you and Sir Conrad.'

The smile faded from Eleanor's lips. 'I am bound to Sir Richard Norton.'

'Ay. And it will mean blood spilt over Highford,' Oswald said ominously. 'The people want a D'Arton to rule them.'

'The people will obey whoever is their overlord, or they will face the consequences,' Eleanor declared and swept past them to return to the privacy of her room.

It was comforting to know that the people still loved her, but she would not be dictated to by them. Too much had happened too quickly. She needed time to think. Time to be alone and be certain that any decision she made would be the right one, both for Highford and Daniel. To stay at Highford would be to play into Conrad's hands. She must seek sanctuary at the priory until Sir Richard came to rescue her.

There was no sign of Griselda in her room and Eleanor

undressed herself and bathed. Later, as she struggled to get a comb through the matted tresses of her wet hair, she became irritated at her maid's continued absence. The castle was in chaos since the fire, but it was unlike Griselda to neglect her duty. Wrapping a towel about her hair and securing the sash of her robe, Eleanor rang the bell on the table to summon a servant. A page answered within moments, but was clearly having difficulty stifling his yawns.

'Where's Griselda?'

'I've not seen her, my lady.'

The boy put a hand to his mouth to hide another yawn and blinked to keep the sleep from his eyes. 'Shall I look for her, or send another woman to you, my lady?'

The page could hardly keep his eyes open; everyone in the castle was exhausted from fighting the fire. She could do without Griselda's attentions for one night.

'No,' Eleanor said gently. 'Get what rest you can.'

Again alone, she sat down on the bed and gave in to the weariness which finally claimed her. She braided her hair into a single plait and lay down on the pillow. Sleep refused to come. Left to tread its own path, an idea slowly formed and blossomed. Eleanor grinned into the darkness. It was the perfect ruse to give her all the time she needed.

At last the castle was silent, except for the distant tread of guards on the roof battlements of the keep. She hoped that they would be too tired for their usual vigilance and she would reach the armoury tower undetected.

She dressed in a plain dark green gown and took a russet wool cloak from the peg on the wall, pulling the hood over her braided hair. In the small hours of the morning the few torches which had been kept alight had burned low, but gave enough light to prevent her tripping over any servant sleeping in the corridors.

Once in the courtyard a watery moon gave enough light through the patches of cloud to guide her around any obstacles in the yard. The ground was cluttered with debris from the fire and discarded water buckets and pitchforks which the weary fire-fighters had dropped as they staggered home to their beds. There were ploughs, wagons and carts dragged from the burning outbuildings and left abandoned. In scattered piles were saddles and harness rescued from the stables.

Halfway towards the armoury tower a guard detached himself from the shadows and confronted her. 'Who's there?'

She saw the D'Arton wolf on the man's sleeve. She tipped back her hood and stood in a patch of moonlight which dappled the cobbled pathway. ''Tis Lady Eleanor. I could not sleep and have come to inspect the damage.'

'There is little to see, my lady,' the man answered gruffly. 'Better return to the keep.'

'In a while. The moonlight gives enough light to show me the extent of the ruins. 'Tis a sad day for Highford. And though I must soon leave I cannot forget that this has been my home for the last eight years.'

It was a tart reminder of her position. The guard stiffened and cleared his throat before adding, 'Some of the structures are unsafe, my lady. You would be wise to return to the keep. Permit me to escort you.'

Eleanor regarded him coldly. 'I did not realise that I was Sir Conrad's prisoner. Am I then not permitted to stroll within the castle confines?'

The man stepped back. 'You are not a prisoner, my lady. But it will be safer for you if I accompany you. My orders were that upon no account were you to be allowed near the armoury tower.'

'Why?' She gave him a look of wide-eyed affront. 'Does Sir Conrad fear I will steal a sword and seek to run him through?'

The moon went behind a dense cloud and the courtyard was pitched into darkness. Eleanor gazed up at the sky. Not a star was to be seen. There would be no more moonlight tonight. She edged away from the sentry.

'My lady, stay!'

Eleanor could hear the guard stumbling over an obstacle to her right as she stealthily made her way to the armoury tower. She put a hand before her to avoid colliding with an unseen object and betraying her passage.

'My lady!' the guard shouted. 'You must return to the keep.'

She grinned at having evaded him. Then her foot trod upon something soft. There was a furious flapping of wings and she was suddenly attacked from all sides by vicious beaks of the geese which she had so rudely disturbed. One pecked her on the knee and another on the hand. She gasped at the pain and backed away from them, straight into the figure of the guard.

'Are you hurt, my lady?' he asked solicitously.

Eleanor was too angry to answer.

'Permit me to escort you back to your chamber, my lady. It will be dawn in two hours and Sir Conrad will be abroad. He may welcome your advice on the damage then.'

She was outwitted. Betrayed by her own geese. To protest too strongly would only arouse further suspicion. If she could not escape by the tunnel she would have to brazen it out some other way. When the portcullis was raised, the villagers would swarm into the castle to begin the clearing work. She had but to dress as a serving wench to make her escape then. Her guard shooed away the ruffled geese and their honking subsided.

The window to Conrad's chamber was thrown wide and his angry voice shouted. 'Guard! What's the disturbance?'

'The Lady Eleanor could not sleep, my lord. She wished to inspect the damage.'

'In the dark?' Conrad snarled.

'I am escorting her back to her room now, my lord.'

The window was drawn shut, but not before Eleanor

caught the mumbled curse from within. 'Damned woman! Will she give me no peace?'

Eleanor permitted herself to be led back to her chamber. Another plan was already forming. She glanced at Conrad's door further along the corridor and smiled to herself. She had no intention of succumbing to the knight's tyranny.

Once inside her room she heard the steady tread of a guard posted at the end of the corridor. Let Conrad's men wear themselves out trying to to keep her caged. There was another way out of her room. And Conrad had shown it to her. She would not remain his prisoner. She had decided she would place her trust in Sir Richard Norton. He would deal with Conrad as justice demanded. Then she must convince Sir Richard that their marriage was impossible.

Now she was in contention with Sir Conrad. It was no longer a question of the rights and wrongs, of who was the true heir to Highford. In truth she acknowledged that his claim had its merits. It was a question of honour. . . Of family pride. . . Of refusing to relinquish what was hers without a fight.

She searched and pushed against the wall until she felt it move. There was a creak and a gust of cold air passed across her feet. A narrow segment of the stonework opened inwards, revealing a black void. She picked up a lighted candlestick and, holding if aloft, peered into the darkness. It smelt unpleasantly musty and of mice. Their squeaks and the sound of soft pattering feet did not deter her, though her flesh shrank from touching the thick dusty cobwebs which festooned the passage. Many hung in shreds where Conrad had recently pushed through them.

Eleanor paused to find the mechanism which would close the opening. Close to the floor was a rusty lever. When the door swung closed, the passage was plunged into near darkness. Eleanor's heart beat frantically as the stuffy atmosphere threatened to suffocate her. It was like entering a tomb and the fine hairs on the back of her neck prickled. That the candle stayed alight proved there was air in the passage, but the light it gave was dim and far from reassuring. It was enough to show her that the passage slanted downwards then turned at right angles, continuing for a hundred paces before ending abruptly at a stone wall.

Discovering a similar level to the one by her chamber at the end of the passage, she pushed it. Nothing happened. Panic swelled in her breast. In the confined space the tunnel became as oppressive as the grave. Her heart banged painfully against her ribs and her spine broke out in a chilling sweat. The chittering of the mice grew louder and something dropped on her neck. She bit back a scream, the tickling sensation turning her blood cold before the large spider dropped to the floor.

Eleanor shuddered. She hated the thought of insects creeping over her flesh. She could feel other spiders dropping down from the roof on to her hair and she smothered a scream. Her efforts became frantic as she wriggled and pulled the lever, which refused to move. When a spider ran down over her face she brushed it off, her hands shaking with the horror of the touch of those creatures. With a shaky sob she hauled on the lever with all her strength and to her relief the rusty mechanism began to move.

Again she felt the paralysis of fear; the grating sound of the opening door seemed deafening to her over-wrought nerves. She had no idea where the passage came out. What if she had walked straight into Conrad's guards?

She blew out the candle and strained her ears in the darkness. There was no sound outside the opening. She slid through it silently, pressing her body flat against the wall to avoid detection. There was the smell of incense and high above her the moonlight picked out yellow and red glints from the figures in the church's stained-glass window.

Her relief was immense. When another spider ran down her neck, she brushed her hands through her hair with a shuddering whimper of disgust. 'Nasty, creeping things. Oh, I hate them. I hate Conrad for making me suffer all this.'

Shaking the last of the spiders from her clothing, she felt calmer and scanned her surroundings. The opening was concealed by the wood-carvings which decorated the back of the pew of the Lord's family. She reckoned there was an hour before the portcullis was raised and Father Hubert would come to the church for the first mass of the day. She would stay here in hiding until then, then slip out amid the general coming and going of servants passing from village to castle.

After only five hours' sleep in three days, Conrad was jolted awake by the sound of his chamber door opening. His hand was on his sword, which through habit he always slept with at his side. He was half out of bed before he saw it was Ned. He laughed and flopped back on the pillow. 'Old instincts die hard,' he said as he dropped the sword on the bed.

'Such reflexes have saved your life more than once, my friend,' Ned returned, but his expression remained grim.

'What trouble is there now?' Conrad asked, wearily swinging his legs from the bed and pulling on his hose.

'The wench—I mean the Lady Eleanor. She's gone. A guard discovered her heading for the armoury tower in the night, but he escorted her back to her room and put a guard in the corridor. No one left her room. A maid discovered her disappearance a few minutes ago.'

Conrad reached for his shirt and tunic. He guessed Eleanor had escaped through the passage behind the tapestry. It had been careless of him to forget its existence. But he had been so exhausted from tackling the fire and so many long hours without sleep that it had slipped his mind. There were guards posted outside the church who should have seen her emerge.

'Surely she did not just ride, or walk out?' Conrad snapped. 'The guards at the gatehouse had instructions.'

'Only the normal workforce from the castle and village have passed through. Of Lady Eleanor there has been no sign.'

Conrad's hands clenched into tight fists. 'She dressed as a page once to get out. She could have adopted a disguise. Have a dozen men join me. I've a suspicion where she could be.'

'You're taking a lot of trouble to keep this wench here,' Ned observed. 'She's trouble. She's bound to Norton. Send her to him with an escort and be done with her. Henry will not consider your claim to Highford while she is a hostage.'

Conrad's face grew rigid and it was with great effort that he spoke below a shout. 'She is a noblewoman under my protection. I cannot allow her to roam the country-side at the mercy of outlaws. Masterless men roam the land in vast numbers, cast loose from Yorkist patrons who are dead or impoverished from the fighting. They scavenge upon unwary travellers. No unarmed man is safe, let alone a woman.'

'Then she should have stayed where she was safe,' Ned said sourly. 'Or perhaps there was a greater danger for her here.'

Conrad looked at him sharply.

Ned sighed. 'It's not like you to let any woman deflect you from your chosen path. She'd better be worth it. You could lose Highford and the King's favour.'

As they rode out of Highford, a peasant woman ran forward, her arms lifted in pleading. 'Find our dear lady, my lord, before harm can come to her.'

It rankled that the people showed such devotion to Eleanor. It could threaten the future security of Highford. Conrad wondered if Eleanor was worth all the aggravation she put him through. He flexed the tired muscles in his shoulders, guiding the destrier with one hand, the other rubbing the ache in his wounded thigh. He could not risk her returning to Norton. She must be found. Despite his antagonism at the trouble she caused him, he could not stop worrying about her safety. For all her proud courage, she was slight and helpless against any attacker. An image of her lying dead in the tatters of her clothing, her lovely body desecrated, her throat cut by outlaws, set his features into rigidity.

He rode towards the priory, certain that was where she would take refuge. To the accompanying drumming of his horse's hoofs, other thoughts plagued his mind. In the heat of her anger she had vowed to die rather than wed him. Yet her blood had responded to his touch, her body yielding to his mastery. And for that he had taunted her. Did not his own blood cry out its need to make her irrevocably his own?

How would that fierce pride react? Would the shame of her response haunt her? Had she fled to cast herself into the depths of the river? Might she even now be floating lifelessly downstream, preferring death to dishonour? A grinding urgency made him touch his heels to his mount's flanks and urge it to a faster pace.

Eleanor had adopted the guise of the goose-girl, who she knew was in the infirmary as one of the victims of burns from last night's fire. She had even appropriated the young woman's dress to aid her deception. Getting out of the castle had been easy, but her progress to the river was slowed by the pace and contrariness of the geese. She had not realised how difficult they were to control, though after her experiences with the creatures last night she should have realised they would be cantankerous. She could not afford to allow the geese to take to the water too close to the castle. Her persistence in driving them forward agitated the flock. The males became aggressive, flapping their wings and making dashes for the river. Twice she was nipped on the leg and once suffered the affront of receiving a vicious peck on her buttocks by the largest gander. It was he who had ruined her escape last night, and the bird had an evil look in his eye. With each bite he gave her, Eleanor found herself regarding him as the next candidate for the cook's pot. And she was convinced he knew it, as he began to mount a perverse assault upon her ankles. Grim-faced, she limped onwards, her eyes blazing as her anger turned upon Conrad. He had reduced her to this wretched state by making her his prisoner.

At the sound of fast hoof-beats approaching, she steeled herself to remember to play the part of her disguise. The goose-girl's gown was high above her ankles and smelt of the peasants' sweat. It also scratched Eleanor's tender skin. From the nips she received with increasing frequency, she suspected it was riddled with fleas. To complete the disguise was a short hood which covered her shoulders. This she pulled low over her face as she stood on the side of the river track.

She kept her face lowered as the horses drew level, but her senses were immediately tuned to Conrad's presence. His voice, harsh with impatience, addressed her.

'Wench, has anyone passed you on the path to the priory?'

Eleanor shook her head and bobbed an ungainly courtesy as she gruffened her voice, using the thick local dialect. 'There were the swineherd taking the pigs into the wood. No one else, my lord.'

The horses began to prance nervously as the geese took exception to having their access to the river blocked.

'Perhaps she did not come this way,' Ned commented. 'Forget the wench, Conrad. You don't need Norton as your enemy. And now that Highford is garrisoned with your men, you should be seeking audience with Henry to secure your title.'

Conrad's destrier pranced as the geese flapped around its hoofs. Conrad spoke a calming word to the horse, but the tone in which he answered Ned was steel-cold. 'You don't win a battle by leaving an enemy free to stick a knife in your back. Once Eleanor is confined at Highford I can go to Court.'

Reining back the destrier, Conrad dug in his heels and set the great horse speeding forward. Eleanor fumed at the callousness of Conrad's plans for herself. So much for the false words of tenderness last night. She had been right not to trust the knave. Her heart sank as the riders headed towards the priory. She could not go there yet. It would mean staying hidden until the patrol returned to the castle. When the riders disappeared from sight she abandoned the geese, who took to the water. She dared not risk staying so exposed to any passer-by. She would use her wits and bide her time.

Conrad sat opposite Mother Benedicta in the guest parlour. The prioress studied him in silence as she listened to his request. At last she said heavily, 'I could not break the right of sanctuary if the Lady Eleanor comes here.'

'You do not trust my motives?' Conrad questioned.

She sighed. 'You are very like your father, in more than just resemblance. The D'Artons are stubborn. You must know it is impossible for me to take sides. My duty and allegiance is to serve our Saviour — not an earthly master.'

'Would you see Highford forever lost to the D'Artons?' he accused. 'None more than you is aware of the history between the castle and priory. The D'Artons founded the priory and we have always been its benefactors.'

Mother Benedicta stood up and there was sadness mixed with the light of battle in her green eyes. 'Nephew, how can you ask that of me? Rarely has a generation passed when a daughter from our family has not entered here. Many, as I have done, rose to be its prioress. Should the Lady Eleanor seek sanctuary I will pray for guidance.'

She rose to dismiss him and at the anger darkening his face she put a hand on his arm. 'The Lady Eleanor is not a conquest of war, Nephew.'

'She is under my protection. If she remains free and stays in the district she is also a danger to my authority at Highford. Once united with Norton she can raise an army to lay siege to Highford. I want no bloodshed, no split loyalties from my people, before Highford has been returned legally to me by King Henry.'

Mother Benedicta eyed him sternly. Her face had none of the hawk-like features of the D'Artons, but their ancient lineage was as proud in her as in Conrad. 'Are you sure that is your only interest in the Lady Eleanor?'

Conrad's voice crackled with authority. 'On my father's death-bed I vowed to him to regain Highford or persish in the attempt. Do you expect me to dishonour such a vow, Aunt?'

Eleanor sat on a boulder overlooking the priory and from a distance saw Conrad and his men ride away. She sighed with relief and climbed down from her vantage point to begin her trek to the safety of the priory. Each step was accompanied by mixed emotions. It would be good to see Daniel again before he was sent to Arnwood. If her own position at Highford were not so precarious she would have found a way to keep Daniel by her side. She wanted to give him the chance to live a normal life. With her own future uncertain that was no longer possible. At least with the monks at Arnwood Abbey he would be tended with the solicitude which befitted his rank.

Unbidden, her thoughts returned to Conrad. He had proved a powerful adversary. Yet she had escaped him. The victory did not give her the pleasure she had anticipated. She closed her eyes to blot out his image, which seemed forever before her eyes. It was branded in her memory, even the smallest details about him. The clear-cut lines of his handsome profile. The way his lips quirked into a smile. The strength in his arms and long lean fingers, which had the capacity to kill, yet could be tender and infinitely sensual when caressing her body. A quiver passed through her as she recalled the potency of his kisses, the intoxication of the demand in his embrace.

Her eyes flew open and she muttered an unladylike curse. It was the ease with which he sought to dominate her which irked her. Surely in the cloistered peace of the priory she would be free of her wayward thoughts? There she would remember only that Conrad was her sworn enemy.

She emerged from the undergrowth at the side of the track leading to the priory. The buildings were dominated by the tall spire of the church and the square turret of the guest quarters, behind which ran the oblong refectory and cloisters. Along one side of the three-sided courtyard was the solid square building of the prioress's chambers, all enclosed by a high flint-stoned wall. A narrow tributary of the river ran alongside the grey stone walls, its banks overhung with willows. Here Eleanor knew she would find peace. Here her prayers would be answered and she would find the solution to her problems.

The last hundred yards of her walk to the gatehouse were exposed. She ran the short distance, looking anxiously over her shoulder as she rapped on the heavy iron-studded oak door. The shutter over the barred window was lifted and she recognised the round face of Sister Dominique, the portress.

Eleanor pushed back her hood so that she could be recognised. 'I must speak with Mother Benedicta. I am in danger and ask sanctuary.'

There was no surprise on the elderly nun's wrinkled face, and the gatehouse door was opened to admit her. Aware that Sister Dominique was bound by her vows of silence, Eleanor had no trouble understanding the nun's gestures for her to follow her to the prioress's quarters.

When she entered the study she found Mother Benedicta kneeling at a prie-dieu, her head bent in prayer. At hearing Eleanor's soft footfall the prioress kissed the crucifix on her rosary before rising to regard her.

'You show no surprise at my visit. But then Sir Conrad D'Arton was here earlier. I hid in the wood waiting for his men to leave. I ask sanctuary until my betrothed, Sir Richard Norton, comes for me.'

The prioress raised an intimidating brow as she regarded Eleanor's attire. 'You arrive here dressed like a beggar. What have you to fear at Highford that makes you take such desperate measures? Sir Conrad is an honourable man.'

Eleanor held her head high and resisted the urge to scratch at the persistent itching the coarse woollen material caused her body. She felt ashamed at appearing before the prioress in such a condition, and it added to the antagonism she felt towards Conrad. 'Sir Conrad would be Lord of Highford. I will not be his hostage.' Under the powerful scrutiny of the nun's green stare, Eleanor dropped her gaze as she added more softly, 'Also, Mother Benedicta, I fear for my virtue.'

'Has Sir Conrad made improper advances?' The prioress was suitably shocked.

Eleanor blushed. The prioress's green eyes were an uncomfortable reminder of Conrad and she had come here to forget the power he wielded over her.

'He is my enemy and I am bound to another. But he is a handsome man, and has a way about him. . .' Eleanor swallowed, her cheeks flaming poppy-red with her shame. 'He desires me. I am still a maid, but. . .'

'The Holy Mother be praised for that. But from your blushes you are not as innocent of men as you should be.'

Mother Benedicta raised a questioning eyebrow, but Eleanor refused to elaborate further.

'This puts a very different light upon what Sir Conrad

told me.' The prioress added sternly, 'In the circumstances I feel that Sir Conrad is duty bound to wed you.'

'I will never marry,' Eleanor declared emphatically.

Mother Benedicta tutted with impatience. 'What nonsense is this? You are betrothed to Sir Richard Norton.'

'That was before I learned the truth about Daniel.'

The prioress crossed herself and muttered a prayer low upon her breath. 'I did wrong in telling you of his illness. Now you worry that your children will be so blighted. That need not be the case.'

'I will not risk it!'

'Marriage and children are your destiny.'

All colour drained from Eleanor's face and her eyes were dark with torment. 'With respect, Mother Benedicta, I have heard this lecture from Father Hubert. My mind is made up.'

'It is in God's hands, not yours, my child.' There was compassion in the gentle voice. 'You are all your mother's daughter, in looks and temperament. There is nothing of Sir Cedric in you.'

'The blood is there. The blood is tainted.' Eleanor held her head proudly though her throat worked against the agony of her decision. 'That is another reason why I am here. I must insist that you answer a most holy vow of silence upon the subject of Daniel's illness. I cannot permit my family's shame to become common knowledge.'

'I take such a vow willingly. Not that I fear Sir Conrad would harm Daniel — I believe that most unlikely — but because of the friendship I bore your mother.' Mother Benedicta folded her hands beneath the wide folds of her habit. 'But in return you must promise me to abide by your duty.'

'You ask too much.'

'I ask only that you place your faith in God.'

Eleanor bowed her head. 'I have never doubted God. My conscience tugs me one way — my faith another. I ask for time to find the truth in prayer, before I can make that promise.'

'And I know you will make the right decision.' Mother Benedicta smiled for the first time since Eleanor's arrival, but a troubled light remained in her disconcerting green eyes.

'How is Daniel?' Eleanor deliberately turned the subject.

'This is one of his quiet days.'

'I would like to see him.'

The prioress looked at her pityingly. 'You will but add to your torment, my child.'

'He leaves soon for Arnwood Abbey and it may be many months before I can see him again. He needs to know that I love him, for any change in his world will unsettle him.'

Mother Benedicta bowed her head in acknowledgement. 'He is by the pond. Sister Mathilde will take you to him.'

'I know the way. I would not take your nuns from their duties.'

Eleanor hurried to the large pond, which was fed by an underwater stream from the river outside the walls. Daniel sat at the pond's edge with a fishing rod in his hands. As he stared into the clear water, he rocked backwards and forwards and did not hear her call his name.

'Daniel!' she repeated. 'It's Eleanor.' Still he did not turn to greet her.

She saw the veins through the paleness of his cheeks and the bones showing through his skeletal hands. He had lost flesh from his frail figure since last she had seen him. Spreading her skirts, she sat on the grass beside him. Even now she was ignored and as she looked at his pinched profile she saw that his eyes were wide and glazed. He was lost in some inner world and was unaware of her presence.

'Daniel,' she said softly, 'do you like to fish?'

He did not answer.

She sat with him as the sun climbed high in the sky and continued to speak in a low voice. None of her words seemed to reach him, but he had stopped his rocking and she guessed her company somehow soothed him. As the heat of the day progressed, Eleanor began to scratch as the peasant's dress irritated her flesh. At midday Sister Mathilde came to take Daniel away for his meal, but Eleanor was not hungry.

Now she was left alone, her thoughts returned to their earlier anguished trail, but her concentration was interrupted by the discomfort of her gown. There was no bath-house within the priory and she could not expect the nuns to wait upon her like servants. The coarse material chafed her shoulders and arms, and suddenly she could stand it no more.

The cool clear water of the pond beckoned invitingly. Her garment offended her fastidiousness and she needed to cleanse herself of its filth and the creatures which infested its cloth. She went to the laundry and found Sister Agnes mopping the suds from the floor at the end of the day's washing.

'Sister Agnes, is there some soap I could use to bathe?' Eleanor plucked at the gown she wore. 'To escape the castle I needed a disguise. This belonged to the goose-girl and is not very clean. I would bathe in the pond and wash it. Perhaps I could borrow a chemise until it dries.'

The nun nodded and, going to the large linen press, took out a towel, but by a negative gesture told Eleanor there was no suitable garment for her to wear. She signalled to Eleanor to wait and went out, her sandals flapping through the wet puddles on the flagstoned laundry floor. Moments later Sister Agnes returned with a linen sheet and a long black cloak. She also held out a small bar of soap.

Smiling her grateful appreciation, Eleanor took sheet and cloak, which would adequately cover her. Anything was better than being feasted on by the fleas from the

coarse gown. With a light step she hurried to the pond.
She stripped off her clothes and stretched as the warm
sun caressed her naked form. Then she ran into the
water, gasping as its coldness lapped over her body.
With a laugh she splashed and dived into its depths,
swimming several strokes underwater before she sur-
faced. The feel of the cool water on her heated flesh was
wonderful. It was years since she had swum, for with the
maturing of her figure it was a pleasure modesty denied
her. She had forgotten how good it felt to lie on her back
and just float and allow the cares of the day to slip away.

Clutching the soap in her hand, Eleanor stood up, the
water swirling around her thighs as she lathered her
body to rid it of the last of the goose-girl's smell. Then
she freed her hair of its pins and washed the last
remnants of the soot and smoke from her hair. Last
night she had needed to rush her toilette; now she could
luxuriate in the warmth of the sun and forget the
problems at the castle. This was the peace she needed to
think, away from the tensions of Highford.

The priory bell rang, calling the nuns to prayers, and
as it fell silent Eleanor rinsed the soap from her hair and
rose up out of the water, smoothing it back from her
face. A movement caught the tail of her eye and she
froze. Then with a squeal of horror, she dived into the
water with only her head left visible. A man was sitting
on top of the priory wall ten yards away watching her.
As she blinked the water from her lashes, she saw the
man was Conrad.

He leapt down to her side of the garden. Eleanor cast
about, but there was no one in sight to aid her. He stood
at the water's edge, watching her with an infuriating
nonchalance. But his eyes told a different story. They
were dark and menacing, with either anger or desire —
she did not know which. Neither boded well for her.

To add to her discomfort the sun went behind a cloud
and her teeth began to chatter with the cold. 'Do you
intend to stand there gawping, or are you gentleman

enough to turn your back, so that I can come out of the water?'

'You've caused me nothing but inconvenience this day. Do I not deserve some reward for the trouble you have put me to?'

Eleanor realised that he was too angry to spare her blushes. He intended to punish her for her disobedience. She lifted her chin and regarded him narrowly as she swam forward several strokes, but kept just out of his reach.

'If I have to wade in and haul you out I will,' he warned.

She believed him. Holding out her hand, she kept her eyes lowered lest they betray her malevolence, and ventured coyly, 'The slope is slippery.'

She rose up out of the water, suppressing the urge to cover her body with her hands. He had seen her naked-ness before and it was a small price to pay before she extracted her own revenge. The bold way his gaze played over her was as blatant as a caress. Desire flared in his eyes as he regarded her and she almost faltered in her resolve. She pretended to slip, and instinctively his hand shot out to take hers to steady her. She was ready. Gripping his wrist with both hands, Eleanor threw herself backwards in the water with all her strength, dragging him with her. As his head broke the surface of the pond, the shock on his face made her erupt with triumphant laughter. 'That should cool your ardour.'

Her merriment was smothered when he made a lunge towards her. With a shriek she turned on her stomach and struck out for the far bank of the pond. Before she had covered a few yards his hand slid around her waist, and she was flipped over in his strong arms to look up at him. She had not expected to find him laughing.

'By all that's holy, Eleanor! You are a sore trial, but an exasperating and provocative one.' His hand slid with possessive familiarity down her spine and over her hips.

She wriggled with fury, splashing him in her attempts

to be free of his loathsome hold. He ducked beneath the
water, drawing her down with him. She swallowed a
mouthful of water and came up spluttering for air.
Without pity, she was caught in his embrace. He smiled
into her angry gaze, unimpressed by her fury. She felt
her anger burn deep within her, together with disappointment and bitterness at yet another failure to escape
him. It was followed by a savage determination to beat
him at his own game. She had learned enough from their
physical encounters to know how to arouse him. This
time she would not be the one manipulated and conquered, it would be him. Once he lowered his guard, she
would make her escape. Besides, the pond was overlooked by the priory buildings. . .*and this was a nunnery*!
She did not believe that even Conrad would force himself
upon her in these sacred grounds.

She made herself relax, allowing the current of the
stream to press her body against him. 'Once more I am
your prisoner,' she said softly, hoping that her voice
conveyed submission and none of her anger.

'You cannot escape me, Eleanor,' he taunted.

The touch of his restraining hands was light upon her
waist, but she knew he would not release her. To try and
overcome his physical strength would be folly. From
their first meeting she had known that he meant to be
master of Highford. He was not a man to deviate from
his chosen path. Yet she suspected that, though Highford was his quest, he had not meant to be entangled in
its mistress's charms. Those she must use to her
advantage.

There was admiration in Conrad's stare as his hand
idly moved along her spine and up over her shoulders,
then slowly down to the swelling of her breast. The
crystal water concealed nothing of her body from his
bold gaze, and it gave her confidence that she could
succeed. But at what cost? She squelched the voice of
caution.

Even that lightest touch from him made her tremble.

She willed herself to remain compliant, dampening her outrage as his mouth lowered with confident dominance to hers. It moved slowly and subtly over her lips, matching the sensuous movement of his hands across her back and along her ribcage. One hand held her head so that she could not escape his kiss, making every pulse in her body leap. Eleanor felt her breasts swell firm against the expanse of hard chest and the rose crests hardened as his calloused hand spread across them. Through the thin fabric of his hose she felt the evidence of his desire.

This was her chance to escape. But her body was trembling and her legs had turned weak at the seductive skill of his touch. Her limbs refused to obey her will, her pride reduced to tatters by the knowledge that again he was in control and she the slave to her senses. Her cheeks flamed scarlet with mortification as he moved against her, and she lost her footing on the slippery pool bed. Their bodies locked together, legs entangled as she fought to regain her balance. His arm was firm about her and there was no escape from the erotic pressure of the subtle rotation of his hips as he twisted in the water, weightless but in control.

'Own that you cannot escape me,' he whispered against her hair. 'I had imagined you ravaged by outlaws.'

Eleanor willed herself to remain detached from his seduction. 'I was perfectly safe. It is only now I find myself in danger of ravishment.' She spoke softly, but clipped out the words as if they soured her mouth.

'Admit I am your lord, Eleanor. Have I not offered you honourable marriage?'

'To win Highford!' she accused, wriggling to free herself from his tenacious hold. His hand slid possessively along her inner thigh, radiating an exciting heat. To her distress it ignited the embers of a scorching fire which flickered in ripples through her body. 'Our destiny is clear. And is it not the will of our people?'

Eleanor gazed into his green, triumphant gaze and saw the promise of forbidden delights.

'My lord, I. . .' She could not answer yea, or nay, and found her lids closing in surrender as his mouth hovered tantalisingly above her lips. Why did her body seem to have no will but his? And why with the strength of his arms around her, and the evidence of his arousal hard against her thigh, did she want him to possess her with a craving which defied reason? She had tried to fight him and lost. There was no strength left in her to resist him further. She shivered, bitterly aware of how expert he was at rousing her beyond coherent thought or reason. Her fate was inescapable. Her arms went around his neck and she heard his low laugh, husky with desire, as he held her in a passionate embrace.

'Conrad! Lady Eleanor!' The voice of Mother Benedicta blasted over them like a whiplash.

Eleanor instinctively ducked beneath the water, but there was nowhere to hide from the prioress's outrage, so she resurfaced. Her hand was taken and she was drawn towards the bank by Conrad, who looked unconcerned, though a faint tinge of pink coloured his cheeks to show his discomfort.

He stood up and shook the water from his hair, but when he bent to lift Eleanor from the pond Mother Benedicta's outraged tones halted him. 'Don't touch her. I will not have her defiled before my eyes.'

Conrad grinned at the prioress with ironic humour.

'Come out of there, Conrad!' she berated him as though he were a small boy.

Despite the chagrin Eleanor felt at her own predicament, she experienced a stab of satisfaction that he was now the one to be discountenanced.

'Stand there, Conrad,' Mother Benedicta commanded sharply. 'And keep your back turned.'

Mother Benedicta came forward, holding out the cloak for Eleanor to wrap around her. Eleanor emerged from the water and covered her shivering figure with the cloak, but was unable to look into the incensed face of the prioress.

'Has either of you any sense of decency?' Mother Benedicta's tone was cold with censure. 'I am shocked. And that you disport yourself so in a place such as this. . .'

She whirled on Conrad, who stared pointedly at the dripping toe of his boot. 'There is but one answer, of course. You will have to be married. And at once.'

'No!' Eleanor protested. 'I came here to escape that fate.'

Mother Benedicta sent her a withering glare. 'Not from what I just saw. A more scandalous scene I could not imagine. At least it solves the question of who inherits Highford. And if I am called upon by the King, I shall tell him exactly why my nephew married the Lady Eleanor. You are well suited.'

'Your nephew!' Eleanor exploded, forgetful of the respect due the prioress. 'Is this some scheme hatched this morning between the two of you to ensure that Highford became the D'Artons' undisputed property?'

Mother Benedicta folded her hands across her waist. 'I am party only to God's will. The circumstances which make your marriage expedient you have brought upon your own head.'

Eleanor was about to cry out that her tainted blood precluded any marriage. Anger at the way she had been tricked made her snap her lips shut. The prioress had betrayed her. Even if Conrad had stolen into the priory without his aunt's blessing, Mother Benedicta should have told her that she was a D'Arton. If they were so determined to win Highford through this tainted marriage, let them. Little good it would do Conrad when he realised the curse her blood brought to the marriage bed. And since Mother Benedicta put propriety above the need to preserve the D'Arton line, let the consequences be upon her pious head.

Eleanor was too angry to think straight. The D'Artons had tricked her and used her to their own ends. She wanted to hurt these two D'Artons as they had hurt her.

CHAPTER TEN

BEFORE Conrad and Eleanor left the priory, a servant was sent to procure fresh clothes for both of them from Highford. Eleanor rode in mutinous silence. They were accompanied on their journey by Mother Benedicta, who proceeded to question Conrad on his years away from Highford.

Conrad was reticent in his answers. His lifestyle had been nomadic, spent serving as a squire to the mercenary armies Sir Lionel hired himself to on the Continent. From time to time he been the companion of Henry Tudor, though this he did not elaborate upon. But one thing in his conversation was clear: everything he had worked for until this moment was to regain Highford.

Eleanor was disappointed that Mother Benedicta did not press Conrad, but the nun would have maintained some contact with her family over the years and would be aware of her newphew's progress.

The extent of the devastation which greeted them at Highford shocked Eleanor. This morning she had been too concerned with her escape to pay much attention to the damage caused by the fire. The entire west-facing curtain wall was black with smoke and a dozen or more outbuildings were reduced to crumpled heaps. Everyone from the village had come to help, except babes in arms, or those incapacitated by age. Several groups of young men and and women were singing as they cleared the black timbers. Young children laughed and giggled as they made a game of searching the ruins for metal items which were taken to the blacksmith for repair. Anything which could be salvaged was put aside for cleaning and repair. That which was beyond saving was being piled on a steadily growing bonfire on the charred grass.

Shaken by the destruction, Eleanor broke her silence to ask, 'Did you learn how the fire started?'

Conrad's eyes narrowed to feral slits. 'The woman Griselda started it. She's under guard.'

He leapt to the ground with an agility which must have pained his injured thigh. As he came to her side to assist her to dismount, Eleanor was aware of the curious glances from the people working around them. Mother Benedicta had dismounted and was standing watching them with her hands folded in the wide sleeves of her habit. The prioress's presence put an end to any suspicion of impropriety in Eleanor's and Conrad's relationship. There was to be no stain upon the D'Arton honour, nor Eleanor's reputation.

Any sign of truculence between Conrad and herself would begin a rift between the people as they weighed old and new loyalties. His expression was affable, but there was a warning in Conrad's eyes that told her it would be dangerous to try and divide the people against him. It was conveyed by a look of such menace that her throat constricted.

With a start she realised she had underestimated him. Until now he had allowed her a measure of freedom, even a momentary feeling of triumph. Each time he had outwitted her and been the victor. Apart from their first encounter, when he had believed her a lad, he had never exerted physical force over her. There had been no need. There was a power which emanated from him which was far more devastating. Even now when she was angry it reached out to touch a core within her. It was an integral part of him — that self-possession conveyed by a languid, but none the less intimidating stride, his intensity of purpose, the keen intelligence and the fearlessness of a wolf. The D'Arton wolf. He was daring, bold and invincible.

As he lifted her to the ground, she studied him closely. There was within his features an austerity of countenance which was strikingly attractive. Though she resented the way in which she had been tricked into accepting their marriage, she now realised it was inevitable. And it was for the good of Highford. His ability to lead men and win their respect and loyalty had been obvious even when he had still been a squire. Now he was knighted, she knew he would be formidable.

She made no secret of her appraisal of him and the light in his eyes changed, first to cynicism, then, as she continued to hold his stare, to the acknowledgement of an equal. A quiver of anticipation roused her awareness, shocking her by its intensity and poignancy. She harnessed the emotion. Once unleashed it would destroy her resolve. Aware of the danger of his close proximity, she stepped back.

'If Griselda started the fire, she did so to save my virtue. For such loyalty she does not deserve to die.'

'A dangerous loyalty,' he warned her quietly. 'Several people are in the infirmary because of her. Extensive damage was caused by the fire to the castle and its provisions.'

She met his hard stare unflinchingly. 'She did it to save my honour and her ploy worked.'

'She must be punished. The people of Highford will face starvation this winter because of her vindictiveness.'

Every word he spoke Eleanor agreed with, but she had to speak for her maid. 'Griselda acted out of love, not spite. I beg of you, do not be too harsh with her. She is no longer young. I promise the people will not starve; grain and provisions will be made available from Arnwood.'

'I cannot allow such an act to go unpunished. It would undermine my authority.'

Eleanor sank on one knee before him, aware that the people had stopped their work and were watching her with shocked amazement. There was a flash of annoyance in Conrad's eyes, but she ignored it.

'My lord, tomorrow we are to be married.' Her voice rose clear for all to hear. She lifted her face to regard

him, her heart quaking at the suspicion revealed by the
set line of his square jaw. 'It should be a time for
rejoicing. . .for the breaching of old grievances. For a
new trust to be forged.' She took his hands, which were
stiff and unyielding. 'My lord, I beg that your judgement
be merciful to my faithful servant.'

'Bring the wench Griselda to me,' Conrad ordered a
guard. He raised Eleanor to her feet, but his expression
was shuttered as he waited for the servant to appear
before them. He would give his answer to her plea before
everyone present.

Griselda was sobbing. Her wimple and veil and had
been lost and her thin grey hair hung loose around her
linen-white face. When she saw Conrad she fell to her
knees, her heavy jowls quivering with the force of her
sobs. 'I meant no one to be hurt. Or for the fire to
spread,' she blurted out. 'A diversion was all I sought.
To spare——'

'Enough of your blubbering, old woman.' Conrad cut
across her words before they could be seized on by the
crowd. 'Tomorrow your mistress and I will be married.'
He raised his voice so that everyone could hear. 'The
Lady Eleanor has a tender and forgiving heart. She has
pleaded for your life. I can refuse my future bride
nothing.'

Griselda looked at him, her chins wobbling as she
pressed her mouth to his hand. 'My lord, bless you.'

Eleanor stooped to help Griselda heave her bulk to her
feet. 'You are fortunate that Sir Conrad has such a noble
nature,' she admonished the maid before turning a
radiant smile upon her future husband. 'My lord, I shall
never forget your generosity. It takes a strong man to
forgive.'

He forestalled her gratitude by taking her hand and
raising it to his lips. When he lowered it he whispered
for her alone to hear, 'And it takes an equally strong
woman to realise that what I do now I do because our
people must realise mercy is not a sign of weakness.'

Turning to face the assembly, he held up a hand to silence their murmurings. Many of them were puzzled and even angry that Griselda had escaped after causing such suffering and havoc to the community. 'I grant Griselda her life, for I do not want my marriage tainted by a death. However, I banish her from Highford. To repent of the suffering she has caused to those in the infirmary, she will spend five years with the good sisters at the priory. Their strict rule of silence and obedience will be penance enough.'

He pronounced the sentence so emotionlessly that it was several seconds before Eleanor realised that she was still to be deprived of the company of her maid. She opened her mouth to protest, but the grim line of his mouth warned her against it. He had spared Griselda's life, and in truth he had been lenient with her.

'Have I your permission to spend an hour in saying farewell to my maid before she must leave?' Eleanor asked.

At her request his eyes widened in surprise. 'You are mistress of Highford,' he informed her. 'You will need the services of an experienced maid to prepare you for our wedding. Griselda will return to the priory with Mother Benedicta after tomorrow's ceremony.'

'My lady, I am so ashamed,' Griselda wailed once they were alone. 'I meant to spare you. Now you have humiliated yourself to that man, and for what? I am to be banished from your side to live in a world of silence.'

'The punishment for arson is death, Griselda.' Eleanor spoke sharply. 'Sir Conrad has dealt with you more fairly than you deserve.'

'It's obvious he's tamed you.' Griselda sniffed her disapproval. 'The shame of this day will echo down the years. It will end in sorrow and pain. Sir Richard Norton will avange the insult you have done him this day.'

'I pray it will not be so,' Eleanor said heavily. 'There is justice in my marriage to Sir Conrad. I will make Sir

Richard understand that. I would have made him a poor wife.' Eleanor could not even speak to Griselda about Daniel. The maid believed, as did everyone at Highford, that the boy had died in infancy. Those had been Sir Cedric's instructions. 'I believe I am barren,' she said by way of explanation.

'That is impossible. Your flux is regular and——'

'I will bear no children.' Eleanor was emphatic. 'Sir Richard is marrying me for an heir. I could not give him that. Sir Conrad is marrying me for Highford.'

Griselda eyed her with concern. 'I don't know what you're planning. But no good will come of it. You are bound to Sir Richard and should honour that vow. Or perhaps D'Arton has some other hold over you. I've seen the way he looks at you. And how your body has changed since first you met him. You have become a woman who is aware of her own sensuality—of the power it can wield over men. Whether you remained a maid or not, your innocence has gone. And it was not taken by Sir Richard. Have a care, my lady. You cannot fight fate. Your mother tried once and it brought her no end of unhappiness.'

Curious at this rare insight into her mother's character, Eleanor asked, 'What happened?'

'It was before I joined the household.' Griselda lowered her voice. She was a born gossip, but she was usually careful to keep the secrets of those she loved. Age was making her careless. Years ago she would never have let such a slip pass her lips, for Griselda had been fiercely loyal to the Lady Isobel. Conrad had been right to banish Griselda to a world of silence. There her wayward tongue could not discredit either of their names.

Something in Eleanor's expression must have alerted Griselda to her indiscretion. The maid shifted her gaze to the floor and her mouth became prim. 'It is not something I would talk about. Lady Isobel showed me nothing but kindness.'

'She was my mother. Have I not a right to know?'
Eleanor could see that Griselda was torn between the
gossip which burned her tongue and her old loyalty to
the Lady Isobel. 'Griselda, you are always telling me I
am like my mother. What if I made the same mistake as
her? Surely you have knowledge which could prevent
that?'

'She was a kind and loving mistress,' Griselda said.
'But she was not happy, though she never spoke a word
against Sir Cedric. That was not her way. She never
loved him. Her heart was given to another before she
wed. It brought her only misery. If she could have loved
Sir Cedric her life would have been easier. Don't be
forced into a marriage without love. Sir Richard cares
for you and you have a deep affection for him. I have
seen it when you are together. Marry a man who loves
you and will make you happy. Don't repeat your mother's mistake.'

'The priest awaits you to perform the marriage, Lady
Eleanor,' Mother Benedicta pronounced.

Eleanor felt the weight of her old fears pressing upon
her. They had given her another sleepless night. Now
love for Highford overrode her anger towards Conrad
and his aunt. Her pleas to Mother Benedicta had fallen
on deaf ears.

'You are strong and healthy and will bear many
children. You must not question God's will.' Her censure
lessened at Eleanor's obvious distress. 'My dear, you put
yourself through unnecessary pain. You and Conrad
must be married. And from the scene I witnessed at the
pond, there will be both love and laughter in your
marriage. Accept what must be.'

'How can you be so calm? Conrad is your nephew.
You've seen Daniel. You know ——'

'I know also that you are your mother's daughter. the
Lady Isobel was my friend. If your mother were alive
now, she would urge you to this marriage. Obedience is

a wifely virtue you would seem much lacking in, Lady Eleanor.'

Eleanor's mind roiled in conflict as she considered Mother Benedicta's words. Was it possible to find happiness with Conrad after all that had happened? In the cave he had declared he would never taint his blood with that of a Twyneham. And that blood was indeed tainted in a way he did not suspect. Would he resent her? Feel revulsion when he learned the truth? He could even use Daniel's illness as a means of getting rid of her.

There was resolution in her blue eyes, which she kept carefully hidden beneath her lowered lashes. Let him try and discard her and he would discover a formidable adversary, for she would fight to remain mistress of Highford.

A knowledge as old as Eve came to her. To keep Highford she must be indispensable to Conrad in all ways. But she must also keep something of a mystery surrounding her. She would surrender, but not be meek and submissive. Her role was clear. It was a dangerous one. But the stakes were high and the challenge excited her.

'I must not keep the priest waiting,' she said, smoothing the pearls at her throat. 'If the deed must be done, best get it over with.'

The prioress smiled wanly. 'Don't let your bitterness mar your chance of happiness. It was the laughter between you and Conrad which drew my attention to the pond. There is a natural affinity between you which is rare between couples.'

Eleanor stood up and spread out the folds of her sapphire velvet gown striped with gold braid sewn with seed-pearls. She held her head high as much from pride as to carry the weight of the low cylindrical bonnet with its stiffened veil framing her pale face.

'My lady,' Griselda whispered as she fussed with the folds of her mistress's veil, 'listen to your heart, not the Reverend Mother. She's D'Arton's kin.'

Eleanor clasped her maid's hands. 'This is how it must be.'

'But you cannot marry that Devil's spawn!'

'That is unjust.' Eleanor was quick to defend Conrad. 'Sir Conrad is your overlord. He spared your life. For that he deserves your loyalty, not your scorn. He could have banished you far from here. Your sister can still visit you at the priory, as shall I.'

'But what of Sir Richard?' Griselda said. 'You love him.'

'No, I never loved Sir Richard in the way you think.'

Mother Benedicta cleared her throat, indicating her impatience at the delay. Eleanor embraced her maid and followed the prioress from the room. When she appeared at the head of the stairs leading down from the keep, the villagers who had gathered below cheered. They at least were delighted with this marriage. Would that she could feel so optimistic. Few couples of their rank achieved happiness. Some formed a tolerance for each other, others hated their partner on sight and were bound in miserable conflict until death released one of them.

That was not what Eleanor wanted. Love within marriage was rare. From what she remembered of the strained tension in any meeting between her father and mother, it had not existed within their marriage. And she had wanted so much more from her own union.

Nothing of her anguish showed on her face as she walked proudly through the parting villagers to the castle church. Conrad was already in the porch with Father Hubert. The elderly priest smiled at her and although Eleanor felt Conrad's stare on her she refused to look at him. Behind them Eleanor could hear the villagers speaking in whispers and as Father Hubert held up his hand an expectant hush fell over the gathering. Opening his prayer-book, the priest began to recite the ceremony in a clear voice.

Each word was like an arrow impaling her martyrd body. Conrad gave his responses without hesitation.

When it was her turn, Eleanor paused, her throat too dry to speak. She could feel the tension mounting in the crowd behind her.

'My lady,' Father Hubert prompted. 'Will you have this man as thy wedded husband?'

'Yes.' Her reply was so low that Father Hubert bent forward, his wrinkled brow frowning.

'Yes,' she repeated loud enough for everyone to hear.

Father Hubert relaxed, but she was now conscious of the tension emanating from Conrad's rigid figure. He rapped out his vows tersely, which puzzled her. He was the one who wanted the marriage. By it he won the undisputed right to Highford.

She kept her voice emotionless as she repeated her own vows. They were like a prison sentence, irrevocable and binding. They made her another of Conrad's possessions. Now that Highford was his, if she displeased him he could banish her to a nunnery. Once that had been her solution to avoid matrimony. Now her pride rebelled at the thought of it. To be so discarded was the ultimate humiliation. Father Hubert had been right. She loved life too much to wish to be shut away from its pleasures. The ceremony had been short and simple, but now only death could abolish it. Conrad kept hold of her hand as they followed Father Hubert into the church for the blessing before the altar.

Eleanor knelt beside her husband. The church was stuffy from the press of people pushing into every corner, eager not to miss any part of the ceremony. The incense-laden atmosphere was oppressive, made worse by the weight of her heavy gown and head-dress. She took deep breaths to stave off the dizziness. When Conrad's shoulder brushed hers, its touch sent a shock wave through her. His closeness was suffocating, making her heart pound alarmingly. The painting of the Last Judgment on the walls of the church began to swirl around her. The demons carrying their souls to hell seemed to grow larger, their fanged smiles expanding to encompass her, mocking the futility of fighting against fate. Unable to prevent it, Eleanor felt her body sway forward. Conrad squeezed her hand and she looked up at him. There was an unexpected gentleness in his eyes, but a dark blond brow lifted in question.

As Father Hubert finished his blessing, her husband's face blurred and she fell forward in a faint. A gasp went through the crowd. Conrad lifted Eleanor into his arms and strode through the people to the fresh air outside. 'Make way, Lady D'Arton needs air.'

He was halfway to the keep before Eleanor stirred. Her eyes opened and her gaze was dreamy as she stared up at him, disorientated. Her hand lay against his chest. She lifted it to touch his clean-shaven cheek. She remembered how she had told him that she preferred it thus, and since his return to Highford he had worn no beard. Then realisation of what had occurred returned and she struggled in his arms.

'Did I swoon? I've never done so before.'

'My aunt said you did not sleep last night, neither did you eat. Two nights without sleep or food was bound to take its toll upon you.'

He did not sound angry that she had disgraced him in public, just concerned at her welfare.

'I am quite recovered now. Put me down, that our people may see that I sustained no lasting harm.'

He grinned. 'I believe they find the incident romantic and I confess the novelty of holding you compliant in my arms is one I could grow pleasantly used to.'

He reached the top of the stairs of the keep entrance before turning to face the crowd, who had hurried behind them.

'Lady D'Arton has recovered.' He lowered her feet to the floor and whispered, 'I think we should relieve their doubts that this marriage was so abhorrent to you that you swooned in horror.' There was a warning in his eyes not to resist him as he bent his head to kiss her before the throng. The cheers which greeted his action were deafening.

Conrad felt Eleanor tense as his arms went around her, goading him to kiss her more thoroughly than he had intended, gathering her to him in a fierce embrace. He felt the shudder go through her body and, judging it to be the passion of which he knew she was capable, he smiled down at her, a mocking gleam in his eyes. It was doused in icy shock. No slumberous passion greeted his gaze, just stark round-eyed fear. He released her abruptly, careful that the expression he showed to his people remained one of affability. Inside he raged. What new trickery was this?

Eleanor recovered herself quickly. The fear she felt was not for him, but for the deep emotion his kiss had drawn from her. She must guard against it, or all would be lost.

'My lady!' He offered her his arm to lead her to the dais, his expression cold. 'Before our people we will act the role of an adoring couple. In private you can hold me in as much scorn as you like. It changes nothing.'

The coldness of his voice smote her. It was not her he cared for, it was Highford. She had always known that, but the knowledge pained her more than she had thought possible. She hid her misery behind a shield of indifference which matched his coldness.

'I am aware of my duties as a wife. Love. . . honour. . .and obedience to your will.' A slow smile curved her lips as she ran her hand provocatively along the length of his arm before resting it upon his forearm. She would show him she regarded this marriage as an enforced transaction, nothing more. 'Love. . .honour and obedience, my lord. You have but to command and it shall be given.'

The rugged contours of his cheeks clenched tighter as she smiled up at him, but he said nothing as he led her to the dais, their wedding guests filing behind them to fill the trestle-tables along each side of the hall.

Throughout the afternoon Eleanor followed the letter
of his command. . .to excess. Every glance she bestowed
upon Conrad was adoring, her laughter merry as they
watched the tumblers and applauded the minstrels who
entertained them. Because of the speed in which their
marriage had been arranged there were no high-ranking
guests in attendance, just Conrad's men, who regarded
her with suspicion. She set out to charm them.

The radiance of her smile never wavered, her wit had
never been more brilliant. She was the most fascinating
and gracious of hostesses, the most attentive, vivacious
and adoring of wives. She captivated everyone.

Toasts were pledged to the couple's happiness and
laughter filled the hall as the guests became steadily more
inebriated. The men's faces were flushed with wine, the
serving maids bolder with their glances, the toasts
becoming more ribald, as they did at all weddings.

Conrad was not deceived. Throughout the meal
Eleanor touched neither her food nor drink. Her face
was a beautiful but frozen mask. When Conrad spoke to
her she answered sweetly and leaned invitingly towards
him. Only he saw that her smile never reached her eyes.
That even in her apparent submission they glinted violet
from an unquenchable defiance. Women! He would
never understand them, and Eleanor was more complex
than most. They had shared intimate moments, promis-
ing a fulfilment which he had never experienced with
another. Now she acted as though his touch were
repugnant.

He lounged back in his chair and surveyed the great
hall at Highford. This was the accomplishment of a
dream, and on this, his wedding-day to so beautiful a
woman, he should be the happiest of men. Instead he
felt the bitter bile of frustration. Outwardly, as he had
commanded, Eleanor was the perfect wife and hostess.
Yet he knew she had withdrawn into herself. Far easier
to deal with would be the anger he knew simmered just
below the surface. He could have tamed her fury, rousing

her to respond to his lovemaking. When she had been his enemy, he had conquered her termagant's fire with passion; now that she was his bride, she was frigid with fear.

He filled the goblet they shared and offered it to her. She shook her head. 'Drink, Eleanor, our people are watching. Would you spoil their pleasure? That we wed in such haste, they believe ours is a love-match.'

'Ay, so it was.' She cloaked her barb with silk. 'You married me for love of Highford.'

Eleanor withstood the storm she saw gathering in his eyes. Her smile was pure seduction as she put her hands over his as they held the goblet to her lips. She drank deeply, holding his gaze over the rim of the cup, her stare defiant. The effect she desired was spoilt by her accompanying hiccup. It brought an amused gleam to his eyes. Too late she realised she had drunk the wine too quickly on an empty stomach.

She turned away to speak with Father Hubert, who sat on her right. The priest was nodding sagely. 'It is a good day for Highford that the D'Artons and Twynehams are united. But how Sir Richard will take the news worries me. He was much smitten with you, my lady.'

He droned on, but Eleanor found her attention wandering. the wine was affecting her concentration. She felt guilty that she had betrayed Sir Richard. She was now Conrad's chattel with no rights of her own. Later she must endure his attentions. And what if there was a child? Her mind froze in horror at the thought. She could not shake the vision of Daniel from her mind. No matter what Mother Benedicta or Father Hubert said, she knew it would be wrong to risk conception. But how could she prevent it? Her heart contracted at the sound of Conrad's deep laughter as he answered a bawdy comment with good humour.

For the marriage to be legal it must be consummated! If it was not, it could be annulled and she would be the pawn of whoever was appointed her guardian. For one night she must endure his attentions; after that she would find the strength to reject his advances. It would not be easy. Already she knew that a single touch would bring her blood to a scorching heat and the inevitable would happen. And if she fought him, her conquest would be even more complete. Even indifference would not work. She remembered the possessive embrace and the mockery in his stare as he kissed her before their wedding guests. She would be at his mercy. They were married before God and man. She could not deny him his rights over her body. Unless. . . She laughed softly.

'Something amuses you, my lady?' Conrad asked.

Eleanor smiled at him and relaxed, assured in her knowledge of sleeping herbs and her ability to trick him.

The meal progressed through its various courses and eventually it was time for Conrad and Eleanor to circulate and receive the good wishes of their people. This she did with graceful enthusiasm, her smile affectionate with warmth as she received their nervous congratulations. She took pains to put each one at ease and took secret pleasure in enchanting the dourest of Conrad's men.

Her trimph was complete when Ned bowed reverently to her. 'My lady, it is an honour to serve you. Your courage, grace and beauty is an inspiration to us all.' The wine had made Ned, newly promoted to captain of the guard, unusually expansive. ''Tis no wonder Conrad is so smitten. There's not a man in this hall does not envy him this day.'

'Thank you, Ned.' The smile she gave him was her most captivating and as he bowed over her hand she saw over his shoulder that Conrad was watching her. A frown marred the arched lines of his brow. He disengaged himself from his companions and as he made his way to join her she skilfully evaded his company. Keeping just ahead of him, she surrounded herself with merry-makers who hung upon her every word as she plied them with her wit.

With each new group of people clustered around her, Eleanor was aware of Conrad's deepening scowl. It exhilarated her. When he came close enough she lifted her voice in praise of him so he would hear, but she was careful to remain just out of reach, delaying the time when they must be alone together. She exulted in her success. He could not complain at her absence from him, for she made certain that the looks they exchanged were suitably adoring. Even the most grizzled of Conrad's men commented upon it. But she could not outman-oeuvre him all evening. When next he moved towards her his step was determined, and she felt a stab of panic. To hide her fear, she took up a horn goblet from the tray of a passing page, lifted it in smiling salute to him, and drank down its contents.

When she laughed and began to relate an amusing anedcdote to Gauthier, she was disconcerted that the young page's face was somewhat out of focus. There was no mistaking his deepening blush, or the way he shuffled his feet with increasing discomfort. But she did not need Guathier's embarrassment to warn her that Conrad had come to stand behind her. Every nerve-end tingled with awareness of his presence. With a sigh she turned from her companions to smile up at the darkening expression on her husband's face.

'My lady,' Conrad took her hand and cut across her conversation. 'It is time for us to retire.'

He tucked her hand firmly beneath his arm, making it impossible for her to refuse him. All eyes in the room were upon her. Suddenly her legs trembled and her stomach twisted into a tight knot. The hall looked vast and at the far end were the steps leading to their chamber. There was a deafening cheer from Conrad's men and Ned, his face reddened from the wine he had drunk, snatched her hand from Conrad's.

'Not so fast, my friend.'

Several men at arms surrounded her and another group circled Conrad. Then she was whisked away from

her husband amid hoots of laughter. She was spun round
from one man to another and on the far side of the hall
the same was happening to Conrad. Several of the bolder
men, such as Ned, and William the falconer's son,
recently appointed steward after Le Gros's death,
planted kisses on her cheek. A shy but drink-embol-
dened Gauthier placed a wet mouth to her hand.

She was giddy and flushed when finally she was pushed
into Conrad's arms and, to the delight of all present, he
swung her up into his arms and mounted the steps to
their chamber two at a time. The stamping of feet behind
them sent a new fear through Eleanor. It was the custom
for the guests to witness the married couple bedded.

Conrad paused at the top of the stairs and addressed
his men with a laugh. 'That's far enough. I need no help
to bed my bride.'

'Come, you'd not deny us our sport,' Ned chortled.
'You'll be getting more than your share of yours.'

Eleanor's cheeks scorched with embarrassment, causing a further round of ribaldry from their guests. Conrad
laughed and sped ahead of his men to their chamber, his
rapid pace unhindered by Eleanor's weight. His soldiers
were too drunk to run fast, and collided with each other
as they jostled for position of being first into the bridal
chamber. There was a shout and a grunt as two men
tripped. They tumbled backwards, causing several
others to topple down the length of the stairs to the
accompaniment of their companions' laughter.

Ahead of Conrad their chamber door was ajar. He
pushed it open with his knee. Carrying her inside, he
kicked the door shut and shot home the bolt with an
ominous thud.

'Put me down, Conrad; my maid must attend me.'

He laughed softly. 'You need no maid but myself this
night. If I open the door, the room will be a swarm with
my men, their intentions well meant, but hardly suitable
for a woman whose life has been as sheltered as yours.'

Seeing her dismayed look, he removed his hand from

beneath her legs, but kept his arm around her as she stood bound in his embrace. When he bent his head to kiss her, she jerked away. He released her and stepped back, frowning.

'You were not averse to my kisses ere we were wed. Why so now?'

'Kisses you forced upon me.' She took refuge in anger. 'Was it always your aim to seduce and compromise me, destroy my reputation, so that I had no choice but to wed you?'

She knew that on this one night she should be meek and submissive, but the fear that she could become pregnant was uppermost in her mind. And there was something else, something she could not put a name to, which laid her plans of revenge upon him to waste. Whatever the consequences, she knew then she must be honest with him.

He saw how violently her body was shaking. This was no attack of wedding-night nerves, or just plain anger. So what was wrong with her?

'You've got what you wanted. . .Highford,' she said coldly. 'And in the bargain won a wife who can never be a true wife to you.'

Conrad rubbed his hand across his jaw, his patience running thin. She had been acting strangely all day and he thought now she spoke out of pique. He knew the passionate side of her nature, and did not doubt his ability to rekindle it to their mutual satisfaction. It was easy to understand her anger—had he not felt likewise that this marriage was forced upon them. Until but a short time ago, he certainly had not considered marrying the daughter of his enemy. Though had she been of any family other than the Twynehams, he would have had no doubts upon the match. But the deed was done and he would make the best of it.

Tonight was his wedding night, and the woman who was his wife was more desirable than any woman he had known. And the most stubborn and contrary. He was

tempted to take her as was his right, but there would be
no pleasure or triumph in that.

His adult life had been far from celibate and he had
known many women. All had been willing: from tavern
wenches, merchant widows, courtesans and even a
French marquise or two. Some he had even thought he
had loved, but the feeling had soon faded with familiarity. Never had one tempted him to cast caution aside as
Eleanor did. Certainly none had given him so much
trouble. He watched her as she retreated to the window
on the far side of the room. She unpinned the head-
dress, and set it aside to massage her temples.

He filled two goblets of wine. Replacing the silver
flagon on the tray, he paused to regard her. His gaze was
captivated by the way the soft candlelight and moonlight
played over her figure to cast it in shades of silver and
gold. Through the folds of her gown where it clung to
her form, he studied the long line of her legs, his heated
imagination visualising the perfection of her slender
waist and full breasts. She was being infuriatingly
remote, detaching herself from what they both knew
must be by a barrier of outraged pride.

'Eleanor,' he said quietly, a huskiness entering his
voice, 'we are married, and I would have you come to
me willingly. If you think to withhold yourself from me,
so the marriage can be put aside as unconsummated, you
are mistaken.'

'And you would not wish to jeopardise your title to
Highford?' she observed with icy bluntness.

He pressed the goblet into her hands. At the way she
flinched at the touch of his fingers, he groaned inwardly.
Right was on his side, and he resented being made to
feel that he was some lecherous ogre. He drank deeply
from the goblet while searching his brain for the best
course of action. Force was abhorrent to him. Whatever
transpired between them this night was the foundation
of their future. Had he not already sampled the delights
her willing passion could bring him? The prospect of a

lifetime of conflict and estrangement was unappealing. There were always mistresses to be had aplenty. Somehow they now seemed second best. The knowledge angered him, fed by frustration and the aching need to make love to her.

Taking her into his arms, he ignored the tension which held her body rigid and unyielding. 'Don't fight me, Eleanor,' he breathed as his lips touched the sensitive nape of her neck.

Stubbornly she did not respond. He pulled the pins and combs from her hair and the dark blonde tresses tumbled over his hands to swirl around her thighs. The fragrance of jasmine filled his senses and fired his need for her. She remained still, as he adeptly unfastened the lacings at the back of her gown. This time when his mouth caressed her shoulder he felt a tremor pass through her.

Eleanor bit her lips to suppress a sigh. Despite her resolve to remain unresponsive, her body was vibrantly alive to the seductive play of his fingers over her bare flesh. How glorious was the heat of his lips as they traced a fiery path to the nape of her neck, their tender and experienced pressure causing her body to respond in a sensual, tingling heat that spread through her veins. The wine she had drunk so quickly earlier was betraying her resolve. She closed her eyes to summon her will to fight as he pulled her against the hardness of his body.

It was a mistake. Her closed eyes accentuated her other senses. He had eased her gown from her shoulders and it fell to her waist. When his hands began to travel over her breasts, gently stroking them through the thin silk of her chemise, their peaks hardened, pushing against the flimsy fabric, her soft moan torn from her parted lips before she could stifle it. She was turned in his arms and his mouth plundered hers, his tongue probing the softness within, before moving to the lobe of her ear and then to the hollow of her throat. The chemise was pushed aside, his lips following his hands to caress her breast. Her fingers dug into his shoulders as her head lolled back, exulting in the pleasure spearing through her from the gentle sucking of his mouth. With a ragged sigh her body writhed in surrender, her blood aflame with fire as she arched against him.

The intoxication of the wine and the ardour of his kisses sent her mind spinning, befuddling her will to withstand his lovemaking. Beneath the onslaught on her senses, her reasoning was no longer clear as to why she must resist. She heard Mother Benedicta's words counselling her to wifely obedience, that all life was governed by God's will. Then there was the sound of Conrad's voice: tender words, subtly persuasive, whispered so beguilingly between his kisses, entrancing her, until conscious thought fled as she was enslaved by the exquisite sensations.

She was lifted and carried to the bed, vaguely aware that they were both naked, their flesh scorching as they lay entwined. Her emotions were in turmoil, fed by the spreading tension which consumed her body. She moaned, her hands raking his back as his caressing fingers sought her inner core, coaxing her to a mindless all-devouring ecstasy until a deep shudder rippled through her and she drew herself up to him. Then he was kissing her with deepening and abiding passion; her arms bound him closer, while the crazy spiralling of her senses resurged as she felt the urgency of his need.

Instinctively, she lifted her hips to accommodate him. There was a sharp stab of pain and her cry was taken in his mouth, his kisses blotting out the discomfort as he moved with gathering momentum. The pain passed, replaced by a new and marvellous warmth that began to grow again deep within her. The bitter-sweet ache spread out from low in her stomach to encompass her entire being. She moved beneath him, wanting the feel of him, indefinably craving something more, beyond the heights to which she had already soared. It was fulfilled, her pleasure expanding in the throbbing possession of her.

She lay in her husband's arms, their heartbeats slowing, kisses becoming slow and languid in the aftermath of their lovemaking. He murmured against her ear, the words unintelligible as drowiness overcame her. With a sigh she snuggled into the crook of his enfolding arm, her legs curled intimately along the length of his. Her last thought was that she was now irrevocably bound to this man for her lifetime.

The rain beat steadily against the grey stone castle, ramming against shutters closed to keep out its driving dampness. Men came awake on their straw pallets; others grunted in pain as they eased the stiffness from their bodies after spending the night slumped over the tables in a drunken stupor. Hands were held to heads which ached, dulling both wits and vision, while whispering servants lit the torches and oil-cressets against the gloom which had settled over the day. Even so, the festive air remained among the Twyneham and D'Arton servants and retainers.

In the chamber above, Eleanor stirred, emerging reluctantly from sleep. A delicious lassitude made her snuggle deeper under the covers. Then her senses were alerted to a tangy male scent, the heat of a muscled leg thrown possessively across her, a hand on her waist holding her captive. Memory returned with frightening clarity. From the ache in her loins she knew herself no longer a maid. Conrad had taken her, spent his seed within her. And from that seed could be a child doomed to spend its life blighted by insanity.

Nervously, she glanced across at Conrad. He was still sleeping. His tawny hair was ruffled and fell forward over his brow. For a moment she stared into his handsome features, and knew her torment was complete. Her body was still bathed in the afterglow of his lovemaking. He seemed not to be aware of the slight chill in the room and had pushed the covers down to his waist, and she could not halt her gaze from playing over the strong, muscled chest with its dark smattering of hair. The yearning to touch him, to feel again the strength of his arms around her, to lose herself in the joy of his caresses almost overpowered her. Therein lay her hell. One touch and she would be lost.

With a sob she snatched up the coverlet before she fled from the bed and the seduction and torment it offered.

Conrad woke up, reaching for his wife. The tender words were never uttered. The bed was empty. He pushed himself on to his elbow and saw Eleanor was on her knees before the wooden cross set into a niche in the wall. She was wrapped in the emerald brocade coverlet from the bed, her dark gold hair falling around her like a shimmering mantle.

'Eleanor,' he said softly, 'come back to bed.'

She appeared not to hear; her eyes were closed, her expression impassioned as her lips moved in prayer. Her piety pleased him, but it was misplaced at such a time as this.

'Eleanor!' It was a light-hearted command. 'A married woman concerns herself first with her husband's needs before her spiritual ones.'

When she turned to regard him, he saw she was unnaturally pale. She stood up, holding the coverlet high to her chin. 'Our bargain is sealed. None can now refute our marraige. I warned you last night that I could never be a true wife to you. You have Highford, but I will never give you a son to inherit it.'

'What the Devil——?' he snapped, all humour gone from his face as he leapt from the bed.

'Stay away from me, Conrad!' Eleanor shrieked as she bolted for the door. The trailing coverlet hampered her and she was jerked to an abrupt stop as Conrad put his foot upon it. The impetus of her flight dragged the coverlet from her fingers and it fell away, leaving her naked and vulnerable to his furious stare. She stood braced to withstand him, her bosom heaving, her golden hair cascading wildly about her body. She glared back at him defiantly, aware of his nakedness, his desire and his ability to countermand her will. 'Heaven help me! Don't touch me, Conrad.'

She stood in the shaft of light from the window, her skin translucent as pearl against the gloom of the chamber. It was an entrancing sight. Conrad paused. Having ensured he had cut off her retreat to the door, he leaned against the portal, regarding her with mingled exasperation and amusement. He had thought that after the evident pleasure she had taken in their lovemaking last night she would be compliant to his will. Trust her to remain unpredictable.

'Eleanor, the role of shrew ill suits you.' He smiled as he approached her with purposeful tread.

She continued to watch him with suspicion, her gaze flickering around the room as she judged her chances of escape. With the speed of an attacking hawk he reached out and pulled her into his arms. She struggled furiously, but his arms were like a vice, clamping her securely to him. He laughed softly at her efforts, his eyes crinkling at the corners in a way that made her heart flutter in panic. He was enjoying himself at her expense, assured of the outcome. With a groan Eleanor stopped fighting him, her body rigid in his hold, aware that doing otherwise only aroused his passions further.

'That is more fitting conduct of a wife,' he chuckled.

Eleanor's enraged cry was strangled beneath his kiss. His hand moved behind her head, forcing her lips to cleave to his. He kissed her long and passionately, his mouth searing, expertly playing over hers, voracious and demanding. She remained tense and unyielding, refusing to surrender to the beckoning excitement of his lips. The building fires which ran like molten lead through her veins she doused with icy control. The pulsating demand throbbing in her loins she somehow found the strength to conquer. Every nerve-end and sinew within her screamed for appeasement. The scorching heat of their naked bodies pressed so intimately together roused a hungering frustration which almost destroyed her sanity. After what seemed an eternity, when every particle of her passionate nature screamed to succumb, but must be denied, he drew away and met the mockery in her gaze.

'I was praying for the strength to resist you. I'll not be a doe to your rutting stag. I prayed that I had been spared conceiving your child.'

She was flung from him, his face set into an impassive mask. 'Damn your treacherous hide! If it's a celibate's bed you want then keep it with joy. There's wenches enough to give me comfort.'

He snatched up his hose and shirt from the floor and began to dress. She had gained the reprieve she sought, but she had never felt so devastated. It was frightening. She felt she was in a nightmare, whirling headlong in a maelstrom of her own making.

Victory was bitter. From the look of loathing he had given her, it would be a long time before he sought her bed. And in the meantime she must bear his censure. The teasing companionship they had shared had also been rent asunder. She had left herself nothing. She had not expected to feel so wretched. Suddenly she knew she could not leave things as they were. Conrad deserved to know the truth.

She wrapped the coverlet firmly around her as Conrad pulled on his boots.

'My lord.' Her voice was a hoarse croak. 'I would explain my words.'

'My lady, they were abundantly clear,' he snarled at her. 'I do not need them spelling out. Besides, as you keep telling me, I have Highford. And for that I must make my reckoning with both King Henry and Sir Richard Norton. Once my title is secure, I will expect an heir, my lady—however distasteful we will both find the proceedings. Your duty on that is clear, and I give you time to accept what must be.'

CHAPTER ELEVEN

ELEANOR was troubled. Her honesty and sense of justice gave her conscience no peace. The anger quickly roused by what she believed was Conrad's callousness had left her by the time she had dressed. It had been fear of her own emotions which had set her against him. Throughout the day her husband avoided her. Whenever she saw him from a distance, he appeared relaxed, clearly enjoying the company of either friend, soldier or peasant. Everyone responded to him with genuine warmth and affection.

When he sent his apologies that business kept him from dining with her that evening, her disappointment was acute. The crowded great hall seemed empty and lustreless without his presence. She retired early to her chamber. When some hours later she recognised his firm tread pass her door without hesitation, and continue to his own room along the passage, she felt desolation rather than relief.

Conrad avoided her again the next morning. Once more she saw him in capable command of the castle, the steward, bailiff and reeve nodding acceptance of his orders as they moved through the castle and its grounds. She had never seen the servants so industrious, the villagers eagerly offering help to repair the damage caused by the fire. They responded to Conrad with open-heartedness.

Obviously he was a worthy Lord for Highford. She was the one who was unfit to rule. Highford deserved an heir. The thought would not leave her. It drove her to despair. She loved Highford and its people too well to deny them a secure future. How could she allow her pride or selfishness to ruin so many lives? Matters could not remain as they were. She sought Conrad in the courtyard. To her astonishment she found him squatting on his heels with a ring of young pages and village boys around him. They were listening raptly to his words, and from his hand movements it looked as if he was describing a battle to them. When he stood up he ruffled several of their tousled heads.

It was not a gesture one expected of a dignified knight. It was the gesture of a man who loved children. No wonder he had been so furious with her. He deserved the truth.

She summoned a page to order the horses saddled, and before her courage deserted her determinedly followed her husband. He was by the ruined stables, studying a plan of the castle spread on the ground, together with William the steward and the carpenter. Other workers — the thatcher, blacksmith, and a scribe — stood near by awaiting their orders. Everywhere else men, women and children were clearing the last of the rubble on to carts to be taken away.

Uncertain of her reception, she sent a page to tell Conrad she wished to speak with him, and waited a short distance away. Conrad paused to listen to the page, and turned to observe her waiting for him. There was a barely perceptible stiffening of his figure. With a quick word to the workmen he excused himself to walk towards her. For the benefit of the curious glances of their people he continued to smile, but Eleanor was aware of the coldness which frosted his eyes.

'As you can see, my lady, I am busy with the rebuilding plans. What have you to say that is so important?' His tone was chillingly polite.

'I am aware that since the fire there is much to repair at Highford.' She swallowed, finding it difficult to go on. 'Not least the misunderstanding between us.'

'There was no misunderstanding. You made your views plain.' His green eyes glittered with contempt.

'This is not the place for such a private matter to be discussed.'

'My lord, I am aware of that.' She refused to be dismissed now that she had begun. 'I ask you indulgence. This is not easy. I owe you an explanation.'

He raised a brow, but his expression remained guarded. 'An apology may be more apt. Or the assurance of your obedience. For now I have more important matters to attend to.'

'The future of Highford is not unimportant!' she challenged. 'Does its future not hinge upon an heir? My opinions on that can never change.'

'Then we have nothing to say to each other.' He began to walk away.

Eleanor flushed at his brutal dismissal. Nervousness had made her careless with her words. Swallowing her pride before her courage deserted her, she ran after him and put a hand on his arm. 'Please let me explain. When you have heard me out you will understand. Nothing is more important than this.'

The look he gave her was uncompromising. 'It is not a subject I will discuss in the courtyard.'

'I ask an hour of your time. Please ride with me to the priory and I will tell you everything. You despise me now, so what have you to lose? What I tell you will free you from a marriage you abhor without risk of losing Highford. Ignore my plea, and you could do Highford irreparable harm.'

She did not stop to hear his answer, but walked to where the two horses were waiting for them. Without looking back, she stepped on to the mounting block and settled herself in the saddle. Only then did she look across to Conrad. He remained where she had left him, staring at her, mystified. If he refused her request she dreaded the consequences.

Her chin lifted with resurging pride. Several people had stopped their work to stare at them. Eleanor would not let them witness her shame at his rejection of her invitation. If Conrad was too stubborn to listen, she would not plead with him again. Whether he accompanied her or not, she would ride to the priory and visit Daniel.

Eleanor wheeled her mare to walk in the direction of the gatehouse. To sustain the stiff carriage of her shoulders and the high tilt of her chin, she drew on the last reserves of her battered pride. The strain was great and, so no one would see the tears starting in her eyes, she set her heels to her mare's sides to gallop to the priory.

The drumming of hoofs over the drawbridge behind her roused no false hope in her breast. Conrad would have sent an escort to accompany her. A horse came level and its rider leant forward to snatch her bridle in his hands and haul her mare to a halt. Conrad threw himself out of the saddle, his expression furious as he glared up at her.

'I don't know what perverse game you are playing, but your excuses for your actions had better be good ones.'

Conrad lifted Eleanor from the saddle, but released her immediately. Anger and suspicion of her motives threatened to destroy his control. Having tasted the pleasure and solace of her submission, the cruelty of her rejection, of her refusal to bear him children, had been a vicious blow. He had not trusted himself to be near her, for he had never felt such rage towards a woman. Or was it a question of wounded male pride? he acknowledged with bitter cynicism. There was something of that, but it was her spite which had cut him the deepest. Could she deny him an heir? He had no taste for rape. Until her determination that there would be no child, he had not realised how much he wanted children. In the days when he had been a wandering exile, his only thoughts had been to win back Highford. Now he saw that his victory was empty, that his purpose was meaningless. Just as he had ached for Highford, he now longed for sons to inherit it. Sons he could teach to ride, hunt and wield a sword and lance. Sons the equal of any man. Sons who would be proud of their heritage, who would bow to no man save their King.

He did not trust himself to speak and waited for her explanation as Eleanor spread her skirts to sit upon an uprooted willow trunk.

Eleanor felt her courage ebb as Conrad remained standing. She could sense his anger and the restraint. But it was the aloofness of his expression which made it so hard to find the right words. She stared out at the river, its beauty for once lost to her. A rasping groan was torn from her as the words welled up and were forced through her stiff lips.

'The suddenness and circumstances of our marriage have been difficult for me to accept. But then it cannot have been easy for you. I admit I was angry, even resentful. My feelings were ignored, and by our marriage you became the undisputed master of Highford. I was the means to a convenient end. A not very flattering truth to come to terms with. Had it not been forced upon us so quickly, my temper would have cooled before such disastrous steps were taken.'

'Then you would fain make the best of a bad lot, my lady,' he rapped out.

Blood rushed into her cheeks. He believed she acted from spite. Her stare lifted to his and she shivered at the contempt in his eyes. Would he ever know the sacrifice she was about to make? Did he even guess that she loved Highford no less than he?

'Our marriage is a mockery, but there is just cause for you to demand an annulment. The people of Highford are devoted to you and your right to Highford is older and more valid than mine. The pity of it is, Conrad, that you did not have to marry me to win it. I am unfit to be its mistress. I am unfit to be any man's wife.'

'Except Sir Richard Norton. You were ready enough to wed him.'

The icy coldness of his voice sent shivers skidding down Eleanor's spine. She had not expected such bitterness from him. 'That was before I knew the truth. I learned it after my betrothal and Sir Richard had left Highford. I never rejected you as my husband out of spite.'

As she beheld Conrad's unyielding countenance her vision became distorted by a a tear-drop. She brushed it away, her voice cracking with her pain. Each word was giving him the power to discard her. Every sentence cast her further away from Highford and all she loved. 'Any son I bear could be tainted with madness. I have a brother, who has been kept shut away at the priory. It is obvious that the sickness has touched him, as apparently it has touched many males of the Twyneham family. The secret was well guarded, hidden from the world so that no one knew our shame.'

Conrad was looking at her with unconcealed horror. It tore through her restraint and with a sob she turned away from him, her shoulders shaking as misery engulfed her.

'And you kept this from me and allowed me to marry you!' Conrad said with a dangerous and unnatural quietness. 'I had not realised what a vengeful bitch you were.'

'The blame is not solely mine. Mother Benedicta knew. She was the one who insisted on our marriage, if you remember.' Eleanor rounded on him, her anger stirring that he reviled her. 'I've told you now. I'm giving you the chance to be free of me. Set me aside. Highford will be yours.'

'And become the butt of every jest at Court?' Conrad sneered. 'I think not, my lady. How do I know this is not some vindictive scheme you have devised? It would suit your purpose well to wriggle out of our marriage and have Sir Richard Norton fight for your cause to win back Highford.'

His words were delivered in cold, stilted tones which

showed her that he was having difficulty controlling his anger.

She had bared her soul to him, told him her innermost secret and fear. . .and he mocked her. Her hands balled into fists; her temper was dangerously close to breaching her self-control. 'I would not lie about such a terrible thing.'

'Would you not? You're a Twyneham. Your father lied and cheated to get Highford. You're his daughter and such a ruse would bring ridicule upon my name.'

'It has cost me dear to tell you this.' Eleanor stood up and in her anger jabbed her finger into Conrad's chest. 'I do not lie. At the priory you will see my brother Daniel. There are rare moments when he is still a loving, if naughty child. But in reality he is a sickly boy of nine, who with each year becomes more violent. The periods grow longer when he retreats to a world where his mind is closed to everything and everyone. Until a few weeks ago I never understood his illness. Each time I saw Daniel acting strangely something inside me seemed to wither and die. Each month which passes he becomes frailer and his tantrums more violent. I suspect he has not long to live. His life has held few pleasures. Do you think I could condemn a son of mine to such a fate?'

Conrad looked down at her finger jabbing into his chest. That he did not trouble to stop her she regarded as a further insult which threatened to send her temper soaring out of control. She had abased herself before him. . .poured out her family's shame, and he believed it all some macabre trick.

His years of training as a knight had taught him to appear outwardly calm and relaxed and yet be alert and in control of both his mind and body. The censure etched into his handsome features was anything but casual; his expression was frightening in its condemnation. But it was his eyes which shocked her most — they appeared neither green nor black, but within them burned all the flames of hell.

'This cannot be true, Eleanor,' Conrad contradicted her fiercely. 'Benedicta is my aunt. She would not have let me jeopardise my descendants.'

Still he did not believe her. Inside, Eleanor felt she was being torn apart. Was not her own wound still raw? Did she not want children? Damn him! She was trying to do what was honourable and he ridiculed her.

'Your aunt is a nun. She could not see past your immorality in attempting to seduce a noblewoman,' she announced grimly, noting his increasing pallor. 'I tried to reason with her and was told not to doubt God's judgement—it was for him to decide the fate of our children. Her answer was to spend the night in prayer.'

Eleanor put a trembling hand to her head. 'I should have come to you before the wedding to tell you, but I was so angry at the way you kept——'

'Forcing my attentions on you,' Conrad finished sourly. 'You were a willing enough victim after your initial affront. Even at the waterfall.'

The stark truth of his words robbed Eleanor of the will to continue the combat. She bowed her head. 'Must you shame me by reminding me? I did not know of my brother's illness then. After that my destiny seemed no longer in my control. My passion was not a lie, Conrad, and in other circumstances I would be proud to be your wife. But this. . .' She hugged her arms about her, unable to go on.

Silence fell between them and she could hear his harsh breathing. He put a hand on her shoulder and gently drew her to him and laid his brow against hers. 'The Devil laughs at our pretensions!' he said gruffly. 'I am to blame for this sorry mess as much as you.'

He eased back and looked into her eyes. 'I wanted you from that day at the waterfall. You were my enemy, but I did not care. Your courage moved me in a way your beauty alone never could. I could not forget your nobleness of spirit in allowing me, your enemy, to enter Highford and honour my father's dying wish.' He spread his fingers along the line of her jaw, his voice becoming husky. 'Somehow you and Highford became irrevocably bound. From our marriage I gained Highford, but it meant I must risk the King's displeasure. Sir Richard Norton will demand satisfaction in combat. Two days ago at our wedding I believed every risk I took to win both you and Highford was worth it.'

'You must hate me now,' she answered hollowly.

His eyes shadowed with pain. 'No. I do not hate you. I don't know what I feel.'

'Numb and angry!' She forced a brave smile.

He shrugged and looked past her to stare at the river. The bleakness in his eyes tore at her heart. 'I'm so sorry, Conrad. So ashamed. . .' Her hands clenched as the emptiness of their lives stretched before her. Words were inadequate to express her heartache. 'It's so unfair.'

He tipped her chin up with his forefinger and stared down into her face. Gently he wiped a tear from her cheek, but his expression showed nothing of his feelings. 'You are the victim, Eleanor. I will not shame you by casting you aside. We will go to the priory and I will see your brother for myself. And Benedicta is right in one thing. Are not all our lives in God's hands?'

Mother Benedicta smiled serenely after listening to Conrad's bombardment of questions. 'I told Eleanor there is nothing to fear. She is worrying unnecessarily. She is overwrought.'

'But Daniel is not the only member of my family to be so afflicted. How can you say that? Why, even my father had the most demonic rages.'

'As have many of our monarchs. The Plantagenets were renowned for their black tempers, which were said to blister a man's skin at twenty paces.'

'But it was not temper I witnessed in Daniel the other day. He did not know me. His mind was in a place where no one could reach,' Eleanor protested.

'He is a sickly child,' Mother Benedicta soothed. 'That

was one of his bad days. Come and see him now. He is very much improved this morning.'

They followed the prioress into the orchard, where Daniel was high in an apple tree, throwing apples down into an apron held out by a nun. He was laughing.

'Daniel!' Mother Benedicta called. 'You have visitors. The Lady Eleanor is here.'

There was a squeal of pleasure and Daniel jumped down out of the tree and ran to her, his face flushed with excitement as he threw his arms around her waist and buried his head in the folds of her gown. 'You came, Elnor. You came,' he babbled. 'It's been so long, Elnor.'

Eleanor took his hands in hers and crouched on a level with him. It was a long time since he had called her by the shortened form of her name, used when as a young child he had not been able to manage 'Eleanor'. It was a long time since he had remembered her name at all. She looked over Daniel's head and saw Conrad frowning and her heart sank. 'Daniel has not looked so well for months,' she explained.

She saw her brother now as Conrad would be seeing him. A dark-haired boy, small for his age and rather skinny, but with clear grey eyes and a healthy glow of colour to his cheeks.

'The child needs the company of children his own age,' Conrad stated. 'Is it not time he was sent to another household to train as a page?'

At the sound of a strange voice, Daniel began to shake and clung tighter to Eleanor's skirts.

Mother Benedicta answered before Eleanor could speak. 'I must admit this is one of his good days, Conrad. As you can see, the boy is terrified of strangers. He can be difficult and has a wicked temper. Sir Cedric had in mind to send him to Arnwood. He is too frail as yet to undergo the rigours of his knight's training. Perhaps later when he is stronger. It is more important that someone with knowledge of his ailment should be on hand to care for him when he falls ill.'

'It was said that Richard Plantagenet was a weak and puny child,' Conrad said. 'That did not stop him becoming an accomplished horseman and skilled soldier. My allegiance was for Henry Tudor, but the Plantagenet had many qualities for a Yorkist king.'

Conrad squatted down to Daniel's height. 'Would you like to train to be a knight, Daniel?'

A single eye peeped out from around the folds in Eleanor's gown. He watched Conrad with distrust. Eleanor said softly, 'Answer Sir Conrad, Daniel. Would you like to train as a knight and have your own horse and sword?'

Daniel sucked his thumb. 'Want horse. Want sword. Kill dragons.'

'Well, there's not too many of those left for us to kill.' Conrad laughed.

Daniel hid his head in Eleanor's skirts and the frown deepened on Conrad's brow. 'The boy has spent too long with women. Sucking his thumb and clinging to your skirts — he would not survive a month among the pages of a strange household. He'll live at Highford.'

Mother Benedicta looked shaken. 'Is that wise, Conrad? The boy can be extremely difficult.'

'Difficult, yes, but he does not have the look of the insane.' Conrad turned to Eleanor. 'If this is all the evidence you have of insanity in your family, my lady, I can see no cause for alarm.'

'But is the best Daniel has been for months.' Eleanor felt her fear returning. If Conrad believed Daniel was normal he would insist on claiming his marriage rights.

Those were exactly Conrad's thoughts. He had not doubted Eleanor's words at the river. She had been visibly upset. But seeing Daniel, he was convinced that her fears were groundless. It was a relief. How could he forget his wedding night? He had been bewitched by her passion, her encompassing warmth. Like a haunting fragrance that memory had never left him. It had beckoned to him, made him crave for more. On that night he had counted his blessings. Newly knighted, Highford once more ruled by a D'Arton, and he was married to a beautiful, passionate and courageous wife. A woman who would be a stimulating companion as well as the mother of his children.

He knew that with courtesy and consideration he could tame the wildness in her. That had been an irresistible challenge. When he had awoken the day after his wedding to discover himself bound to a virago, with a spiteful and vengeful disposition, his illusions had shattered. Yet it was the memory of the softer woman he had roused to passion which had plagued his dreams and given him no peace.

'The boy will come with us to Highford,' he commanded. He smiled reassuringly at the lad, but received a scowl in return. As they approached the horses, the boy shrieked in terror at the sight of the chesnut destrier Conrad rode. Conrad spoke kindly to the boy. 'The horse will not harm you. And you will be safe riding before me.'

Daniel pulled back as Conrad reached out to pick him up. He began to scream in earnest and as Conrad clasped him around the waist he received two painful kicks on his shin.

Eleanor saw Conrad's lips draw into a tight line of pain when Daniel's foot struck his wounded thigh. The attack loosened Conrad's hold and Daniel broke free and threw himself on the ground. There, to the shocked silence of the three adults, he drummed his heels into the grass, his face puce as he howled and thrashed about.

Eleanor was the first to recover, and, ignoring the kicks and scratches, took Daniel into her arms. 'Daniel, there is nothing to fear. Sir Conrad means you no harm. He will teach you to be a knight. You will live with us at Highford. You will live with me. Won't you like that?'

He appeared not to hear; his eyes were wild and his body was convulsed with fury. Conrad put Eleanor aside and to her horrified gaze smacked Daniel lightly across both cheeks. The boy's mouth gaped open and his screams stopped.

Eleanor wailed. 'How could you be so cruel?'

'The boy is more shocked than hurt. It's the only way to treat hysteria.'

Eleanor saw that only a faint tinge of pink coloured Daniel's waxen cheeks. Conrad picked the now calm Daniel up in his arms and put him on the saddle of his horse and swung up behind him. Daniel pouted sullenly, but Conrad ignored the boy's ill humour and spoke quietly to him. 'Now if you are going to be a knight and fight dragons, first you must learn to sit on a horse straight. It's no good slumping forward or you will fall off. You hold the reins like this, which leaves your other hand free to wield a sword or lance.'

Daniel's sullenness was gradually replaced by interest, and Eleanor saw that he was relaxed and listening to Conrad. The tantrum had tired him and Eleanor was frightened by the pallor of his skin. It was almost transparent as it stretched over his cheeks. Before they had travelled half the distance to Highford, Daniel had fallen asleep against Conrad's chest.

Conrad looked across at her. 'The boy needs a firm hand. The nuns have ruined him. Fresh air and exercise will bring the colour back to his face and put flesh on his bones. When he learns that he will get nowhere with his tantrums, he will begin to act more rationally and normally.'

Eleanor was not convinced. But Conrad's genuine concern for her brother roused a warmth of feeling within her towards her husband. If Daniel remained shut away, Eleanor was the heir to all Sir Cedric's lands. Instead of being master of Arnwood, Conrad had unselfishly taken on the role of its guardian, and that of the guardian of an unstable child.

Throughout the evening meal she was conscious of Conrad's gaze repeatedly upon her, of the touch of his thigh or his arm as they brushed her own. The tension between them relaxed as they both laughed at the antics of the jester.

'Do you find him amusing, my lady?'

'Yes, and now the mummers have come into the hall. I sent for them especially to entertain you, my lord.'

He smiled in a way that was as intimate as a caress. His face was only a few inches from her own and there was no mistaking the golden sparkle which brightened his eyes. His hand covered hers and her heart leapt in quick response. 'My lovely wife, tonight all I wish for is to be alone with you.'

The fear which leapt into her eyes turned them to darkest indigo. She stood up and was visibly trembling. 'You know that cannot be.'

She left his side quickly, causing many curious glances to watch her departure from the hall. When Conrad rose to follow her, he heard Ned laugh and say to the soldier at his side, 'Conrad is hot for his wife and can you blame him?'

Ribaldry was a common part of his companion's banter, but this time Conrad did not find it amusing. Eleanor had not hurried from the hall in excited antici-pation — she had all but run from it in terror. That smote his pride. It was outside his experience for a woman to be repulsed by his attentions. As a companion of Henry Tudor he had spent many years living upon the suffer-ance and tolerance of powerful magnates. His life had become enmeshed with conflict, with plans for invasion and the need to do battle to win both the Tudor's throne and his own birthright. He had not envisaged that his own marriage would become a battleground, and he had no intention of allowing it to be so. After years of wanderings, he wanted a home, a family. . .and peace.

When Conrad entered Eleanor's chamber he found her surrounded by her women. They had removed her head-dress and were in the process of loosening the laces of her gown. Her thick hair was free of constraint and its seductive curls framed her oval face, making her look young and vulnerable.

'Leave us,' he commanded the women.

Eleanor did not demur but she sat very still, biting her lower lip and refusing to look at her husband.

Conrad sat down on the bed. 'My wound needs tending. You have greater skill than my squire in such matters.'

She visibly relaxed. 'Of course, I will get my box.'

Eleanor went to the carved coffer and took out a small tray, placing on it what was needed. Her hand also closed upon a small pouch of specially mixed herbs. They were a powerful sleeping draught. When she returned to the bed she was dismayed to discover that Conrad had propped himself up on the mattress and leaned back at ease upon the pillows. He had removed his thigh-length doublet but had not divested himself of his boots or hose. Clearly he expected her to play the role of a devoted wife in every respect.

Placing the tray on the table by the bed, she dealt with his boots. The matter of his hose was more difficult and a more intimate operation. She knelt on the bed and bent over him, her fingers shaking as she unfastened the points of his hose tied to the inside of his short tunic. The heat from his body and the masculine scent of him permeated her senses, swirling like a cloak around her to steal the chill from her body. She worked quickly, though her mind and body craved for her every touch to linger and feel the power and strength of his body. Not once did she look at him, but her flesh burned from the intensity of his gaze, which never left her.

The wound had healed well and no longer needed a poultice or bandage. She rubbed in the salve, her fingertips savouring the texture of his muscled thigh. The sound of his indrawn breath warned her of the danger of continuing the massage. She snatched her hand away, but it was caught in his and raised to his lips. The touch of his mouth sent a *frisson* of pleasure through her fingers and arm. Her gaze lifted to meet his stare. The heat of his touch matched the smouldering desire which darkened his green eyes.

Eleanor closed her eyes, unable to contain the shudder of longing which shook her form.

Conrad misinterpreted the movement as fear. Throughout her ministrations he had resisted the urge to run his fingers through the silken strands of her hair. As she bent over him the low neck of her loosened gown gaped open, revealing an enticing display of her breasts. It had proved a sore trial as he felt his loins tighten uncomfortably, and he wondered how long he could remain in this position as she continued to tend his wound before his arousal became obvious. He had reached his limit of restraint and taken her hand to his lips as a preliminary to lovemaking. That shudder of revulsion and the fear which shone in her eyes made him release her.

There was no tenderness in his eyes as he regarded her coolly. 'I'm sorry that you find my touch abhorrent. I've no wish to spend my nights with an icicle who sees her duty as a form of martyrdom. But if I must, I shall take you, willing or not, to ensure an heir for Highford. I will not see all I have striven for destroyed because of your wish to remain barren.'

Eleanor kept her eyes tightly closed. To open them and witness his pain would be her undoing. She must be strong; her determination was based on a deep-rooted fear which she knew was not misplaced.

'You have not seen Daniel as he can be,' she said brokenly. 'Can't you understand I am trying to spare you? What use would a lunatic heir be to Highford?'

'Daniel is spoilt, not insane,' Conrad informed her harshly.

'Then what of my uncle, whom my father spoke of to your aunt? Locked away at Arnwood for his own protection and that of others. He killed a servant for spilling wine over him.'

'If that is madness, then a third of our nobility must suffer from it. The Plantagenet blood had been well spread among them in the three centuries that Devil's brood has reigned. Henry VI was mad. But he certainly did not kill people in a rage. He gibbered like a child and believed himself to be a monk instead of a king.'

His voice gentled, subversively cajoling. 'Eleanor, would you see our marriage doomed before we have given it a chance?'

Her eyes opened at his words and he saw in their tortured depths not fear, but wretchedness and pain.

Eleanor bowed her head. He had spoken of taking her to ensure an heir for Highford; he had not spoken of loving her. The barrenness she must endure was not only that of the womb, it would be of the heart.

'I learned a few weeks ago of the taint upon our family. It has shocked me deeply. I believe it. A few words of reassurance from you is not enough. You have not seen how Daniel can change when the sickness takes control of his mind.' She pulled back from him and left the bed. It was easier to express her feelings without the pull of his male attraction clouding her thoughts. 'But you wrong me if you think I act from some sense of vengeance. I consider you to be a worthy Lord of Highford. But what use am I as your wife if our children are unfit to inherit?'

She could not go on; it was too painful upon wounds still too raw and newly inflicted. 'I have not yet come to terms with the fact that I must remain barren. Do you think I don't want children? But not like Daniel. . . Never!'

The plea in her voice pierced Conrad. He came off the bed to stand apart from her. For several moments he continued to regard her. She was beautiful, her figure long-limbed and perfect. No man could look upon her and not desire her. And, God help him, she was his wife, but, if he allowed his hunger to enjoy the delights of her body to control him, it would destroy their marriage.

She needed time to come to terms with the blow her father had dealt her. With Daniel living at Highford she would soon realise that her fears were groundless. His patience would be sorely tested, but since thier marriage had been so hasty she deserved that at least.

'Go to bed, Eleanor.' He sat on the chair before the unlit fire. 'I will not force you. And I will try to be patient and give you time. But you are a desirable woman and my patience is not inexhaustible.'

She remained wary. 'Why do you not retire to your room?'

'And have every inhabitant of Highford speculating as to why we sleep apart after only two nights of marriage? Last night I took pains to work into the early hours with the steward and bailiff. A second night spent away from your bed would give rise to gossip that you displeased me as a wife.' He gave her an ironic look. 'That is not yet the case.'

Eleanor poured two goblets of wine and for a moment her hand paused over the pouch of herbs. What better safeguard was there that Conrad did not make love to her? Yet she pushed it away; his consideration moved her. Few men would sacrifice their marriage rights and she knew he desired her. When she had been tending his wound she had been uncomfortably aware of his arousal. She feared that their marriage was doomed, but for his consideration she owed him honesty and trust.

She held out one goblet to him and tipped hers in salute to him. 'To Highford. May God in his mercy prove I am wrong.'

She sipped the wine and, turning her back to him, stepped out of her loosened gown. It was her custom to sleep naked, but tonight she modestly retained the silk chemise.

Conrad inwardly groaned as he watched her dive beneath the covers. The clinging silk of the chemise left nothing to his imagination, and the glimpse of long, perfect limbs was almost too much for him to withstand.

He sat back in the chair and finished his wine. Sleep was impossible as he conjured the memories of Eleanor in his arms, Eleanor responding to his touch, Eleanor crying out in passion. And, to his dismay, Eleanor staring up at him in uncontrollable fear.

The night was long advanced before the restless movements from the bed finally stilled and he heard Eleanor's soft, measured breathing. He left his chair and, removing his clothing, slid under the covers of the massive bed and kept far away from Eleanor's beckoning warmth.

CHAPTER TWELVE

ELEANOR awoke to the soft touch of a hand upon her hair as Conrad stirred in his sleep. Cautiously, she peered at him through her lashes, careful not to wake him. Her emotions were mixed: relief that he had kept his word and had not made love to her; disappointment and yearning that he lay so close, but so irrevocably out of reach. If he opened his eyes now, how would he regard her? With belligerence, mockery, or with desire? The thought tightened her throat.

When had he come to bed? She had lain awake for hours, fighting her awareness of him in the room and of his self-denial. Would his restraint be as strong when he awoke and discovered her so easily within reach? She was not prepared to wait and find out. Slipping from the bed, she dressed quickly, plaiting her hair into two simple braids and covering them with a filigree caul. Her glance fell upon the wine goblet and pitcher by the chair Conrad had sat in, waiting for her to fall asleep. Obviously, he had not trusted himself to take his ease beside her. It was another self-sacrificing gesture and brought a fond smile to her lips as she looked back at his long, powerful figure sleeping so soundly. The empty wine pitcher attested that his thoughts had not been mellow ones. Her husband was an exceptional man. A dull ache settled over her heart as she looked down at him, the need to reach out and touch a firm, muscled shoulder all but overwhelming her. She steered her thoughts away from that precipitous path before her resolve faltered.

Leaving the bedchamber, she went first to Daniel's room, stepping over the page who slept outside his door. Her brother was fast asleep, his thumb in his mouth.

Last night before the banquet she had stayed with him until he slept. The strange room had upset him and, though exhausted, he had sobbed himself to sleep. Daniel was so frail; another hour or so of sleep would do him no harm. Nothing must upset Daniel in his first days here. More than anything, she wanted him to be happy and begin to lead a normal life. It would not be easy. So much of the future remained uncertain.

She closed the door silently and suddenly needed privacy to enable her to think undisturbed. She climbed the stairs to the battlements on top of the keep. Ignoring the two sentries patrolling the crenellated walls, she walked along the parapet which overlooked the steep ravine and halted by a favourite corner which gave her views of the river, water-meadows and sweep of hills. She frowned. Beyond those hills were the roads leading east to London or northwards to the Welsh border, where Sir Richard Norton would be preparing Belrise to receive her as his bride.

Never had she felt so wretched. What would be his reaction to her marriage to Conrad? Such a matter of honour could only end in bloodshed. Guilt pitted her. She could not bear the thought that either knight would be hurt, especially Conrad. He had fought so hard to win Highford. Her sympathy for her husband surprised her. But it was true. It had been easy to stir her indignation and anger against Conrad when he had used her so callously. Last night had changed that.

She still did not trust him, but his consideration had chiselled beneath her defences. It would be easier if she found her husband unattractive and without charm. But he had both in abundance, and other strengths and qualities which she discovered with each passing day. Not least that, though her mind might rebel against him, her body responded with treachery to his touch. Even his first kiss had stirred her in a way that Sir Richard Norton had failed to do, despite the respect and warmth she felt for the older knight.

She rested her brow against the rough stonework, trying to make sense of the tortured writhings of her mind. It was not in her nature to give in to fate. She was a fighter, but how could she combat the inheritance of her blood?

Troubled, she paced the battlements. When she reached the far side, she was saddened to see the full extent of the fire damage. Turning away from the destruction, she let her gaze roam absently over the oldest part of the castle, which was built on the promontory of steep cliffs where the river flowed into a ravine. Here more work was needed. The walls were crumbling and so dangerous that no guard patrolled the parapet along that side of the outer wall. It angered her that Sir Cedric had neglected Highford and had never spent a groat on its maintenance. That would all change now that Conrad was Highford's lord. But she knew her husband was not a rich man.

Though she was the heiress to a Yorkist supporter, her marriage secured her inheritance. She doubted Arnwood would be confiscated from her family. It was time the wealth of Arnwood paid for the repair of Highford. Yet how would King Henry view a marriage made without his consent?

She was heartened by the rumours that the King was planning to end the years of conflict between Yorkist and Lancastrian by marrying the Princess Elizabeth, the eldest daughter of Edward IV. A marriage uniting the two opposing houses would make the children of Henry and Elizabeth the undisputed heirs to the throne. Especially now it was rumoured that Elizabeth's brothers, Edward and Richard, had died in the Tower of London while under the protection of Richard Plantagenet. Eleanor shuddered. She refused to believe that King Richard had had his nephews murdered to secure the throne for himself. There had never been any question of his loyalty to his brother, King Edward, and Richard had been a man who delighted in having his family around him. Such a man as that would never condone the murder of children, especially his own nephews. Though, of course, there were men who had been close to King Richard who would not have hesitated to take such steps — with or without the King's knowledge or consent.

Eleanor did not want to speculate about the fate of the young princes, tragic though it was. If King Henry was set upon uniting the houses of Lancaster and York as a matter of policy, it followed that he would seek to bury old enmities by encouraging his subjects to do the same. Was not her marriage to Conrad the ideal solution to end the conflict of the D'Artons and Twynehams over Highford? Or would have been if Sir Richard had not fought for Henry at Bosworth. . .

Again her thoughts completed their tortuous circle without finding a resolution. She leaned against the wall and stared down at the river tumblng over jagged boulders a hundred feet below. The scenery began to revolve and Eleanor brought her head up quickly and mastered the giddiness she always felt when confronted by vast heights. She hated the weakness which had overtaken her at the waterfall.

A bitter-sweet pain clutched at her heart as she recalled every incident of her hours with Conrad that first day. From that moment her life had changed. Her expression became wistful as she remembered the afternoon she had spent with Conrad when he came to Highford disguised as a pedlar. It had been a time of truce, the only time in their relationship that there had been no antagonism between them. And its sweetness unexpectedly haunted her.

You are mellowing, Eleanor, an inner voice mocked her. Conrad was charming to you that day because you had given him what he wanted — admittance to Highford. He still forced this marriage upon you. It's Highford he loves — not you. Her pride rebelled to admit the acid truth. It chased the mellowness from her heart to erect a barrier against Conrad's treachery.

A movement on the horizon caught her attention. She frowned as a line of horsemen appeared out of the mist. Several of the riders carried the black and white quartered pennons of Sir Richard Norton. Her rescue had come. Sir Richard would not tolerate the manner in which Conrad had manipulated their marriage. Sir Richard loved her. He would free her from this marriage.

She ran from the battlements, hearing the sentry crying out that riders approached. Halfway down the stairs she heard the tocsin bell toll, calling the guards to their posts. The guards were not allowing Sir Richard entrance to the castle. As she emerged from the stairwell on a level with her chamber she saw Conrad, sword in hand, and clad only in hose and boots, run into the passage.

'Sir Richard Norton is at the gates,' she cried in triumph. 'Now you will answer for your knavery.'

Conrad scowled at her. 'Have you not learnt by now that I relinquish nothing which is mine by right?'

He ran past her down the stairs to the hall below, rapping out commands to his men. Buffeted by those tersely delivered words, Eleanor stared after her husband. It had not been anger in Conrad's voice, but the fierceness and pride of possession, and with sudden clarity she knew they included herself as well as Highford. The knowledge left her weak and shaken. How much easier it was to fight Conrad believing it was just Highford he wanted, and that she was the means to win it. To that end he had abducted and seduced her. Until now she had not considered that he could possibly cherish her as well.

To give in to such reasoning was dangerous. She must not weaken. Sir Richard was here. Sir Richard would free her from a marriage based on trickery and deceit. And Conrad had barred him from entering. She ran to the courtyard in time to hear the end of Sir Richard Norton's challenge.

'Highford is mine!' the older knight proclaimed. 'Eleanor Twyneham is mine by right of contract. Both your marriage, D'Arton, and your possession of Highford is a mockery of the law. Are you man enough to fight for that which you would steal like a thief in the night?'

Eleanor felt the fine hairs on her arms rise in dread. Conrad stood in the centre of the drawbridge, exposed to Sir Richard's bow-men, though the portcullis remained lowered.

'Are you prepared to fight man to man for the right to be Lord of Highford?' Conrad returned. 'I will not barter my people's lives in a drawn-out siege. This is between us, Norton. It is the only way it can be settled. My allegiance to King Henry is not questioned. But I will not surrender Highford, or the Lady Eleanor, even to his will. My death alone will give you possession.'

'No!' Eleanor's voice ran out. She was appalled at these new events. 'You may feel justified in fighting like carrion over Highford. But I am no man's possession. I am the true mistress of Highford until King Henry decrees otherwise. For no man will I become a prize of conquest.'

'Stay out of this, Eleanor,' Conrad ordered.

Eleanor moved past her husband to address Sir Richard. He was mounted on his destrier halfway across the drawbridge. That he was dressed in court clothes, not armour, was proof he had not known of her marriage. 'You deserve an explanation for what has passed here. It is not something to be discussed in public, to become the gossip of my people or your men. Whichever knight wins, I become the butt of common gossip and ridicule. I will not be humiliated this way. If you are to be my champion, Sir Richard, let it be to release me from an unlawful marriage. . . From any marriage.'

At his frozen expression, her voice broke with anguish.

'It is to spare you further pain that I ask so much of you. Again it cannot be discussed before so many. In that I ask for your trust.'

Sir Richard stared down at her icily. 'It is a question of honour, my lady. My honour. I cannot permit any man to steal that which is mine, or usurp my authority.'

It was the code all knights lived by. The ancient rule of survival: the law of conquest. As a woman she was unimportant. Bitter resentment roiled through her. In that moment she hated them both for their callousness and pride, which made her feel as nothing. But she was powerless. A woman had no rights. She was the property of man.

The Devil take them both! She felt doubly betrayed. With Conrad she had always known that Highford came first, his desire for her second. She had thought Sir Richard different. There had been an affinity between them. She had felt a warmth and comfort in his friendship that no other had roused. Yet he, too, put his pride before her feelings. Both had betrayed her for their own greater glory.

Even as the thought formed, she knew she was being unjust. Only the strongest survived in this harsh world of constant conflict. They were both men who made their own destiny, who would lay down their lives for a cause they believed right. She was wrong to condemn them for it. Theirs were the strengths and resilience Highford needed in its Lord.

An inhuman howl from the direction of the keep claimed everyone's attention. At once Eleanor knew its source, and her body went cold with fear. How could she have forgotten Daniel? He would be terrified at waking to find himself in an unfamiliar place and surrounded by strangers. The demented wails became louder, accompanied by the sound of smashing furniture. Then, like a demon from hell itself, Daniel ran screaming down the steps of the keep. He was naked, his eyes wild, and his hair sticking out like a hedgehog's spines.

'Stop the little fiend!' William the steward bellowed from inside the building.

Eleanor sped towards the keep. A village boy ran up the stairs to bar Daniel's way. The lad was a head taller than Daniel and twice his build. Eleanor heard him laugh, ridiculing her brother. Daniel's face twisted and spittle sprayed from his mouth as he lunged at the lad. With a strength Eleanor could not believe he possessed, Daniel shoved the villager out of the way. The boy cried out, his arms thrashing in the air as he pitched sideways over the side of the steep steps. There was a sickening thud as his body hit the cobbles, then lay ominously still.

Daniel ran on, his hand jabbing at anyone who tried to stop his progress. The servants jumped aside as Daniel approached. As Eleanor neared him, she saw that he was stabbing at them with a dagger. The blade was already red with blood and several of the servants were holding a slashed arm or side.

'Daniel, stop! There's nothing to fear. It's Eleanor.'

The glazed wildness in his eyes told her he was beyond hearing. He was making horrible animal noises, and lunging at anyone who came close to him. Eleanor was horrified at what Daniel had become. This was what she dreaded would happen to a child of her own. There was no hiding Daniel's insanity. He was a danger to himself and to anyone who came close to him. One boy was already seriously hurt and several people wounded because of her brother's madness. She had to stop him.

'Daniel!' She gentled her voice as she ran to cut off his flight across the courtyard. No one now dared come close to him. Eleanor grabbed at his shoulder. 'It's Elnor. You remember me. We are friends. No one will harm you.'

He spun round, those grey eyes wild and unfocused with madness, his lips curled back over his teeth in an animal snarl. He struck her twice with the dagger in her arm and shoulder, the pain making her drop her hold. Unheeding of her wounds, she staggered after him.

'No, Eleanor!' Conrad clasped her waist to stop her. And then he was chasing Daniel across the courtyard and up the narrow steps to the battlements.

Eleanor watched with gathering horror as Daniel sped like a hunted deer. And like all hunted prey he instinctively sought isolation. Daniel was now running along the crumbling parapet to the oldest, deserted part of the curtain wall. A stone dislodged, bouncing off the steps down into the courtyard.

Conrd was gaining on him. Eleanor's eyes widened with fear. Did Conrad know the extent of the danger to any who trod those broken walls? How could he?

'Conrad, stop!' she shouted as she began to race after them. 'The parapet is unsafe.'

Conrad ran on. It was likely that Daniel's manic screams had drowned her warning cry. When Conrad shouted at Daniel to stop, the boy whirled to face him. Their figures were outlined against a bleak charcoal sky and the fractured crenellated wall. Eleanor stumbled on the smooth steps, her breathing harsh and stilted as her fear for their safety mounted. She could not take her eyes off the two figures just ahead.

Conrad was now within reach of Daniel, but her brother began to back away, gibbering and salivating. Seeing Daniel hurl the dagger at her husband, Eleanor screamed. The parapet was too narrow for Conrad to side-step. She shuddered, convinced the blade would embed itself in Conrad's heart. The dexterity achieved from long years of combat training saved his life. Conrad flattened himself against the wall and twisted his body to avoid the blade's lethal flight. The dagger passed perilously close to Conrad's side. For a moment it was outlined against the clouds as it winged over the wall and dropped out of sight. There was a dull ring of metal as it hit the rocks below.

Failure to bring Conrad down drove Daniel to a greater frenzy. He leapt up and down with rage, but, to Eleanor's relief, Conrad no longer advanced. He stood still, holding out a hand to the boy, talking in a soothing voice as he would to an unbroken colt to calm Daniel's terror. It made no impression. Daniel clawed wildly at his own face, drawing blood as he again retreated.

Eleanor came level with Conrad, saying jaggedly, 'He fears you. Back away. Daniel may listen to me.'

When Conrad lifted a hand in protest, she shook her head. Her gaze was riveted upon her brother. His cheeks were bloodied, as was his chest, from the wounds he had inflicted on himself and others. He was like a wild, cornered beast. His nakedness showed her how frail his body had become. The veins were clear along his puny arms and the skin almost transparent as it stretched over his ribs and bony chest.

'Come to me, Daniel.' She held out her arms. 'Come to Elnor. Let me hold you. There's nothing to be frightened of.'

Daniel backed away from her. Eleanor advanced slowly, terrifyingly aware that Daniel was close to the most unstable part of the wall. She was familiar with every inch of the castle and the extent needed of its repairs. The wall behind Daniel was cracked. There had been some fault in the cement which bound the stones in this section of the wall, and it had eroded. Each winter the snow, which could lie for weeks, further damaged the crumbling mortar, and during a tempest five years ago the stones had started to fall down into the ravine.

Behind Daniel, Eleanor saw the broken segment of wall. Through it she also saw the spread of rocks far below. It made her head begin to spin. Angrily she fought it. This was no time to succumb to her fear of heights. She edged closer to Daniel, who now had his back to the unstable wall. Her weight caused a flagstone on the walkway to shift beneath her feet. It sent a shaft of terror through her body. At any moment the parapet could give way. Her body shook as the sky and crenellated wall began to revolve slowly around her. Concentrating solely on Daniel's cringing form against the wall, she put out a hand to pull him to safety. He flinched back. Again as she stepped forward, the parapet shifted. Daniel too felt it move. Giving a demonic shriek, he leapt to his feet and threw himself against the wall.

Eleanor heard the grating of the stones. Heedless of the danger to herself, she reached forward. Her hand touched Daniel's wrist. For a second his eyes cleared.

'Elnor!' he cried.

Then the stones shook. Even as her fingers closed over Daniel's wrist, the wall behind him began to collapse. She screamed. Her hold lost its grip. In slow motion she saw his hand fall away. Then Daniel was no longer before her. His body pitched into space—a white blur among the falling stones—to be smashed on the jagged rocks below. Trees and rocks in the valley far below spun before Eleanor's horrified stare.

A vibration through her feet warned that the section of parapet on which she was standing was about to give way. The stones moved. Fear paralysed her. Her body chilled with terror as the walkway cracked beneath her weight. There was a moment of terrifying weightlessness. Then as her body began to drop, her ribs were simultaneously crushed as an arm clamped around them, and she was heaved back several yards to safety.

She clung trembling to Conrad, feeling the hard beat of his heart beneath her cheek as she sobbed out her terror and grief. Conrad held her close; his words were incoherent to her numbed mind. Gradually the tenderness in their tone penetrated her consciousness and her sobs began to ebb, the trembling which gripped her figure subsided.

'You did all you could for the boy, Eleanor.'

She shook her head. 'I should have stayed with him on waking. I should have realised he would be frightened. Instead I. . .I put my own troubles before his welfare.'

'His death was inevitable. If not today, then it could

not have been far off.' He tilted her chin to force her to look into his eyes. 'You must not blame yourself.'

'I should have stopped you bringing him here. Several of the servants are wounded and one boy seriously. But I did not realise it would be so bad.' Her voice broke. 'Even in my worst nightmares, I did not fear it would be so bad.'

There was pain and understanding in Conrad's eyes as he regarded her bleakly. 'You did warn me. I did not listen. I could not believe that there was insanity in your blood.'

Eleanor regarded him tiredly. 'Do you believe it now? Do you finally understand why I would rather be barren than risk bearing a male child?'

The fight drained from her as she looked up at him. Her heart was aching. 'I beg you do not fight Sir Richard because of me. I'm not worthy of any man's bloodshed. Let King Henry decide who owns Highford. I will not contest your title. Highford needs heirs. If I enter the priory here and take holy vows you will be free to take another wife.'

There was nothing in his expression to convey his thoughts to her. It was as devoid of emotion as the effigies on his family tombs. Did he care so little?

He frowned as he looked at her shoulder. 'You are hurt.'

Eleanor stared down at the blood on his hands. Her gown was slashed across the shoulder and it hung in tatters over her forearm. There were two long slashes across her skin which had already stopped bleeding. 'They are but scratches. I have fared better than others Daniel attacked.' She turned to retrace her steps to the courtyard, willing her shaky legs to carry her forward. 'I must tend them.'

There was an edge of defiance in her tone that Conrad could not define. It was evident in the tilt of her head, the way her eyes slanted and their depths coloured to deepest indigo traced with violet. An unusual combination, and seen only when their combat had been at its fiercest and she stubbornly refused to admit defeat. Death before dishonour was the maxim which came to mind. It was there in her eyes.

Conrad frowned as he walked in silence at his wife's side. What had conjured those words? They were the maxim of Sir Richard Norton if he was not mistaken. Was it an omen that he would be vanquished on the tourney field tomorrow? Conrad squashed the thought. The defiance in Eleanor's eyes had always stirred him from the first moment he had come upon her like a sylvan nymph in the woods. An ill-fated meeting, he reflected wryly. It had changed the course of both their lives. And now it put in peril the future of Highford.

He had witnessed many violent deaths. Not always during his exile had he been with Henry Tudor. There had been the years when he had accompanied Sir Lionel as his squire when his father hired his sword to any who would pay a mercenary's price. Many of those deaths had been gruesome, but the madness which had accompanied Daniel's had appalled him. Had he the right to condemn a son of this marriage to that end?

When he gazed at Eleanor, he knew only that Highford would not be the same without her, neither would his life. Yet she had made no secret of her preference for Sir Richard, though he'd stake his reputation that they were not the protestations of a woman in love. He studied her grief-stricken face. There were lines of strain as she battled to remain calm before their people. She would put her duty before her personal pain. But what was she really thinking? He had to admit that his years of training for knighthood gave him no insight into a woman's complex mind.

Before the curious glances of their people he could not take her into his arms to reassure her. It surprised him that his first instinct was to protect her. This morning all his dreams for Highford had been dashed. There would be no son to come after him. Neither would he put Eleanor aside. She did not deserve that shame.

His jaw hardened with resolution and he forced all emotion out of his voice. 'I will fight Sir Richard at noon tomorrow,' he announced as they approached the crowd gathered around the injured boy on the ground. 'It is a matter of honour. If I survive I will give you the freedom to decide whether you wish to remain my wife or enter the priory.'

'Sir Richard should know the truth about Daniel. To him Highford is no great prize. He will be willing enough to disavow our betrothal once he learns I bear tainted blood. Let me speak with him.'

'The fight is not yours, Eleanor,' Conrad answered tersely.

'There you are wrong. Do you think I want either your or his blood on my conscience? By marrying you I have shamed him. He did not deserve that.'

'You care for him?'

The words were flung at her in accusation.

'Yes.'

The lines about Conrad's mouth tightened in a way that cruelly wrenched Eleanor's heart. There had been so many misunderstandings between them. This was too important an issue for her to be less than honest. 'Sir Richard is a great knight and a worthy lord. He treated me with respect, kindness and consideration. I enjoyed his companionship and was proud to be chosen as his wife. I had no reason to believe that our marriage would not have been a happy one. But during the short time we were together I did not know the truth about Daniel. That would have changed everything.'

'As our marriage apparently changes nothing!' The accusation was rapped out with such vehemence that Eleanor winced.

Conrad marched away from Eleanor before she could reply. She opened her mouth to call him back, but she was suddenly surrounded by a clamouring press of people all talking at once. The sight of Conrad's stiff, censorious figure left her bereft, following as it did upon her brother's death. On the battlements he had been so tender and considerate. Now he walked away as though he hated her.

And why should he not? There was no disputing Daniel's insanity, nor that any son she bore could be so afflicted. Tomorrow Conrad fought for Highford. Once the victor, he would give her the choice of remaining or leaving. Not because he loved her, but through misplaced chivalry. Conrad would know that she was too proud to live here upon his pity and sufferance. Pride would give her no choice but to leave.

And go she would. Hot upon her resolve came a harrowing revelation. She laid a clenched hand against her heart to ease the agony which lacerated it. She would leave because she loved Conrad. Loved him enough to set him free. Loved him beyond selfishness—beyond honour. Loved him too much to watch the condemnation grow daily in his eyes that Highford would pass from his line.

Through her misery she saw a group formed around the boy whom Daniel had pushed from the steps. Here was someone who needed her, and a means to keep at bay her own pain and wretchedness. The unconscious boy's chest rose and fell. She recognised him as Guy, the blacksmith's son. There was an ugly bruise on his temple and the blood spreading across his leather jerkin showed that Daniel had stabbed him. From the angle of his leg it looked as if it was broken. The resetting must be done without delay while the boy was still unconscious to spare him further agony.

'Bring a board to carry him to the infirmary,' Eleanor ordered.

'My lady, I will tend the wounded.'

Eleanor looked down at Eadgyth's wrinkled face and shook her head. 'It is my fault they were injured. I should never have allowed Daniel to be brought here. I will tend them.'

'But you are hurt yourself,' Eadgyth protested.

Eleanor lifted the torn shoulder of her gown, which was covered in blood. She felt little discomfort, for the two cuts were not deep.

'My lady, have you not considered that there is another who needs you more than Guy?' Eadgyth admonished with a severity the wise-woman had never used to her before. 'Sir Conrad saved your life today. Tomorrow he fights Sir Richard for Highford. A man should not go into battle with bitterness in his heart, especially when he fights for the woman he loves.'

Eleanor took no offence from Eadgyth's manner, for the old woman was a respected member of the village, but her reply was unusually tart. 'You are growing old, wise-woman. Sir Conrad loves Highford, not me.'

Eadgyth looked at her with the intolerance of the old at another's stubbornness. 'If you believe that, then for all your learning you are a fool. He may not as yet have acknowledged it, but to him—you and Highford are irrevocably bound.' She stared into Eleanor's eyes with unnerving calculation. 'Look into your own heart, my lady. Tomorrow may be too late.'

'You are impertinent, Eadgyth.'

'Yes, my lady.' The old woman smiled, unrepentant.

Could it be that Eadgyth was right? Eleanor felt a blaze of hope consume her. Before it could take hold she quickly snuffed it. Better not to listen to an old woman's day-dreams. All of Highford rejoiced in her marriage. It was a romantic ideal for the people to believe that she and Conrad were in love. It had clouded Eadgyth's judgement.

To keep her mind from loitering on the impossible, Eleanor concentrated on tending the wounded. All the patients had been cared for when a page came to inform Eleanor that Daniel's body had been brought into the castle and was now lying in the church. She allowed

Eadgyth to dress her shoulder and changed out of her ripped gown before going to the church. The first shock was beginning to wear off. Daniel's death had all the horror she had envisaged could fall upon any male child she might herself bear.

The blue Twyneham standard with its white cockerel had been placed over her brother's body as it lay on a trestle between four candles. Eleanor prayed for Daniel's soul. The numbness of spirit and body remained with her as she maintained her silent vigil. Not all her prayers were for Daniel. Many were for Conrad. Throughout the day she fasted and prayed, dimly aware of the people entering and leaving the church, but she paid them no heed.

It was night when a familiar assured footfall approached.

'Come away, Eleanor. You will make yourself ill. The servants tell me you have eaten and drunk nothing all day.' Conrad put his hands beneath her elbows and gently raised her up. 'Do you wish Daniel to be buried here at Highford or with your father at Arnwood?'

Eleanor emerged from her stupor with a start. 'Is Father buried at Arnwood? I had not realised.'

'Did the Lady Clemence not send you word? His body was sent there after the battle at Bosworth.' Conrad frowned, then he shrugged. 'I forget the battle was less than ten days ago. Much has happened since then. It is likely that Sir Cedric's body has only just reached Arnwood.'

Eleanor stared at her brother's corpse. 'Daniel was frightened of strangers. His place is not here among the D'Artons, or even at Arnwood. The only home he truly knew was the priory. Perhaps Mother Benedicta would allow him to be buried in his favourite place in the garden.'

'I will have word sent to her. It will be as you wish. The funeral shall be after the combat tomorrow.' His expression remained solemn. 'Eleanor, if I perish on the field, it is my wish to be buried here. And I ask you to honour my vow to Sir Lionel that his body will be brought here to be laid to rest beside my mother.'

The calm way he spoke of death frightened Eleanor. A fierce pain pierced her numbness to plunge through her heart. She had begun to think of Conrad as invincible. But he was mortal. Her love for him laid waste her grief. Life would be unendurable if Conrad was killed. Her hands tightened convulsively over his arms. 'Your wishes will be obeyed. But it will not come to that.' Her gaze anxiously scanned his face. 'You and Sir Richard cannot mean to fight to the death. It is barbaric.'

'There is no love lost between us,' he declared with cold finality. 'When I vowed that the D'Arton standard would once again fly over Highford, I expected no less a contest between myself and your father. I will die before I see another fly in its stead.'

So emphatic an avowal could not be reasoned against. She should not have expected less from Conrad. Nevertheless she had to try to prevent the combat. 'Sir Richard has no right to Highford. If he has a quarrel it is with me, not you. I'm the one who betrayed my troth. Let me explain matters to him. He's a reasonable man. Once he understands there will be no need for you to fight.'

'There is every reason. Sir Richard fights to win the woman he loves.'

'All the more reason why he should know the truth. He believes I was forced into this marriage. If he knew the taint I would bring to his name he would think himself well rid of me. For you it is Highford which is important. Sir Richard has many castles. He needs an heir, and that I can never give him.'

Beneath her hands she felt a tremor pass through her husband's body. Conrad drew a deep breath and wrenched away from her, his expression frozen as he stared at Daniel's broken body. She saw his throat jerk as he swallowed. It was easy to guess the bitterness of his thoughts and the sight of his stiff, dignified stance devastated her. Eleanor was suddenly cold, her body stippled with icy prickles, and she had never felt so empty, so totally wretched in her life.

When at last he spoke, his voice was low and gruff with an indefinable emotion. 'Norton has never shown an inclination to wed until now. Such a man does not choose a wife lightly. If he loves you he will not give you up. You underestimate your worth as a beautiful and passionate woman. And you seem to have forgotten that you are now a wealthy heiress. As Sir Cedric's eldest daughter, you will inherit Arnwood. There are also other smaller estates.'

She shrank from him at his words. 'Is that why you will not let me go to him—because of the lands I have brought you in marriage? You fight for a high prize on the field tomorrow.'

'I fight for honour and to keep what is mine.'

'You risk your life unnecessarily. You are Henry Tudor's friend. This is your ancestral home. I am the interloper. I will not contest your right. Let it end here.'

He did not reply, but turned his gaze upon the tombs of his family, visible in the candlelight. She stood tense and miserable behind him. Then she saw his blond head lower as his gaze returned to her brother's corpse and he rubbed a hand across his chin.

'I would not be worthy of Highford if I were not prepared to lay down my life for it.' His expression remained closed to her, but there was nothing of anger in his tone, just the fierce ring of pride and possession. 'You are my wife, Eleanor; you are not an interloper.'

At last he faced her, his lips curving into a wry smile. 'It is time you learnt to obey my will.'

He took her hand and she jumped in response. Today had been a nightmare. Never had she needed his strength more to ease her pain. The lure to throw herself into his arms almost overwhelmed her. She fought it. There would be no peace in Conrad's embrace. A touch was enough to rouse her blood to a fiery heat, an embrace would ignite their passion and consume them both in the furnace of hell. She pulled back from him, her eyes wide with her unmasked fear.

He frowned, feeling the tremor which vibrated through her body. 'Eleanor, do you hate me so much?'

Recovering, she shook her head. She searched his face to gauge his feelings, for his voice had conveyed nothing. The gloom of the church showed only the clenched line of his jaw and the bright accusation in his green eyes.

'Nay, my lord, I do not hate you.'

He ran his thumb over her fingers as they trembled beneath his touch. 'Then what is it?'

There was no mistaking the gentleness in his voice nor, as he drew her closer, the look of concern on his handsome face. She could feel the quickening of her heartbeat, the betraying warmth insidiously spreading through her veins. With a strangled sob she tore herself free from him, her body growing cold and frigid as she stared at Daniel's corpse.

'Tomorrow you fight. And I do not want us to quarrel. But I beg you, let me send a letter to Sir Richard. You can read it, for I will tell him only of the truth about my brother. Fight for honour if the two of you must. But not for me. I am not worthy.'

'There you wrong yourself. You are more noble in spirit than any woman I have known.' He placed his hands along each side of her face and tipped it up to meet his forceful gaze. 'Write if you wish; it will serve no purpose. As you say, it is a question of honour. Yours as well as mine.'

'Because I am your wife. Yet you seek from me only submission to your will.'

'I seek your willing submission, my dear. There is a wealth of difference,' he murmured hoarsely. 'Tonight you mourn your brother and I ask nothing from you but a truce.'

His thumbs reverently circled her jaw, and the tenderness of his touch plucked at her heart. Tomorrow he faced death. She could not let him go with bitterness in his heart. She lifted her lips to his. They parted under the warm pressure of his mouth, yielding and trembling with a need she could not put into words. She clung to him, desperate that he understood that she bore him no ill will. She could not speak of her love, for she feared that would place an added burden upon his conscience. He answered with an urgency which left her weak and breathless. His kiss gentled as he restrained his passion. He raised his head and gazed into her eyes, which were shimmering with tears. Tenderly he touched his lips against their moistness.

'God grant I be given time to be worthy of your tears, my love.' He put his hands over her wrists and gently but firmly took her arms from his neck and held her away from him. 'We both have a vigil this night — you to mourn your brother, and I to make my peace with God and prepare for tomorrow's fight.'

He laid a swift kiss upon her fingers and marched from the church. She lifted a hand to call him back, but let it fall, her plea unspoken. An understanding had passed between them this night which transcended physical love.

CHAPTER THIRTEEN

ELEANOR spent the first daylight hour composing a letter to Sir Richard. With a groan of frustration she screwed up the eighth attempt and hurled it in disgust across her chamber. This was not somethng she could write about. She must speak with Sir Richard. Taking up another sheet of parchment, she wrote a note to Conrad explaining why she must speak with Sir Richard and that she would meet the knight under the gatehouse with the portcullis lowered between them.

She chewed her lip as she sanded the letter. Then she cut a thick tress of her hair and threaded it through a brooch bearing the Twyneham device. She wrapped it into a length of silk which already contained the title deeds of Highford which she had gifted over to her husband, before adding some final words to her missive to Conrad.

> Highford is yours. I relinquish all claim to it. And no man should go into combat without wearing the favour of his lady. God be with you this day, most noble lord.   Eleanor.

She rang for a page and bade him give the letter and package to Conrad. She then called for a second page to follow her and walked determinedly to the gatehouse. Ordering the portcullis raised high enough for the boy to duck beneath, she told the lad to seek out Sir Richard to give him her letter. It seemed an eternity passed while she paced the castle precincts waiting for a reply. From the corner of her eye she saw Conrad leave the keep for the stables. He stopped to watch her as Sir Richard approached on foot over the drawbridge. To Eleanor's relief Conrad made no move to prevent the meeting. He signalled his men to keep back from the gatehouse to afford Eleanor the privacy she needed. With a curt nod in her direction he entered the temporary enclosure which replaced the burnt-down stables.

'My lady!' Sir Richard faced Eleanor through the iron struts of the portcullis.

'Sir Richard,' Eleanor answered, finding it difficult to hold his gaze. She forced herself to do so. His face was furrowed with lines of hauteur, but when she smiled nervously at him the expression in his blue eyes softened.

'It is good of you to come, Sir Richard,' she said with warmth. 'I'm sorry it has come to this, but Sir Conrad is not wholly to blame.'

'You are loyal to your knight.' His tone was colder than she had ever heard it.

'How can I not be, since we are married? I cannot right the wrong done to you. I do regret it, and ask your forgiveness. You are the most noble and chivalrous of knights. I have always held you in high regard.'

She saw his jaw tighten and her throat constricted as she forced herself to continue. 'Since our betrothal I learned something about my family. It has been kept secret for generations. There is insanity. . .' Her voice broke as she pictured Daniel's broken body lying in the church. 'It affects only the males — not all of them. . . Sir Cedric and some of his cousins have been spared.'

Sir Richard stepped forward and gripped the bars of the portcullis, his knuckles white. 'This cannot be!'

'I do not lie, Sir Richard. It was wrong of my father to permit our betrothal. When I learned the truth I was horrified and resolved never to marry.'

'You expect me to believe that, when you and D'Arton are wed?'

Eleanor notched her chin higher as she faced his anger. The thought of this man whom she liked and respected fighting with Conrad slashed through her like a knife. 'Circumstances made my marriage inevitable. Sir Conrad has been wronged as much as you.'

His glare was uncompromising. She stepped forward, compelled by the affection she had felt for him to ease his wounded pride. 'Sir Richard, yesterday you allowed the body of a boy to be brought through your men. From your camp you may not have seen what happened.'

'I saw enough,' he answered icily. 'Especially the tender embrace between you and D'Arton.'

He turned to go. Eleanor panicked. He looked furious; she had made matters worse. 'The boy was my brother,' Eleanor called frantically after him. To her relief Sir Richard halted, and, though his expression remained suspicious, he retraced his steps. 'It must have been obvious he was deranged. Any son I bear could be so tainted.'

She held his glacial stare. 'It is not easy to speak of my family's shame. And I regret that my marriage to Sir Conrad should be at the expense of your honour. See it not as dishonour,' she implored, 'but as a reprieve. I could never have given you what you need most — a son.'

'My fight is with D'Arton, not you, Eleanor.'

His tone told her further discussion was useless. Failure bowed her proud head and brought a droop to her shoulders as she turned away.

'Lady Eleanor. Do you love D'Arton?'

She looked at him in silence and saw his face become pale as he saw the answer in her eyes.

'You have all the perfection of your mother's beauty and the spirit she lacked.' He spoke more to himself than to her and it was hard for Eleanor to catch his words. When he saw the puzzlement in Eleanor's face, his expression turned cynical. 'The Lady Isobel was the only other woman I have ever considered marrying,' he stated drily. 'She was bound to Twyneham and had not the courage to face the censure from her family. I was young and arrogant, and that cut my pride. Since then I have enjoyed the freedom of my bachelor status. Until I met you. Now D'Arton has taken what was mine. For that he must pay the price!'

Eleanor was still staring at him in astonishment as he twisted on his heel and marched away.

With each hour that passed before noon Eleanor became more wretched and desperate. She had watched from a distance as Conrad did an hour's sword practice with Ned then began an inspection of the castle grounds, stopping often to speak with his people. Every part of her cried out to be at his side, but she knew this was something he needed to do alone. Highford was what he was fighting for. When she saw Conrad return to his chamber to don his armour for the contest the strain became unbearable and she went to his room.

At her entrance, Gauthier, who was acting as his squire, finished fastening the straps of Conrad's breast-plate and stood back from his master. Conrad dismissed Gauthier with a curt nod. Once they were alone Eleanor crossed to her husband. He looked magnificent and imperious.

'My lord, I come to pay you homage as Lord of Highford and ask your forgiveness.' She had deliberately worn the sapphire and gold gown she had been married in and its full skirts spread over the rushes as she sank to her knees before him. Placing her hands together in the accustomed fashion, she lifted them to him as she reverently bowed her head.

His fingers closed over hers, their warmth and strength sending a pleasurable jolt through her.

'What is there to forgive?' He raised her to her feet.

Conrad looked down into her oval face, his heart clenching as he saw the unshed tears which brightened her indigo eyes.

'There is no lord more worthy of Highford than you,' she said huskily. 'I wanted to tell you so.'

He saw her lower lip quiver and her eyes change from indigo to violet as she submitted to his will, though there was still a part of her which remained defiant. Her mouth tipped up at the corner in the taunting challenge he knew so well. But she said nothing and the violet light in her eyes faded as she said softly, 'God be with you, my lord.'

She picked up his tourney helm from the table and handed it to him. As she did so her glance fell upon the tress of dark blonde hair and Twyneham brooch knotted into the white plumes which hung down its back. The sight of it destroyed her fragile serenity. He would be wearing her favour. Again her eyes moistened as she stared up into his face. Rising on tiptoe, she kissed him swiftly on the lips, then fled the chamber before her control snapped completely and she threw herself at his feet, begging him not to risk his life.

As the sun reached its zenith in the sky the portcullis was raised and Sir Richard Norton rode into Highford. Following the ceremony already agreed by the D'Arton and Norton heralds, Sir Richard was escorted to the tiltyard. A chair had been placed under a canopy for Eleanor to watch from, and Sir Richard's men and the people of Highford ringed the roped-off area. At each end was a rack of lances.

When Eleanor took her place, she saw that both knights were already mounted at their respective ends of the field. Father Hubert came forward to announce the rules of the combat. As a priest he had been chosen as a neutral party to act as marshal. His voice carried clearly to all present.

'This is a combat of honour between Sir Richard Norton and Sir Conrad D'Arton alone. No soldier from either side is to take up the fight, on penalty of death. The contest will be decided by the drawing of first blood.'

Eleanor let out her breath with relief. It was not to be to the death. Then Conrad's words in the church last evening came back to her. He would not relinquish Highford while he lived. And there had been no mercy in Sir Richard's eyes when he spoke of the coming fight.

She closed her eyes against a wave of pain and fear. It would be to the death.

Both knights rode forward to receive Father Hubert's blessing. Eleanor's hands gripped the arms of her chair as the two men saluted her before snapping shut the visors of their helmets. She knew that Conrad during his years in exile had been fêted for his prowess in the lists. Gauthier had once told her that without the prize money he would have starved. But Sir Richard was nearly twenty years his senior and vastly more experienced. Throughout the reigns of Edward and Richard he had been unbeaten in the lists.

All her prayers were for Conrad, the man she loved, but she did not want Sir Richard harmed. Her feelings for the older knight had always confused her. It was a strange kind of affection, deeper than friendship, born of respect and something she could not explain — it was just there. Her life would have no purpose if Conrad died on the field, but if Sir Richard perished she knew that it would leave a deep scar.

'Blessed Jesu, let both of them live.' Her lips moved, repeating the silent prayer as the two knights trotted their horses to opposite ends of the field.

Each man took up a lance and couched it against his side. When Father Hubert dropped his hand the two destriers leapt forward in a muderous charge. A hush fell over the crowd. Eleanor felt her heart pounding in time to the drumming hoofs. Her mind saw everything in slow motion and with cruel clarity. There was a sickening thud as Conrad's lance stuck Sir Richard's wooden shield. Sir Richard's lance had missed its mark, but Conrad's strike knocked his opponent backwards. A roar went up from the crowd, and Eleanor held her breath as Sir Richard rocked in the high-backed saddle. He had recovered his balance by the time he reached the far end of the lists.

A second lance chosen, both destriers again galloped towards each other. The two knights rode as though they were moulded to their mounts. The destriers' caparisons, emblazoned with their master's arms, rippled in the air, stirred by their furious pace. Eleanor saw not the beauty and spectacle; she saw only the deadly tips of the lances drawing closer to their target with each leaden heartbeat. The clash was deafening. Both lances had struck their mark. At seeing Conrad reel in the saddle, Eleanor started forward. The great destrier went down and she was terrified that Conrad would be crushed beneath his weight. He was too experienced for that. Throwing down his broken lance, he agilely leapt free of the horse and rolled on the grass. Staggering under the weight of his armour, Conrad rose to his knees. The charge had taken Sir Richard further down the lists, which gave Conrad a moment to recover his breath. He heaved himself upright and drew his sword, his figure braced for his opponent's attack.

Sir Richard trotted towards Conrad. The unseating of an opponent usually ended the contest. But this was no court tourney for the entertainment of their peers. This was in earnest. Conrad's defiant stance told Eleanor that her husband would not cry off. Father Hubert was advancing towards the knights. The priest was satisfied that Norton was the winner and the matter settled. There was an outcry of shouting from the crowd. The people of Highford wanted Conrad as their lord.

Before Father Hubert reached them, Sir Richard dismounted several paces from Conrad, slapped his mount on the rump to speed it from the lists, and, to an accompanying loud gasp from the crowd, drew his sword. An expectant hush descended over the ground and Eleanor found her legs trembled so violently that she sank back on to the chair. Swords raised, the knights began to circle each other, taking the measure of their opponent. Sir Richard was two or three inches taller than Conrad, but there was little between them in weight. Skill alone would determine the victor of this day.

Suddenly they rushed at each other. Father Hubert's

protest was lost against the loud ring of steel. Making the sign of the cross and closing his hands in prayer, the priest backed away from the knights. Their swords moved so fast that Eleanor could not count their strokes. There seemed nothing between them in skill or agility. Both men were pressing hard, awaiting the slightest lowering of a guard to finish the attack. Sir Richard struck a mighty blow. Conrad caught it on his shield, but the force behind it was so great that he staggered. Another ferocious blow brought Conrad to his knees.

Eleanor cried out and leapt up out of the chair, her knuckles thrust into her mouth to stop a scream. Conrad parried each downward stroke as he tried to rise to his feet. A blow to the side of his helmet made him reel and lose his balance. To Eleanor's horror he fell full-length to the ground. Sir Richard swayed as he stood over him. His tiredness was apparent. The hesitation was enough. Conrad brought up his shield and foot, caught Sir Richard in the middle, and sent the knight somersaulting on to the grass.

The spectators went wild with excitement. Eleanor shook so violently that she could barely stand, and nausea roiled in her stomach. She held her breath as Conrad rolled over and straddled his winded opponent. He snatched off Sir Richard's helmet and placed his sword point at his enemy's throat.

Sweat was running down Conrad's face and his breathing was laboured. 'Yield or die, Norton!'

He found himself staring into the knight's eyes—brilliant blue irises that remained defiant even though he was beaten. Then he saw them change as the corner of Norton's lip tilted. The furious eyes he now stared into were indigo flecked with violet. His own eyes widened with shock. The lapse of concentration was his undoing. Norton threw his weight over and reversed their position. It was Norton's sword which now poised over Conrad. With the same deliberate intent he removed Conrad's helmet.

There was a scream from the crowd and into his line of vision Sir Richard saw Eleanor running towards them. All his hatred for the man who had stolen her flooded him. Not only hatred for D'Arton, but for Twyneham, who had denied him the Lady Isobel as a wife. Twyneham had fallen at Bosworth by Richard's hand; now it was D'Arton's turn. He had dared to steal Eleanor, who surpassed the Lady Isobel in beauty, wit and courage. Eleanor possessed the intelligence, grace and passionate nature he had spent twenty years seeking.

Sir Richard's eyes narrowed as he drew back the sword. He had a reluctant admiration for the way D'Arton had risked his sovereign's wrath by daring to reclaim his ancestral home and take Eleanor as his bride. He felt a pang of remorse that the young knight had to die. D'Arton would never rest until Highford was his. They were irrevocable enemies. 'Die, D'Arton, and know that both Highford and Eleanor will be mine.'

'Eleanor can never be your wife,' Conrad snarled at him. 'She's your daughter, man.'

Sir Richard had not expected that. Conrad saw the hesitation and struck. Breathing heavily from his exertion, he again found himself straddling the older knight. Their sword hilts locked, first wavering down to one knight's throat then up to threaten the life of the other. Both men were breathing heavily, their face muscles corded as they forced out their speech while resuming their deadly fight.

'Such a tale will not save you,' Norton rasped as they rolled across the ground in the struggle to gain supremacy.

'Is it?' Conrad grunted as he stared at the knight again beneath him. 'The Lady Isobel was reputedly beautiful. Few such beauties missed your attention. Your mistresses have been legion. Was the Lady Isobel one of them?'

From the challenging look in Sir Richard's indigo eyes, Conrad knew he had hit upon the truth. When the older knight caught his lower lip between his teeth as he considered the point, Conrad was certain.

'Eleanor is your daughter,' Conrad persisted. 'She has your eyes and mannerisms.'

Still Norton was not convinced, but Conrad eased back from his attack. 'Pax. I've no wish to kill my wife's father.'

He felt the tension lessen in the older knight's sword arm and cautiously Conrad lowered his weapon. The blades rested on Sir Richard's chest as the knights laboured to regain their breath.

'Look at Eleanor,' Conrad said. 'Her colouring is all her mother's, but she has your eyes, Norton. She's even biting her lip in the same way you are now. Why do you think I hesitated to kill you when I had the chance?'

In mutual agreement they both rolled aside and stood up. Then Sir Richard feinted, and before Conrad could retaliate Norton touched his sword point against Conrad's throat. 'You fight well, D'Arton, but never trust an opponent until you've disarmed him.'

A dubious glitter still lingered in the older knight's eyes. There was a cry of protest from Eleanor as she reached them. Both men looked at her and Conrad saw the recognition dawn in Norton's eyes.

Eleanor put out a hand towards the sword which was an inch away from stealing Conrad's life. 'Please, Sir Richard, I beg you. Spare my husband.' She was unaware that tears were streaming down her cheeks, that her eyes were large and luminous, indigo flecked with violet—eyes which stared back at Richard from a looking-glass each time he shaved.

He shook his head to break the spell of incredulity which had settled over him. Lowering his sword, he clamped a gauntleted hand down on Conrad's shoulder.

Eleanor stood staked to the spot as she looked at both men, relieved, but still wary and puzzled. The crowd remained quiet, sensing the tension within the lists. Conrad was looking secretly pleased with himself, but it

was Sir Richard's expression which disconcerted her
most. He stared at her intently and then his lips twitched
and his eyes sparkled.

'I think, my dear,' Sir Richard said with what sounded
like misplaced amusement, 'we had better seek the
privacy of the solar. This is a day of celebration for us
all.'

'I don't understand.'

'Have patience, my love.' Conrad grinned as he began
to pull at the straps of his breastplate. 'We will rid
ourselves of our armour and then talk.'

Patience had never been one of Eleanor's virtues. Now it
was tried to its limits. Both knights left her and for half
an hour she paced the solar with such agitation that she
rubbed a blister on the sole of her foot. An impatient
glance through the window showed her that the people
had not dispersed back to the village. Trestle-tables were
being set up in the courtyard. No doubt Conrad intended
to celebrate his undisputed lordship of Highford.

Conrad arrived first at the solar. The relief Eleanor
had felt that neither man had been injured in the combat
had withered, replaced by antagonism that they had
hatched a conspiracy in which she had no part.

'It would seem Highford is yours, my lord.' Eleanor
voiced her agitation. 'What bargain did you make with
Sir Richard?'

His smile was infuriatingly assured. Sir Richard
arrived before she could question him. Eleanor tilted her
head and her lip curved up as her anger simmered
beneath a polite façade as she addressed them. 'It is good
that your differences were settled without bloodshed.'

When the two knights exchanged a secretive and
amused look, what little remained of her restraint
snapped. 'Will one of you kindly inform me what was
resolved by your combat?'

Conrad nodded to Sir Richard, who stepped to her
side. 'These last weeks the fates have mocked us all.

What I learned today was both a shock and a pleasant surprise. It would seem, Eleanor, that you are my daughter. D'Arton saw the likeness.'

'But that's impossible.' Eleanor stared at him as though his wits had left him.

He cleared his throat and an embarrassed flush darkened his cheeks. 'It is very possible. I checked the date of your birth with Father Hubert to be certain. There's no doubt in my mind. The Lady Isobel and I. . .' He spread his hands in an expansive gesture and dropped his gaze from her candid stare, before continuing. 'The Lady Isobel had been betrothed to Sir Cedric since she was five, but had never met him. When she came to Court prior to her wedding I was captivated by her grace and beauty. Sir Cedric was delayed; he had succumbed to an attack of measles. A month later he arrived at Court to claim his bride and our brief relationship ended.'

'You did not contest Sir Cedric's right?' Eleanor queried. 'Surely if you and my mother were in love. . .?

Sir Richard coughed, clearly discomfited. 'I adored your mother for her beauty, and if I loved anyone it was her. But I was young and proud. Isobel was terrified of her father, too frightened to disobey his wishes. I despised her for her lack of spirit. The reason why I remained unwed for so long was because I sought not only beauty in my wife, but wit and courage. Sir Cedric arrived at Court and they were married within a week. Afterwards Isobel left Court and lived in seclusion on Twyneham's estates. I never saw her again. Neither did I know that she had given birth to my daughter.'

Eleanor was shocked at her mother's conduct, then her honesty made her feel guilty that she should pass such judgement upon her. Had not she been attracted to Conrad from the first moment they met?

'How could you possibly be certain that I am your daughter?'

His eyes crinkled with confidence and affection.

'D'Arton noted a likeness in our mannerisms and in our eyes. That you were born just eight months after Isobel married confirms it. I am your father, not Sir Cedric.'

The news stunned Eleanor, but it explained so much. There had been little affection between Sir Cedric and her mother. How could Lady Isobel have loved Sir Richard and not fought for her right to marry him? Eleanor knew she would have done as much for the man she loved. But Lady Isobel had been a truly gentle woman. She would not have had the courage to rebel against her family's wishes.

Eleanor looked at Sir Richard with greater insight and understood the natural affinity she had felt with him. No wonder Mother Benedicta had been convinced that she was a fitting wife for Conrad. Lady Isobel must have confessed to the prioress that her daughter was not Sir Cedric's child. But over all this one thought conquered all else; it was mirrored in the happiness which illuminated her face and eyes. 'Then my blood is not tainted with the Twyneham madness.'

'It would seem not.' Sir Richard looked down at her with open affection. 'You have your mother's beauty, which first attracted me to you. But it was your spirit which set you apart from other women. It made you worthy to be my wife. It makes me very proud to be able to call you daughter.'

He took Eleanor's hand and placed it into Conrad's. 'And D'Arton has proved himself a worthy husband to my only child. What we have learned this day will remain our secret. I would not shame the memory of the Lady Isobel by acknowledging you to be my daughter. But I hope we can see each other often.'

'You will always be welcome in our home,' Conrad said as he poured a goblet of wine and held it towards Sir Richard. 'I am proud to be aligned with the Norton family.'

Conrad filled two more goblets and came to Eleanor's side to place one in her hand.

Richard nodded and smiled at them both. 'Today is indeed cause for celebration. Now I will leave husband and wife alone. And give you my blessing on your marriage. We will meet again at the feast tonight. Then I think we all have some explaining to do to our sovereign. Not least that I intend to make one of my grandsons my heir. At five-and-forty I find I enjoy my bachelor life too much to easily relinquish it.'

He raised his goblet in toast to them. 'To the Lord and Lady of Highford. May their days be long, their coffers full, their nursery filled with strapping sons.'

He downed his drink and with a wink at them both departed.

Eleanor became suddenly self-conscious in her husband's company. He was watching her, his muscles seemingly coiled and tightened, his breathing carefully measured as though he fought to control it. Conrad made no move to touch her, but his gaze brought a tingling to her limbs and a quickening to her breath. It was more profound than a caress.

She lifted her hand palm up towards him, her voice husky and breathless. 'My lord, my father has given his blessing upon our marriage, but it is for you to decide whether I shall stay or live within the priory.'

He did not move and all pride was stripped from her; she knew her eyes spoke her love, but did not care as she silently prayed that he would not renounce her.

His hand took hers, his fingers warm and assured. 'Come here.' He drew her into the Lord's chamber behind the solar. Once the door was firmly shut against the outside world, he took her into his arms.

'Wife, I have no intention of allowing you to shut yourself away in the priory.'

'Forceful green eyes stared deep into hers; they were commanding, resolute and tender, but that was all. Her heart wrenched. There was no light of the love she craved to see blazing there. She sighed softly, lowering her lashes over the expression in her eyes as she sought the courage to speak with bitter honesty, to find the strength to give him his freedom if that was what he wished. 'Our marriage was based on a lie. I am not even legitimate — though I no longer carry the burden of the taint of madness running in my veins.'

A soft chuckle made her look up at him, perplexed. His lips curled with secret amusement. 'Our marriage was based on no lie, my love. Except the lie we told ourselves. It was inevitable. Founded upon our mutual passion and built upon by respect and fashioned by my love.'

She gazed at him with awe, her cheeks flushing with remembrance of their passion, an insidious heat spreading through her body, a sweetness which his nearness always roused invading her bones.

'I fought for the right to call you wife, but I cannot command your love, my darling,' he said hoarsely. 'I wanted you from that first day by the waterfall. There's not been a single day when I have not wanted you since. Even Highford became unimportant if you were not part of it. When I thought we could not have children it made no difference to what I felt for you.' His green eyes lit with an iridescence which humbled her. 'I love you, Eleanor. You are more important to me than Highford, more precious than even life itself.'

She uttered a soft cry as her arms went around his neck, pulling his head down to meet her ardent kiss. His lips covered hers, taking the whole of her mouth. . . thirsting.

How long had she been fighting him, denying the call of her blood? Always his mastery had subdued her. This time was different: he did not seek dominance, but equality.

He covered her face with kisses and she found herself laughing and crying as the torture of the last days ended. She clung to him. With a delighted laugh he lifted her into his arms. Her heart soared as he carried her to the bed. Their clothing was quickly dispensed with, their fingers impatient in their hunger. They lay naked side by side and Conrad leaned over her. For the space of several heartbeats, he hesitated, gazing down at her, his desire held in check as he sought to assuage a moment of doubt.

'Is this of your own free will, Eleanor?' he whispered, offering her a last chance of freedom. His fingertips feathered across her cheek, caressed the outline of her lips. The sensuous touch continued along her throat to pause just above her breast. 'If you prefer life in the priory to that of my wife, you have but to say.'

She smiled enticingly, as his hands continued their seductive circling, making her burn deep inside with longing. She arched against him, her eyes shimmering with happiness and love, her hands sliding over his back as she received his kiss. She whispered a vow against his ear. 'I am yours, Conrad. . .always.'

He made love to her, suspending them in a haven of pleasure. The afternoon stretched lazily ahead of them as they discovered the meaning of two bodies and souls blending as one, each giving and receiving pleasure, heightened by the new awareness of trust, unhampered by inhibitions or regret. They marvelled in the pleasure they gave each other, words of love mingled with soft cries of rapture. She moved with him, breathless in her declaration of love as she wondered at the magnitude of her emotions. Where he led, she eagerly followed, an apt pupil to the erotic secrets he taught.

His tongue played around her ear and her lips seared into his shoulders. The surging tension built into a passion which engulfed them both, bursting with explosive intensity into a final and simultaneous relief which left them satiated.

The fire which had blazed between them even now was slow to die. Conrad held her against him, tangling his fingers in her hair. He rolled on to his back and lifted her across him, her hand pressed against his chest, and when their eyes met their depths were filled with the soft sparkle of languorous rapture.

'Oh, Conrad, tell me this is not a dream. That I will not wake and find I must deny myself children — that, worse, you do not love me at all.'

'I love you.' He smiled. 'This is no dream — but the reality of our future. And there is so much more. . .'

'More, my love? I cannot believe that possible.' She spread her fingers across the hairs on his chest to caress his neck and touch the softness of his mouth.

'Believe me, there is so much more.' He nipped the tip of her finger with his teeth. 'And I shall teach you everything.'

She felt a blush steal across her entire body at the bold promise in his stare and with a bewitching chuckle she leaned down to kiss him with returning passion.